The Wooing of Wistaria

The Wooing of Wistaria

Onoto Watanna

MINT EDITIONS

The Wooing of Wistaria was first published in 1902.

This edition published by Mint Editions 2021.

ISBN 9781513271538 | E-ISBN 9781513276533

Published by Mint Editions®

 MINT
EDITIONS

minteditionbooks.com

Publishing Director: Jennifer Newens
Design & Production: Rachel Lopez Metzger
Project Manager: Micaela Clark
Typesetting: Westchester Publishing Services

Contents

I

When after a life that had never lacked variety the Lady Wistaria came to the years of tranquility, she was wont to say, with the philosophy that follows dangerous times: "No one, man or maid, ever really began to live before the time to which the first memory reverts."

The first recollection of the Lady Wistaria goes back to an earlier childhood than that of most mortals. This she ascribed to its terrible and awful import. She could scarcely do more than move with the uncertain direction of babyhood, when her father, always now in her memory as gaunt, lean, haggard, tall, had taken her upon a long journey. They had travelled partly by kurumaya, and, towards the end, on foot. That is, her father had walked, carrying her on high in his arms.

When they halted at Yedo they stood amid a vast concourse of people, who remained silent and respectful against the background of the buildings, while in the centre of the road marched steadily and pompously a great glittering pageant.

Wistaria had clapped her hands with glee and delight at the mass of color, the glimmer of shield and breastplate, the prancing, snorting horses. But her father suddenly had raised an enormous hand and in a moment had stopped her delight. Wistaria lapsed into an acute silence.

Instantly she was awakened from her painful apathy by her father, who moved her higher in his arms, and turned her head slowly about with one hand, while with the other he pointed to a shining personage reclining in a palanquin borne high on the shoulders of ten stout-legged attendants.

"My daughter," said her father's hollow voice in her ear, "yonder rides the man who killed your mother. It is through his crime that you are orphaned and have no mother to care for you and love you. Look at him well! Hush! Do not weep or shake with fear, but turn your eyes upon him. Look at him! Look! Look! Yonder rides your mother's murderer. Do not forget his face as long as you live. It is your duty to remember it!"

Whereupon Wistaria, who, in obedience to her father's commands, had stared with wide eyes fixedly at the reclining noble, set up a most extraordinary cry. It was unlike that of a little child—a wild, wailing shriek, so weird and piteous that the by-standers started in horror and fear. The noble raised himself lazily on his elbow, staring across the heads of all, until his eyes rested upon the man with the child held on high. He fell back with an uneasy shrug of the shoulders.

That was the Lady Wistaria's oldest memory. There were others, but none so vivid as this, the first of all. Even later, when she had ceased to be a child, she had been unable to pierce the mystery of her father's life, or indeed her own.

One half of her earlier years had been spent in a small, whitewashed cottage, built on the crest of a little wind-blown hill, far enough removed from the dwellings in the village below to be entirely cut off from them.

There was a touch of the uncanny and weird about the little village, whose slender streets, ascending and descending, zigzagging up and down, disappeared among hillocks and bluffs, though built in reality in the hollow outskirts of a flourishing city at the foot of a small chain of mountains. Though the land here was green and beautiful at all times of the year, there came no one from the great city beyond to this solitary settlement, whose inhabitants bore the impress of toil, pain, and oppression.

Why her father, who, she had been told, was of noble blood, resided here on this hill-top, isolated even from the strange people who dwelt in the silent village below, the Lady Wistaria had never learned. When she had questioned her uncle and aunt, she had been frigidly informed that curiosity and inquisitiveness were degrading traits, which a maiden should strive with all her strength to overcome. Neither did she ask her father, who, taciturn and cold during her brief residence each year in his house, gave her no opportunity for winning his confidence. His love Wistaria had never dreamed of possessing.

Nevertheless, whenever she went to her father's house, a wistful longing and yearning for him possessed her whole being, and when she departed she would hide her face in her sleeve, weeping silently, not knowing why she should weep, and scarcely conscious of the fact that she wept for lack of her father's love.

In her father's house there were no servants, no maids, no attendants— only one weazened, blind, and infinitely old woman, who wept tears from her sightless eyes upon her arrival, who sang and crooned to her at night in a sobbing, sighing voice, that was as sweet and pure as a girl's.

She addressed the old woman as "Madame Mume," and preserved always towards her the reserved and dignified attitude of the mistress to the maid. Yet her father addressed her as "Mother." Wistaria knew the old woman was not his mother, and she could not believe she was even akin to them; for had she not always been taught that the family from which she was descended was one of the oldest and noblest in Japan, while old Madame Mume, though gentle and good, wore the garb of the poor heimin.

The other half of her childhood had been spent at the home of her uncle. Here were countless retainers and servants, besides a host of samurai, petty vassals, soldiers, peasants, and citizens, who lived upon his land and owed their direct allegiance to him.

The garden walls surrounding her uncle's palace were tall and of massive structure, built of solid stone. Its gates were guarded by handsome, bold samurai clad in thick armor. The steel upon their breasts and shoulders glistened with a sinister sheen, and beneath their blazing helmets fierce eyes burned out their unswerving allegiance and loyalty to their lord and their scorn and defiance of all his enemies. Their coats, all emblazoned and embroidered with golden dragons, bore two crests, that of the Shogun Iyesada, and that of the powerful Daimio under whom they served, the Lord of Catzu, uncle of the Lady Wistaria.

Here in her uncle's palace Wistaria was watched over, cared for, nurtured, and refined. Lackeys and servants were about her on all sides, ready to spring to her service. As a child she had attended a private school, kept by an old samurai, where with half a dozen other little girls she had squatted on small, padded mats before writing-tables but twelve inches high, and had been taught the intricacies of the language. Two gorgeously liveried attendants always accompanied her to and from the school-house, carrying her books, her writing-box, her kneeling-cushion, and her little table.

When she grew older she attended the elementary school. After she had left this, a silent woman of perfect manners and exquisite appearance had come to her uncle's palace and attached herself entirely to her. With the coming of this governess, Wistaria ceased to pay her annual visits to her father's house. He himself came to the palace instead, once every year. Upon these occasions Wistaria was brought into his presence. He would put a few stern questions to her concerning her knowledge of her duty to her parents, to which Wistaria would respond with expressions of filial submission to his will in all things.

From the governess, Wistaria learned the elegancies of conversation and how to act on meeting great personages at court. She had even been drilled in certain graces which should not fail to enchain her lover, when he, the proper one, should be chosen for her.

Now that she had reached the age of fifteen years, this perfect person had departed from the palace to teach maidens of younger years. The Lady Wistaria had arrived at an age when she could be said to have been graduated from her governess's hands as competent to pass the rest of her life without further instruction, save that constant restraint exercised over her by her aunt, the Lady Evening Glory of Catzu.

II

The education of a Japanese maid is not alone a matter of cultivating the mind; it is an actual moulding of her whole character. The average girl under such discipline succumbs to the hereditary instinct of implicit obedience to her dictators, and becomes like unto their conception of what she should be. But the Lady Wistaria was not an average girl. That is the reason her appearance at the court of the Shogun in Yedo created a furore. Her fresh, young beauty, her grace and bewitching charm, were a revelation to the jaded court.

The Lady Evening Glory, who had spent years of thought and preparation for this event, had warned her repeatedly that upon such an auspicious occasion she was to tread across the vast hall with downcast eyes and an attitude of graceful humility. She was on no account to look about her. While all eyes might gaze upon her, she must see no one. And this is how the Lady Wistaria carried out her instructions.

When first she began the slow parade towards the Shogun's throne, my lady's head was drooped in the correct pose, with her eyes modestly downcast. She had proceeded but a few paces, however, when she was thrilled by the intuition that the spectacle was worthy of any sacrifice necessary to see it. Her small head began to erect itself. Her eyes, wide open, with one great sweep viewed the splendor of the picture—the graceful courtiers, the lovely women in their costumes of the sun. A sharp pinch upon the arm brought her back to the exacting presence of the Lady Evening Glory beside her. Down drooped her head again. Gradually the eyelids fluttered. My lady peeped!

There was a low murmur throughout the hall. The waving of fans ceased a space. The Lady Evening Glory recognized the significance of that murmur, and then the hush that ensued. A tremendous fluttering pride arose in her bosom. Her experience of many years assured her that her niece's beauty was compelling its splendid tribute.

Then the Lady Wistaria was presented to the Shogun. Her prostration was made with inimitable grace. Her beauty and charm called forth words of praise from the Shogun himself to her uncle.

A young noble, more daring and ardent than all the others, separated himself from the assembled company, and, crossing to where the Lady Wistaria stood, kissed a hyacinth and dropped it at the girl's feet.

The Lady Evening Glory could have shrieked aloud with fury at the action of her niece, due solely to her innocence. She had no thought whence it had come. A flower in her path was not something she could tread upon, or even pass by. There in the centre of the gorgeous hall she stooped tenderly and picked up the pleading flower.

"Wild girl!" cried her aunt, in a suffocating whisper.

Wistaria started with a little cry of genuine dismay. She had forgotten in one moment the instruction of years. In her confusion she stopped short in her progress across the hall. As if impelled by some great subtle force within her, helplessly the Lady Wistaria raised her eyes. They gazed immediately into the depths of another pair, afire with an awakening passion. The next moment the young girl had blushed, red as the tints a masterful sun throws to coquetting clouds at sunset.

All the journey through, to their temporary palace in Yedo, her aunt abused the Lady Wistaria. The training of years wasted! Ingratitude was the basest of crimes! Was this the way she repaid her aunt's labor and kindness? Well, back to Catzu they should go. It would be unsafe to remain longer in the capital. Certainly her niece had much to learn before she could continue in Yedo longer than a day.

The Lady Wistaria sat back in her palanquin, pouting. What, to be taken from the gay capital one day after arriving—before she had had the chance to meet or even speak to any one! Oh! it was cruel, and she the most stupid of maidens not to have comported herself correctly at her presentation!

"Dearest, my lady aunt," said she, "pray you, do let us continue in the capital for the season."

"What! and be laughed at by the whole court for our shocking and magnificently bad manners? People will declare that you have been reared in the fields with the peasants."

"Do not, I beg, blame me for an accident, dear, my honorable aunt. It was not, in truth, my own fault."

"Indeed!"

"Indeed, I do assure you it was the fault of that honorably silly flower."

"Tshh!"

"And of that magnificent and augustly handsome courtier who dropped it."

"Dropped it! My lady niece, I saw the impudent fellow throw it at your feet!"

"What! You saw! Oh, my aunt, then it is you who are jointly guilty with me!"

"What is that?" cried the aunt, angrily.

"Why, my lady, your honorable eyes were improper also."

The Lady Evening Glory turned an offended shoulder.

"We will start to-morrow for home."

"Oh, my lady!"

"I have spoken."

"But, dear aunt—"

"Will you condescend to tell me, girl, who is guardian, thou or I?"

With the Lady Evening Glory, "thou" was the end of discussion.

The following day, therefore, the returning cortège set out for Catzu. As fortune would have it, the Lady Evening Glory travelled in her own train, while her niece had also her personal retinue about her. Consequently the journey was joyous for the Lady Wistaria.

When first the cortège began to move through the city a strange little procession followed in its wake. It was made up of the love-sick suitors, who, having but once gazed upon the beauty of the Lady Wistaria, wished to serve and follow her to the end of the world. The following was quite large when the cortège started. A number dropped off as they reached the city limits, then gradually the hopeless and disappointed swains with drooping heads turned back to Yedo, there to dream of the vision of a day, but to dream hopelessly.

Wherever the Lady Wistaria's personal train travelled there lay scattered upon the ground, and blowing in the air above and about her, tiny bits of white or delicately tinted and perfumed paper. They were, alas! the love-letters and poems penned by the ardent lovers, which the hard-hearted lady, tearing into infinitesimal bits, had saucily tossed to the winds. It was thus she tossed their love from her, she would have them believe.

Hopeless, and finally indignant, therefore, backward turned these erstwhile hopeful suitors.

Sir Genji, the big samurai, who had especial charge of Wistaria's train, reported to her, with a smile of satisfaction, that she would suffer no further annoyance, as all save one of her suitors had finally retreated.

"Bring closer your honorable head," said the lady to Genji, who strode beside her norimono, ever and anon ordering and scolding the runners.

He brought his ear closer to the girl's lips. She leaned over and whispered, while a pale pink flush came, fled, and grew and deepened again in her face.

"Tell me," said she, "which of the honorably bold and silly cavaliers is it that remains?"

"The one, my lady, who, not content with despatching his love-letters and tokens to you by underlings, has had the august impertinence to deliver them himself in person."

"Yes—ye-es—of course," said Wistaria, blushing deliciously, "and that was honorably right. Do you not think so, my brave Genji?"

"Perhaps," admitted the astute samurai, frowning at the same time upon a portion of the parade belonging to the Lady Evening Glory. Wistaria laughed with infinite relish.

"Well," she said, "if my honorable aunt or august uncle were to learn of his boldness, I fear me they would command that the curtains of my insignificant norimon be drawn so tightly that I should surely suffocate."

"Fear not," said Genji, "I shall take immediate measures to prevent such an occurrence, my lady."

Wistaria pouted, and frowned as heavily as it is possible for bright eyes and rosy lips to do. She toyed with her fan, opening and closing it several times.

"You are honorably over-zealous, Sir Genji," she said.

"My lady," he replied, "know you aught of this stranger?"

"He has a pretty grace," said Wistaria, "and the bearing of one of noble rank. Have you not noted, Sir Genji, the beauty and richness of his magnificent attire?"

"I have, my lady. It is of that attire I would speak."

"Do so at once, then."

"It is the attire, my lady, of the Mori family."

"The Mori! What! Our honorably hostile neighbors?"

"Exactly," said Genji.

"Oh, dear!" murmured Wistaria, as she sank back in her cushions in troubled thought. After a moment her little black head again appeared.

"Gen," she cried, "come hither once more."

"My lady?"

"A little closer, if you please. So! Know you not, Sir Gen, that my lady aunt, and indeed also my own august father, once served this odious Mori prince?"

"I have heard so, my lady."

"Well, then, truly *all* of the members of this honorable clan cannot be augustly bad!"

Sir Genji could not restrain a smile.

"Indeed, my lady, this Choshui people have many worthy and admirable qualities."

"You are a very clever fellow, my dear Sir Gen," said Wistaria, smiling engagingly now, "and I shall bespeak you to my honorable uncle. And now—now—if you would really wish to serve me, do you pray show some kindness—some little insignificant courtesy to this unfortunate Mori courtier. Perhaps he may have some good attributes."

"Undoubtedly, my lady."

"And do be careful to allow my lady aunt to know naught concerning him, for she, having come from this Mori, is actually more sour against them than we, you and I, Sir Gen, who have not indeed."

Just then my lady heard a familiar tramp to the left of her norimono. There were but few horses in the cortège, and most of them had gone ahead with her father's samurai. Consequently the beat of a horse's hoofs was plainly to be heard. The Lady Wistaria wavered between lying back in her carriage and drawing about her discreetly the curtains, or sitting up and feigning indifference to the horseman.

The rider had fallen into a slow trot behind her norimono, and seemed to be making no effort either to overtake or ride beside her. For the space of a few minutes the Lady Wistaria, with a bright, expectant red spot in either cheek, waited for some sign on the part of the rider. His stubborn continuance in the background at first thrilled, then irritated, and finally distracted her. My lady put her shining little head out of the vehicle, then, leaning quite far out, she looked backward. Instantly the rider spurred his horse forward. In a flash his hitherto melancholy face became luminous with hope. A moment later he was beside the lady's norimono. Before her officious maid had time to draw the curtains a love-letter had fallen into my lady's lap.

It was possibly the fiftieth appeal he had penned to her. Hitherto he had borne the bitter chagrin of seeing the torn bits of paper fall from a little hand that parted the silken curtains of her gilded norimono and scattered them to the winds.

The lover rode within sight of his mistress's palanquin until the first gray darkness of approaching night crept like an immense cloud over the heavens, chasing away the enchanting rosy tints that the departing sun had left behind.

Undaunted by the fact that his letter received no response, encouraged rather by the fact that it had not shared the fate of its predecessors, the lover now set himself to the task of composing more ardent and flowery epistles. What time was not occupied in eagerly watching for the smallest glimpse of the little head to appear was spent in writing to her. He wrote his love-letters and poems with a shaking hand even while his horse carried him onward. He wrote them by the light of the moon when the train halted for the night. He wrote them in the early dawn before the cortège had awakened. And he delivered them at all hours, whenever he could obtain opportunity.

Though the Lady Wistaria by this time must have acquired a goodly quantity of useless literature, she took no measure to relieve herself of the burdensome baggage. Nevertheless the lover began to despair. A few hours before they reached her uncle's province he delivered his last missive. It was really a very desperate letter. At the risk of his life—so he wrote—he would follow her not only to her uncle's province but into the very grounds surrounding his palace—into the palace itself if necessary. He besought her that she would send him one small word of favor.

He waited in impatient excitement for a response to this last fervid appeal. He felt sure she must at least deign to express her wish in the matter. But when they reached the province he saw her carried across the borders without having given him one sign or token.

In his despair he dismounted, and was divided between returning to Yedo or continuing his hopeless quest.

As he remained plunged in his gloomy reflections and uncertainty of purpose, an enormous samurai touched him sharply upon the arm. In his irritation he was about to resent the fellow's familiarity, when he perceived a little roll of rice-paper protruding from his sleeve. Stealthily the samurai reached out his arm to the lover. The latter seized the scroll eagerly.

III

The palace, and indeed the whole domain of the Lord Catzu, presented the appearance of being constantly armed as though for attack, a not uncommon thing in the latter days of feudalism. The Shogun had been artful in his disposal of the various lords of the provinces. Families attached personally to him were stationed in provinces lying between those administered by families friendly to the Emperor. Thus none of the Emperor's friends could meet to revolt against the Shogun.

So it happened that while the Lord Catzu was one of the most intimate and confidential of the advisers of the Shogun, his neighbor, the old Prince Mori, Daimio of the province of Choshui, desired to see the Mikado once more, the real, instead of the nominal, ruler of Japan.

Consequently the two neighboring clans, while displaying extravagant courtesy towards each other in public, were in reality unfriendly. Only during that portion of the year when the Shogun's edict ordered a Yedo residence for all daimios, did the lords of the provinces meet one another, and that under the Shogun's eyes in his Yedo seat of government. In the capital they simulated suavity and cordiality, but once back at their provincial capitals they preserved towards each other an attitude of polite defiance which made all intercourse between them impossible save that of the sword, when their respective samurai and vassals, coming in contact with one another, fought out their lords' political differences.

Imbittering still more the feeling existing naturally between the Mori and Catzu clans, there was a personal element in the situation. When Catzu had first been made lord of the province he had met on a visit to the Shogun's Yedo court the Lady Evening Glory, whose brother and guardian (she being an orphan) was a young samurai in the service of the Prince Mori. Having fallen a victim to the lady's beauty and charms, the lord of Catzu was determined to have her for wife despite the opposition of the Mori Prince. Bold, brave, fearless, and with a grand contempt for the power of his rival, the Lord Catzu had carried off the fair lady from his neighbor's dominions, though it was generally understood that both the lady herself and her samurai brother lent their assistance to the young lord. The young samurai, incurring thereby the deep displeasure and enmity of his Prince, was deprived of his title and estates and sent into exile upon the first convenient pretext. Strange tales told without shadow of authority diversified the nature of the crime for which the samurai had been exiled, but the two lords remained silent. All who had been concerned in the affair were commanded to the same silence by the Shogun.

Whatever were the many reasons responsible for the constant attitude of antagonism of these two clans towards each other, the lords carefully guarded their lands—more particularly those in the vicinity of their palaces—with all the rigor of a fortress prepared for the fiercest onslaught. Seemingly unapproachable and impenetrable as were the grounds of the Catzu palace, yet there must have existed at some spot in their watchful walls a vulnerable point, the heel of the stone Achilles.

A courtier, by his dress and demeanor plainly a member of the Mori household, lingered in the private gardens of the palace. The day had long since folded its wings of light, but an early March moon was enveloping the land in an ethereal glow. The courtier remained under the friendly shadow of a grove of pine-trees. His eyes were cast upon the stately Catzu shiro (palace). It seemed as though the moon-rays had singled out the graceful old castle and was bathing it tenderly in a halo of soft light.

It was cold, not bitterly so, but sharply chill, as it is at night betwixt the winter and the spring. But unconscious of the chill, erect and graceful, the courtier leaned against a tree-trunk, his arms crossed over his breast, his eyes full of moist sentiment, drinking in the beauty of the night scene, which had an added enchantment for him, a man in love.

All about him, before, behind, and around him, graceful pine-trees raised their slender, pointed heads up to the silver light. In the distance, like a strange, white mirage set in the moonlit sky, a snow-capped mountain seemed hung as in mid-air. The grass beneath his feet was young and intensely soft, with dewy moisture upon it.

A nightingale on the tip of a tall bamboo sang with such passionate sweetness that it brought the lover out from the shelter of the shadow. Quivering with emotion, his soul responding and vibrating to the song of love, he strode into the light of the moon. Unmindful of the danger of his exposure to possible observation, he drew forth from the bosom of his haori a little roll of rice-paper. Once more he read it through, and yet once again.

My Lord,

I write this augustly insignificant letter to you, trusting that your health is good. Also the health of all your honorable relatives and ancestors.

"I have received your most honorably magnificent compliments. Accept my humblest thanks.

"Now I deign to write unto you, beseeching you to abandon so foolhardy a purpose as to follow me to my uncle's home. I would feign warn you that my uncle's guards are fierce and ofttimes cruel, and to one wearing the garb of a hostile clan, I fear they would show no mercy. Therefore I beseech you, do you pray abandon your honorable purpose.

"Also condescend to permit me to add, that if you must indeed truly attempt so hazardous an undertaking, I would beg to inform you, that though the grounds are surrounded by such great walls that I fear me not even a tailless cat might climb them, and also the gates are guarded by the fiercest samurai, nevertheless, on the south there is a small river. Mayhap you will hire a boat. Then do you come up this honorable river, keeping close to the shore, and I do assure you that you will discover a break in the south wall, which leads into the gardens surrounding the palace.

"My lord, my uncle's guards are not so vigilant before sunrise, as I myself have ofttimes remarked when I have arisen early of a morning and have looked from my casement, which is also on the south side of the palace, facing the river and the outlet thereto."

The nightingale paused in its song, and then broke out again, its long, piercing trill filling the night.

The lover returned to the shelter of the pine grove, and, throwing himself upon the grass, drew his cape close about him. Leaning his head upon his hand, he gave himself up to his dreams.

IV

The Lady Wistaria arose with the sun. Without waiting to pin back the long, silken hair which hung like a cloud of lacquer about her, she stole softly to the casement of her chamber.

The perfume which stole up to her was sweeter and stronger far than that wafted from the trees laden with the dews of the early morning. Yet the trees were bare of blossoms and would not bloom for a month to come. Nevertheless the ledge of Wistaria's casement was piled with the living spring blossoms of plum and cherry. She could not but caress them with her hands, her lips, her eyes, her burning cheeks. With little, trembling hands she searched among them and found what she sought—a scroll—a narrow, thin, wonderful scroll, long, yet only a few inches in width, with golden borders down the sides, and the faint, exquisite tracings of birds and flowers intertwined among the words that leaped up at her almost as though they had spoken. It was a poem to her—her grace, beauty, modesty, loveliness, its theme:

> *"A stately shiro was her home;*
> *In royal halls she shone most fair,*
> *From tiny feet to golden comb,*
> *In her sweet life what is my share?*
>
> *"Oh, lovely maid, my moon thou art;*
> *O Fuji san, thou hast my heart!"*

There were many other verses, but the Lady Wistaria was too much moved to have either the vision or the mind to read beyond the first stanza. As became her rank and the painful tuition of years, she should have pushed very deliberately the flowers from her sill and torn the scroll into ragged pieces, a chastisement prescribed by every etiquette for the temerity of a presumptuous lover.

But the Lady Wistaria did nothing of the sort. She gathered the flowers tenderly and took them in. Then she came back to the casement, and, leaning far out, gazed with piercing wistfulness out into the little garden below. For some minutes she waited, the patience of her caste fading away gradually into that of the impatience of her sex.

A voice beneath her casement! She leaned farther over. A young man's eager, glowing face smiled up at her like the rising sun. Again the Lady Wistaria forgot the training of years. Her trembling voice floated down to him:

"Pray you do consider the perils in which you place yourself," she implored.

"I would pass through all the perils of hell so I might reach you in the end," he fervidly whispered back.

"Oh, my lord, look yonder! See, the sun is pushing its way upward above the mountains and the hill-tops. Do you not know that soon my uncle's guards will pass this way?"

"Under the heavens there is nothing in all this wide world worthy as a gift for you, dear lady. That you have deigned to accept my honorable flowers and my abominably constructed poem has given me such strength that I am prepared to fight a whole army of guards. Ay! And to give up readily, too, my life."

"And if you love me," she replied, "you will guard with all your strength that life which you are so recklessly exposing to danger."

"Ah, sweetest lady, can it be true then that you condescend to take some concern in my insignificant existence?"

She made no response other than to pluck from the climbing vine about her casement one little half-blown leaf and drop it at his feet.

As he stooped to pick up the leaf a form interposed itself, and a half-grown man looked him steadily in the face. With a little cry the Lady Wistaria vanished from her casement.

Meanwhile the intruder, instead of being the aggressor, was defending himself against the flashing blade of the infuriated lover. Too proud to call for aid, the youth opposed to the lover found himself outmatched before the skill and fire of the other. So thinking caution better than valor, he flung his sword at the feet of the lover. The latter, picking it up by the middle, returned it to his opponent with a low bow of utmost grace. Then with one hand on his hip and the other holding his sword, he addressed the youth.

"Thy name?"

"Catzu Toro. And thine?"

"Too insignificant to be spoken before one who bears so great a name as thine," returned the other, bowing with satirical grace.

"How is that?" cried Catzu Toro—"insignificant? What, one in thy garb and with thy skill of swordsmanship?"

The victorious one, shrugging his shoulders imperceptibly, again bowed with a smile of disclaimer.

"May I be permitted," he said, "to put one question to you, my lord, and then I am perfectly prepared to give myself up to your father's guards, though not, I promise you, without a struggle, which I doubt not your vassals will long remember." And he blithely bent the blade of his sword with his two hands.

"Nay, then," cried the youth, impetuously, "You do me injustice. I am ready to swear protection to one who has acted so bravely as thou. But a question for a question, is not that fair?"

"Assuredly."

"Very well, then. You serve the Prince of Mori?"

"In a very humble capacity," returned the other, guardedly.

"In what capacity?" inquired the young Toro, quickly.

"Ah, that is two questions, and you have not even deigned to listen to my one."

"Speak," said the youth, curbing his curiosity and impatience.

"The Lady Wistaria—she is your sister?"

"My cousin," answered the other, briefly.

"Will you tell me how it is possible for one unfortunately attached to an unfriendly clan to pay court to your cousin?"

"Two questions, that!" exclaimed Toro, promptly, whereat they both laughed, their friendship growing in proportion to their good-humor.

"Now," said Toro, "I will answer whatever questions you may put to me, if you in return will only satisfy my mind concerning certain matters which I am perishing to know."

"A fair exchange! Good!"

"Then," said Toro, unloosening his own cape from his hips, "pray throw this about you, for I fear you will be observed by my father's samurai. Even my presence," he added, with a sigh, "could hardly protect you, for I, alas! am under age."

"Is it possible?" said the stranger, with such affected surprise that the boy flushed with delight.

"Now, my lord"—he hesitated, doubtfully, as though hoping the other would supply the name—"now, my lord, let me explain to you why I truly sympathize with you in your love for one who must seem impossible."

"Not impossible," corrected the lover, softly, thinking tenderly of the Lady Wistaria's fears for him.

"I, too," confessed Toro, "am in the same plight."

"What!" cried the lover, in dismay; "you also adore the lady?"

"No," replied Toro, shaking his head with sad melancholy; "but I have conceived the most hopeless attachment for a lady whom I may never dream of winning."

"Then I am much mistaken in you. I thought, my lord, that you were not only a brave man, but a daring knight."

"But you cannot conceive of the extremity of my case," cried the youth, piteously, "for consider: the lady I love not only belongs to our rival clan, but is already betrothed."

"Well, but betrothals have been broken before, my lord, and the days of romance and adventure are not altogether dead in the land."

"Ah, yes, that is true, but my rival is not only more powerful, but in every respect more prepossessing and attractive."

"Indeed? Well, all this interests me very much. Still, I must say, my lord, that though I am in the service of the Mori, I have not seen the knight or courtier who could prove so formidable a rival to you, either in graces or rank—for are you not the son of the great lord of this province?"

"And has not our neighboring lord a son also?"

"Wh—what!" cried the stranger, darting backward as though the youth had dealt him a sharp and unexpected blow; then scanning the other's face closely, "You do not mean—the Prince—?"

"Yes—the Prince Keiki. That swaggering, bragging, noisy roustabout, who bears so many cognomens."

"Hum!" said the other. "They call him the Prince Kei—, truly—"

"Yes," said the youth, jealously, "and also 'Hikal-Keiki-no-Kimi' (the Shining Prince Keiki)."

"You have told me strange news indeed," said the Mori courtier. "I did not know of the betrothal of our Prince. It is very sad, truly."

"Sad! To be betrothed to the Princess Hollyhock sad?"

"For you, my lord," replied the other, with a slight smile.

Toro doubled his hands spasmodically as he frowned with the fierceness of a samurai, that the other might not observe the soft moisture of a woman in his eyes.

"Now let me tell you a secret," said the stranger, touching his arm with confidential sympathy. "Upon my word, the Princess Hollyhock is not betrothed to the Prince Keiki."

"My lord, you do not say so! Are you sure?"

"As sure as I am that I am here now."

"Oh, the gods themselves must have sent you hither!" cried the youth. "Will you not accept my protection and constant aid in your suit for my cousin?"

"You are more generous than—"

"Your Prince, you would say," interrupted Toro, bitterly.

"—than the gods, I was about to remark," said the other, gravely. "Now let us form a compact. You on your side will promise me protection and aid here on your estates, and I will swear to you that you shall win and wed the Princess Hollyhock."

"I have a small house yonder, my lord," cried the impulsive youth, excitedly. "It is kept by my old nurse. Come you with me thither. I shall lend you whatever clothes you may require and you shall remain here as long as you wish. I will introduce you to my family as a friend—a student from my own university in Kummommotta. Then you can make suit to Wistaria, and, having once wed her, who can separate you, let me ask?"

"Not the gods themselves, I swear!" cried the other.

"And your name—what shall I call you?"

The courtier hesitated for the first time.

"My name is insignificant. It is a Mori name, and therefore dangerous in your province."

"You must assume another, then."

"Hum! Well, what would you suggest, my lord?"

"How will Shioshio Shawtaro do?"

"Not at all. It has a trading sound."

"Ho! ho! How about Taketomi Tokioshi?"

"Too imperious."

"Fujita Gemba?"

"No, no."

"Then do you choose yourself."

"My lord, waiving aside all our political differences, do you not think it would be loyal for me to take the name of one of my own people?"

"What, a Mori name? You are very droll, my lord. Why not keep your own name, then?"

"Ah, but it is not the Mori family name I wish to assume, but a surname."

"It might be dangerous."

"Oh, not without the family name and title attached. Suppose I take the name of Keiki?"

ONOTO WATANNA

"What! The name of my rival!"

"My prince, my lord," said the other, bowing deeply.

"Nevertheless my rival."

"Not at all; and if he were so, why not grant him this little honor, seeing you are to worst him in the suit for the lady?"

"That is true."

"The name will sound vastly different with another family name attached. Suppose I assume the name of Tominaga Keiki? That is somewhat different from Mori Keiki, is it not?"

"Somewhat."

"Then Keiki is my name."

"Kei—Very well. Let it be so."

V

The Lord of Catzu received his son's friend with hospitality dictated by his fat and good-humored nature, beseeching him to consider the Catzu possessions as his own. Keiki (as he had called himself), on fire to make use of the advantage he had now gained at the outset, was met by two unexpected obstacles.

In the first place, the Lady Wistaria was hedged about by an almost insurmountable wall of etiquette and form. Though the lover blessed all the gods for the privilege of being in her presence each day, yet, impetuous, warm-blooded, and ardent, he could not but chafe at the distance and the silence which seemed impassable between them.

Wistaria, he thought, might just as well have been a twinkling star in the heavens above him as to be placed at one end of the guest-room, her lips sealed in maidenly silence, while at the other end, in the place of honor, must sit he, the august guest, inwardly the burning lover. Between them interposed her honorable relatives and certain members of her uncle's household, separating the lovers with their extravagant politeness and words of gracious compliment and hospitality.

In the second place, the pilot upon whom he had relied for safe conduct through the icy forms which kept him from his mistress had deserted him perfidiously. Toro, the reckless and foolhardy, his imagination fed by the daring and sang-froid of the Mori clansman, his own heart aflame with as deep a passion as his friend's, had borrowed his dress and departed for Choshui, there to risk all chance of danger with the bravery, but without, alas! the wit, of the Mori courtier.

To offset these two hardships, the lovers saw a gift sent by the gods in the indisposition of the Lady Evening Glory. After the long and tedious journey from the capital, the lady, who was of a delicate constitution, retired to her apartments with a malady of the head and tooth. In point of fact, the Lady Evening Glory suffered from neuralgia. The lovers prayed that her illness might be long and lingering, though Wistaria, having besought her to keep to her bed as long as possible that relapse might be avoided, tempered her prayer with a petition to her favorite god that her aunt's illness might be unattended with pain.

With the Lady Evening Glory, the vigilant mentor of Wistaria, safely out of the way, the girl found no cause for despair. This was the reason she returned her lover's pleading and ofttimes reproachful glances with smiles, which, but for the joy of seeing them, he would have thought heartless. The joy of Wistaria's smile almost compensated for the pain of her lover's poignant surmise that her heart had no pity for the woes of her adorer.

And, indeed, at this time there was little else in the girl's heart save a singing joy, a rippling flutter of new emotions and thrills, which she, too innocent as yet to recognize their full import, cared only to welcome with delight, to encourage, to foster and enjoy to the uttermost.

Between Wistaria and her uncle there was utmost confidence and love. The young girl occupied that place in his heart which would have been held by the daughter denied him by the gods. The mantling flush, the ever-shining eyes, now bright with joy that would overflow, now moist with the unbidden tears that spring to the eyes when the heart is disturbed with an emotion more sweet than expression; these—the change which young love alone can produce in a maiden—he was quick to perceive.

The Lord Catzu's own marriage had been most romantic, and if his lady had lived down frigidly to the world, her husband at least had retained his sentimental remembrance of the adventurous escapades attending it.

Such were the opportunities of life to the daimio of a province at peace that, to all outward appearances, Catzu was too indolent, too listlessly, luxuriously lazy and preoccupied with his own pleasures to observe his niece's condition of heart. But the Lord Catzu, with all his placidity, was astute. Beneath his lazy eyelids his own small eyes missed little that passed before him.

In fact, it was not long before he became aware of the attachment between the young people. The courtier, he knew, bore an assumed name, for Toro had labored with awkwardness when he endeavored to invent a lineage for the friend whose appearance at the Catzu palace without the customary retinue of servants or retainers had convinced its lord that he had discovered a tinge of that delightful mystery which but added to the favor of the unknown in the eyes of the sentimental Lord of Catzu. In addition, it was the mode for young nobles of the realm to undertake courtship over an assumed name, so that an air of romance might be lent to their love affair. As to the young man's rank there could be no question, since his manners and breeding, his grace of person and charm of speech, were caste characteristic. Looking secretly with high favor upon the young man, Catzu considered how he might aid the lovers.

Slothful and deliberate in all he undertook, Catzu might provoke impatience, but his gradual accomplishment of his ends was gratifying. Just as he took his time in the serious business of life, so was he leisurely in the pursuit of his pleasures. As a consequence the lovers for a time were kept in an agony of waiting and suspense.

Keiki, maddened and irritated by the constant presence of the smiling Lord Catzu, who in his opinion stood between him and his heart's desire, once more fell to writing imploring letters and poems to the Lady Wistaria which made up in epithets of endearment what they lacked in rhetoric. He prayed her to find some means by which he might be with her alone, if only for a fraction of a minute. The one word "Patience," written upon a little china plate, so minutely that he could scarcely decipher it, was the reply brought by the Lord Catzu, with the information that the Lady Wistaria herself had painted the plate for their august guest.

Meanwhile Catzu, cognizant of every sigh, every appealing expression, every significant motion, laid his plans carefully for the impatient suitor's happiness. Certainly within the walls of the palace itself there was no hope of solitude for the lovers. Pretexts for out-door pleasure-parties were never wanting in the warmer season. Local fêtes, the birth of each new flower, family events—all these were sufficient invitation in themselves for such convivial parties as delighted the soul of the Lord of Catzu, and could not have failed in their chance opportunity for dual solitude.

At this time of the year, alas! there was neither snow nor moon nor flowers to serve a pretext. A series of heavy rainfalls, most distressing and persistent, was the only fugitive before approaching spring. Yet even the rain-gods have a limit to their tears, and, after all, the rains preceding the first month of spring are ofttimes the very means by which the land is cleansed ere it bursts into beauty and bud.

Not so interminable as it seemed to them was the lovers' waiting. Three short days—yet how long!—and then the sun which had struggled for ascendency over the troubled heavens rose up proudly triumphant. The thunders retreated into tremulous growls of defeat; the gray-black clouds rolled away before the blinding flashes of the sun-rays, flitting like ghosts before the dawn. An immense rainbow, spanning the entire heavens, sprang out of the skies, a signal of the sun-god's victory.

What mattered it that the land was barren as yet of flowers? The grass was green and the trees almost bursting in effort of emulation.

Catzu, having satisfied himself that the moisture on the grass was but the dew of spring, forthwith devised a small party. It consisted of his lady niece and the august guest of the household, who was graciously entreated to accompany them, and who accepted with an alacrity almost lacking courtesy.

With but two attendants, the party set out from the palace. Taking a small boat, they made a swift pilgrimage up the graceful river to a small island where a picturesque tea-house and gardens, with twenty charming geishas, made a fairyland for lovers.

To receive so early and unheralded a visit from the august lord of the province threw the geishas into a delighted panic of excitement. Their attendants were seen rushing hither and thither throughout the place, hastily making it suitable for the reception of the exalted guests.

Hastening down to the beach, the chief geisha herself apologized for the island's condition. The Lord of Catzu went to meet her. For his guest to be received without preparation, he explained to Keiki, would be unfitting. Consequently he begged him to remain on the beach, while he himself proceeded with the chief geisha to the tea-house to issue instructions.

The stolid and indifferent lackeys who had attended the party returned to the boat, where they fell into conversation with the oarsmen.

At last the lovers were alone.

For a long moment Keiki and Wistaria looked into each other's eyes. They were safe from all observation, for the gardens, and indeed the whole island, was of that rock-and-pebble-built variety favored by the Japanese. Behind and around them they were screened by quaint, grotesque rocks of natural form and immense size, carried from a mountain to this tiny island, placed there in miniature to simulate nature.

Nevertheless Keiki, the impatient and ardent, now at the crucial moment, had naught to say. He had confessed his love in his letters; she had admitted tacitly her own. Still they did not embrace, or even touch each other. Culture is strong in Japan, where also is the fire of love. So these two but looked into each other's faces, all their hearts' eloquent passion in their eyes. Wistaria's eyes did not fall before his tender gaze. Only a rose-red flush crept softly like a magic glow over the oval of her cheeks, tingeing her little chin while accentuating her brow's whiteness.

Without a word her lover dropped upon one knee, lifted the long sleeve of her kimono, and buried his face within its fabric.

Five minutes later, hand in hand, they were standing on the same spot. They were watching the river, swollen by recent rains, as it burst over the rocks beyond, bounding down the river-bed, rolling swiftly along, twisting, curving, and winding about the sinuous form of the island's shore, holding it in the grudging love of the water for the land. The water was blue-green in color, save where the sunbeams reflected its own light in glistening gleams of quicksilver, ever moving, ever playing, while the shores on either side threw shadows of their trees and rocks upon it. As it ran busily, merrily along, now and then lapping the shore and leaping to their very feet, it seemed a living thing which babbled and laughed with an inward knowledge of their joy, and also sighed and wailed with a prophetic undercurrent of coming woe.

The touch of their hands close clasped together made them tremble and quiver. Their eyes met to droop away and meet again in the vivid recognition of their own innocent happiness. They could not speak, because their hearts had laid claim to their lips and sealed them in a golden silence.

Then, after a long interval, Keiki found his voice. If he spoke of the flowing river at their feet, it was not the river itself that absorbed his mind, but because in it, as in all things beautiful in life, he now saw reflected the image of his beloved.

"The honorable river," he said, "flows high at this season, but before the summer dies it will be but a thin line, very still, very quiet."

"Yes," said Wistaria, tremulously, "but the lotus will spring up in its honorable waters, and if the river should continue to rise and rush onward like this, I fear me the water-flowers would perish and the noise of its ceaseless flow would drown the voices of the birds, which make the summer speak."

"That is true," said Keiki, "but when the summer passes then the flowers must still die, and we may no longer hear the singing of the birds. Then still the river will be silent and motionless—perhaps dead."

Keiki sighed with the moodiness of love attained. A gentle depression stole from him to the Lady Wistaria.

"Alas! my lord," she murmured; "it is so with all things in life that are beautiful. They vanish and die like the flowers of summer."

"Then," said Keiki, "swear by the god of the sea, by whose waters we now stand, that our love shall never die, and that for the time of this life, and the next, and as many after as may come, you will be my flower wife, and take me for your husband."

"By all the eight million gods of heaven, and by the god of the sea, I swear," said Wistaria.

VI

The air was balmy, the sky of a cerulean blue, the Dewdrop gardens were sweet with a strange charm and mystery all their own. Pebbles, sand, and stone, were cunningly displayed and mingled to create the illusion of an approach to a giant sea. In themselves the wondrous rocks were so fashioned as to form a landscape wherein neither foliage, trees, nor flowers were necessary. Small, grotesque bridges, made of rare rocks in their natural form, undefaced by hammer or chisel, spanned the miniature rivers, which, snakelike, crept and threaded their way in and out of the rock island. Suddenly appearing caverns yawned wide agape, only to show on closer approach that they were naught but gigantic rocks, hollow within.

Though the gardens were bare of foliage, yet the spot shone out like a jewel set in a magic river. Here was the perfection of art, that art so complete that without the very things of nature which seem necessary to a landscape, the cunning hand of man had fashioned the like out of the hard and jagged substance of stone and rock. And in this the hand of the Creator had aided, since the very rocks which formed this precious and priceless island, the pride and wealth of the Lord of Catzu, had been untouched by the tool of the artisan, for, having been gathered together from all parts of the country, they were planted in their natural form upon this island jewel.

Across the narrow river the shores were green, while beyond the silent surface of the moats the granite walls of the Catzu palace rose to a height, white and stately, tipped with golden towers and peaks that were taller than the cedars and the pines centuries old.

A stir of expectation thrilled the Dewdrop tea-house, and then a clear, shrill voice cried aloud:

"The Lady Wistaria passes into the honorable hall."

The twenty geishas prostrated themselves at my lady's feet. Gracefully she returned their courtesy, begging that they would serve her and her august guest, the Lord Tominaga Keiki, with refreshment.

The geishas, at this period in history occupying a high and dignified position in society, expressed their wish to serve their lady for the rest of their lives.

They brought the lovers fresh fruit, shining and luscious, and drink from a well of sweetest and purest water. Humbly apologizing for the honorable meanness of the refreshment, the chief geisha prayed that they would condescend to pardon her, for not even in her dreams had she imagined that the gods would favor her so soon in the season with such august guests.

But the lovers only smiled benevolently upon her, and insisted that never, no, never in all the honorable days of their lives, had they been blessed with more gracious refreshment. Whereat the geisha, with many low, grateful obeisances, retired.

The lovers sighed as in one breath.

"Once more alone," said Keiki, blissfully reaching over the little table and laying his own hands softly upon those of the girl. "How gracious the gods!"

"Of a truth," said Wistaria, smiling up at him; "we must repay the gods."

"We must, indeed. What shall we do? Build a thousand temples to— well, which one?"

"I consider!" quoth Wistaria, thinking very seriously. Then, suddenly, with a little, silvery laugh: "I have it. Let us deify my own august uncle. Is he not the god who befriends us?"

"Not consciously," said Keiki, "for I doubt not my Lord of Catzu would fume and curse me roundly did he know I took advantage of his honorable disposition to sleep."

Wistaria laughed softly.

"Now I am quite ready to swear," she said, "that of late my honorable uncle is perfectly conscious when he sleeps."

"Pray tell me," cried Keiki, starting.

The girl nodded merrily.

"Will you tell me, then, how it is possible for one to fall asleep in a small, rocking boat? Could you or I do so, my Lord Keiki?"

"Oh, not you or I; but your honorable uncle is divinely lethargic."

"Then, my lord, he is but lately afflicted."

"But I do not understand, then—you cannot mean—Oh no, it could hardly be so!"

"And why not, my lord? To me it seems that even the gods must needs favor you, much more an honorable mortal."

"Your uncle favor me! It cannot be possible."

"It is possible. It is so."

"But he has been acquainted with me only for the past six days."

"And does it take a year for favor to grow, when love—"

"Awakens in a day—an hour," finished Keiki, rapturously. "No, I can see how it is possible, but I could not at once realize my good-fortune. Moreover—"

Suddenly he broke off as a melancholy shadow crept across his brow, troubling his eyes. In a sudden depression he bent forward.

"My lord is troubled? Speak to me quickly."

"Troubled? Yes, that is so," Keiki sighed.

"Then do, I pray you, speak your trouble to me," said Wistaria. Immediately she threw herself at his feet, resting her hands upon his knees and raising her face upward to his. Keiki took her face in his hands. He looked deep into her love-lit eyes.

"Yes, I will tell you, little Wistaria," he said, "though I fear you are already acquainted with my secret."

"I am not, indeed," she denied.

"You do not know," he asked, sadly, "that I am of the Mori clan?"

"Of the Mori clan! And is that all that troubles you, my lord?"

"And is not that sufficiently serious?"

"No."

"But surely you must be aware of the feud existing between the Mori and Catzu clans?"

"My lord, you and I do not constitute the Mori and Catzu clans."

"You and I," he repeated, slowly, "do not constitute the Mori and Catzu clans." Then, after a silent moment: "Alas, my lady, I fear we do!"

Wistaria snatched her hands quickly from his and arose. Certainly he could not love her, she thought, if he allowed so small a thing as that to distress him.

"If that be so—if that is what you think, my lord, deign to inform me why you have condescended to make suit to me?"

"I was forced to make my suit in secret," he said, almost bitterly.

"But your love is honest, is it not?"

"Oh, my flower-girl, can you ask that?"

She was contrite in a moment. Once more she was at his feet, kneeling, and pressing both his hands with her little, slender, nervous fingers.

"Nay, then, do not look so sad, my Keiki. It troubles me that you should allow so silly a thing as the differences of our respective clans even for a fraction of a moment to come between us."

"They cannot truly come between us," was his fervid reply, "for no power on earth can actually separate us now. Are we not sworn to each other for all time—for all eternity?"

"Then why be so sad? You, who are so brave, cannot fear the dangers that may beset our union."

"No, no, it is not that. But—I sigh for the tears of others—our honorable ancestors and parents."

"Then do cease to sigh at once, if you please. Why, it is not such a terrible crime to marry a Mori, surely!"

"No, I hope not," said Keiki, smiling now.

"No, indeed, for my own honorable uncle committed that same fault."

"Fault?"

"And I believe that if we were to go to him, and tell him the honorable truth, he would gladly assist us."

"Not if he knew all," said Keiki, sadly. "No, he must know nothing yet."

"Indeed," said Wistaria, "I did not know the feeling of the Mori was so bitter against us, and I do assure you that in Catzu the prejudice exists not so much against your clan, as against your lord and prince."

"Alas, that is too true!" answered Keiki, half under his breath.

"Well, a courtier's loyalty to his Prince need not at all be shaken if he marry the insignificant niece of a rival clan. My own honorable father was of that very clan himself. Know you not that, my lord?"

Keiki groaned suddenly. Whereat the girl placed her hands on his shoulders and forced him to look into her eyes.

"My lord," she said, "do you know aught of my father's history?"

Slowly Keiki drew himself up from her clinging hands. Placing one arm close about her, he drew her to his breast.

"Let us no longer talk of these distressful matters."

"Nay, I have asked you a question. Do, I beseech you, answer me."

"What can I say?" His voice was very low.

"Tell me of my father—pray tell me," she implored, almost piteously.

"Of your father? But surely I can tell you nothing that you do not already know?"

"I know naught of my father, save that he was a Choshui samurai, and for some honorable offence was banished by that wicked and cruel Prince of Mori."

Keiki was silent.

"I have questioned every one about me—my uncle, his samurai, the very servants about the castle—but none will make answer to me, whether from ignorance or by command of those in authority over them, I know not. Do you, then, my lover, answer me."

"My little flower-girl, I do not know the offence of your honorable father, nor do I know why or wherefore he was sent into exile. I was but a child of five when this penalty came upon him."

"Then wherefore did you tremble and turn away your eyes when I spoke of my honorable parent?"

"Because I know that injury of some sort was wrought against your honorable parent by my—by the Mori, and since then so implacable an enmity exists between our families that nothing but blood alone can ever wipe away the stain. Think, then, of the wrong I do your father in loving his own daughter!"

"No, no—dear Keiki—it is no wrong, I do assure you. If there be a feud existing between my father and the Mori Prince, truly you and I, who are innocent, cannot be implicated in any way, and, indeed, it is not as if I were about to wed one of the Mori family itself, but—"

"In that case," he interrupted, quickly, "if I were indeed of this Mori family, what then?"

For a moment the girl recoiled, shrinking backward, and regarded him with frightened, shocked eyes.

"That—would—be—impossible," she said, and she shivered with apprehension.

"If it were possible?" said the lover, hoarsely.

"It could not be," she insisted, "for the Mori princes are proud and ill-favored, while you—"

"While I?"

"—You are more beautiful than the sun-god."

"But you have not answered me. Suppose it were—Prince Keiki, the heir of Mori, who wooed you?"

"I cannot, my lord. Oh, the Prince is otherwise occupied than in wandering with love," replied Wistaria, smiling at the thought. "Why, he is the head of a wicked party of Imperialists, I have ofttimes heard my uncle declare, and is the most cunning and base fermenter of intrigue against our august Shogun in the whole empire. Indeed, he has no time or inclination for dallying with love."

"But—if I were indeed he, what then?"

"Why, then—then," said the girl, slowly rising, and regarding him with shining eyes, "then still I would say, 'Take me.' What have we to do with the quarrels of our ancestors, the wrongs or the rights of our honorable parents? You and I are under the sheltering wings of the god of love. We recognize no law of country, lord, or kindred. Let us go into the mountains together and find refuge in a cottage where we can live and love in peace."

"Oh, thou dear one!" he cried.

"But why suggest such a horrible possibility?" she continued, tremulously. "Thou art not that base and traitorous Prince? Thou art—"

"Thy love! That is all," he said.

VII

In the joy and sunshine of Wistaria's nature, which would have driven sadness from the soul of a hermit, Keiki's melancholy was evanescent. Her lover's fears at the mere possibility of their being forced apart were soon dissipated by her.

A week passed—sped like so many minutes. The pale green of the spring grass was deepening in hue and the trees were in leaf. The lovers lingered in the paths that led down to the little boat-house, whence each day they sailed slowly down the river to the rock island. There in the lazy, drifting boat, the drowsy Lord of Catzu dosed back against his padded seat, while the lovers looked into each other's eyes, or furtively pressed each other's hands.

Meanwhile their short hours of happiness were being slowly ticked off by the god of love, at whose shrine they had offered the whole wealth of their hearts. The days of their joy were numbered. That strange honey of bliss they sipped so greedily was soon to be snatched from their lips.

The Lady Evening Glory was recovering slowly from her indisposition. Because the lady herself had contracted a most wilful and romantic marriage, she was perhaps the more suspicious of the culpability of others. She trusted neither youth nor maid, but Wistaria bore the weight of her suspicions.

While gossip and idle chatter had stolen into the lady's chamber concerning the charms and grace of their whilom guest, Wistaria's almost extravagant solicitude for her set my lady at first to thinking, and then to acting.

The Lady Evening Glory was no believer in the worship of the sun. Nevertheless, some garrulous maid having carried to her the innocent remark of her niece that she enjoyed viewing the rising of the sun, a few mornings later found the Lady Evening Glory not only arising before the sun, but wending her way through the silent corridors of the palace until she was before the chamber of the Lady Wistaria. Without so much as a tap for admission, she softly pushed aside the sliding shoji.

With the keenest of lover's ears. Wistaria heard the faint shir-r-r made by the sliding doors. In the same instant down went her own shutter. So when the Lady Evening Glory entered the chamber she found her niece sitting on the floor, her back set stiffly against her casement shutter, and a deep rosy coloring all over her face. Her guilty eyes fell before the cold glare of her august aunt.

The next thing the Lady Evening Glory's sharp eyes fell upon were the flowers. They lay in a great, tumbled mass all about the Lady Wistaria. There was no mistaking the meaning of those tell-tale blossoms. The Lady Evening Glory's lips became a thin, pursed line.

"The flowers? Whence came they?"

"From the honorable garden," answered Wistaria, trembling.

"There is no tree in all the garden with blossoms in full bloom. They are only commencing to bud, and will not blossom before the first of April."

To this undeniable fact Wistaria made no response.

"Answer when thou art spoken to," prompted her aunt, sharply.

"My lady—I do not know what to say."

"Then you leave me to my own conjectures. You have a lover."

"Oh no, indeed!"

"What! Flowers fresh with the morning dew in your chamber, and you with your hair unbound! Pray when did it become an honorable fashion for ladies of our rank to venture out to purchase flowers before sunrise—and in such scanty attire?"

"My aunt, you are killing me."

"Your health appears to me to be far from feeble."

"I am innocent of any wrong," said Wistaria, with a flash of spirit.

"Then you will not object to inform me who presented you with these flowers?"

"An honorable gentleman," said Wistaria.

"Indeed! And what is this honorable gentleman's name, may I ask?"

Wistaria hesitated. Then a sudden idea came to her. She smiled mysteriously.

"But I do not know his name," she said, which was quite true, as she was unaware of her lover's true name.

"You do not know the name of your lover!" cried her aunt, incredulously.

"Indeed, I wish I did."

"Yet you accept his gift! You are entirely without shame, girl!"

"Oh, lady! the flowers were so beautiful I could not resist them."

"Beautiful!" shrieked her aunt. "And because flowers are beautiful, is that an excuse for accepting the love of some impudent adventurer?"

"Accepting the love!" repeated Wistaria, faltering.

"Yes, indeed, and you need not pretend ignorance of my words. They are quite clear to you, I have no doubt."

"But—"

"You are well aware that by accepting the flowers you also accept his despicable love, and practically betroth yourself to this fellow. He shall be flogged for his impertinence."

"Flogged!" cried Wistaria, becoming very pale.

"Flogged, I repeat," said her aunt, coldly.

Wistaria shivered with apprehension. She had not until now grasped the real seriousness of her position.

"Your father," continued the Lady Evening Glory, "shall be sent for this day. We shall see what those in authority over you think of your conduct."

The aunt had but to mention the father to fill Wistaria with fear. She sprang to her feet and stood trembling among the scattered blossoms.

"I am guilty of no wrong, I do assure you, my lady aunt. But I arose to enjoy the sun's awakening, and—and I did find these honorable flowers on my sill, and indeed they spoke to me of—of the coming summer, and so many things, dear aunt, that I was fain to take them in."

"Then do, pray, my little dove, inform me what you know concerning this presumptuous fellow who placed them on your sill."

"Oh, my lady, he is indeed honorably noble."

"Indeed!"

"I do assure you. He is—" she broke off, painfully debating in her mind the wisdom of confessing the truth to her aunt.

"He is—?" repeated her aunt.

"Our own august guest."

"Ah—ho! Then, if that is so, you spoke a lie just a moment since when you said you did not know your lover's name."

Wistaria attempted to speak, but broke off, faltering and stammering piteously.

"May I inquire, then," continued her aunt, relentlessly, "whether you are unacquainted with the honorable name of our august guest?"

"Oh, my lady, I do believe that—that he assumed another—only— just for the innocent romance of wooing me under an assumed title."

"So! And pray how comes it, then, that my son's honorable guest should also happen to be your lover? If in order to woo you he came hither under an assumed name, then it would seem that you had some previous acquaintance with him?"

ONOTO WATANNA

"He followed our cortege from Yedo, madame," confessed the unhappy girl.

"What! You do not mean to tell me that he is that insolent Mori courtier of whom I heard only after my arrival home?"

Wistaria pressed her hands tightly together. She seemed overcome. Then suddenly she raised her head with almost defiant bravery.

"He is of the Mori clan, madame," she said.

"The Mori clan!" The lady's voice rose shrilly. "How came he, then, to enter our grounds?"

"He came, my lady, by the south river, where there is a break in the wall."

"But how could he know this? Answer me that at once."

"I—"

"Will you deign to inform me whether you condescended so far as to answer the love-letters of this young man, for I have no doubt he favored you with many?"

"I wrote only one insignificant reply," said Wistaria.

"And what, pray, did you say in this reply?".

"I implored him to follow us no farther. I besought him to give up the impossible exploit of entering our grounds, and, knowing what would be his fate if he attempted to do so, I also informed him that if he must indeed enter, to do so by way of the south river, that a portion of our grounds ran down to this honorable river and was unprotected by the walls, which otherwise surrounded us on all sides."

"So it seems that you have betrayed to our enemy the weakness of our condition?"

"Not an enemy, lady! He is not, indeed."

"And may I ask how your redoubtable lover, having gained entrance to our grounds, also contrived to wedge his way into the palace and become a guest of our hospitality?"

"Toro—" faltered Wistaria.

Her aunt's face flamed.

"Toro, he discovered him the first morning, and—and—they became friends at once."

"My son!"

"Oh yes, madame, and on my two knees, I am prepared to beg you to show him mercy."

"Keep your knees, my young lady, to beg mercy for yourself. You may have need of it ere long," said her aunt, with chilling irony.

VIII

From the insinuations and threats of the Lady Evening Glory it might seem as if Wistaria's lover were in imminent danger, and that the Catzu family might be expected to hasten instantly to cast him out from their province or have him imprisoned as a trespasser and impostor. But Japanese craft is more subtle. Besides, the right of judgment lay in the hands of the father of Wistaria, who was her natural and legal guardian. It was necessary, therefore, that the young man should, for the time being, gather no suspicion of their discovery. Consequently the Catzu family redoubled their expressions of good-will and friendship for their guest, while the only one who could have warned him was placed where she was helpless to do so.

With excessive sweetness, the Lady Evening Glory informed the courtier that she had heard such good reports of him from her honorable husband that she had risen prematurely from her bed of sickness in order to greet him and assure him of her solicitation for his comfort and pleasure during his stay in Catzu.

All these marks of friendship and compliment from the honorable lady of the house, besides the increased cordiality of the Lord of Catzu, would have been very delightful to the lover, but for the fact that almost coincident with the return to health of her aunt it was announced that the Lady Wistaria was unable to leave her apartments because of a sudden illness. The lover, therefore, in an agony of apprehension for the health of his mistress, had no heart or ears for the words of compliment pressed upon him by her family.

He spent his time roving restlessly about the grounds of the palace in the neighborhood of Wistaria's casement, but the blinds were drawn tightly, morning, noon, and night, and there was only the memory of the girl's exquisite face at the window to torture the lover.

The arrival of Shimadzu, the father of the Lady Wistaria, created no stir in the Catzu palace. He came silently at night. If any of the servants or members of the household knew of his presence they were dumb concerning the matter. The lover, consequently, was wholly unaware of his coming.

Shimadzu was closeted for some hours with his sister and brother-in-law. The Lady Evening Glory was bitter against her niece. Not merely the fact of the indelicate and unconventional manner of the courtship, nor even the fact that the lover was a member of their rival clan, and through his residence among them must have acquired information concerning their province which would be of value to his prince—not these things infuriated her so much as the thought that her son, the pride and joy of her life, the heir of Catzu, had been led by this stranger into an undertaking both perilous and shameful, the outcome of which was most uncertain.

The Lord of Catzu was milder and more lenient towards the guilty parties, possibly realizing in his inmost soul a measure of the responsibility. He endeavored to palliate their offence.

As for Shimadzu himself, he had not one word to say. He listened to the separate speeches of his sister and brother-in-law, and when they had concluded he simply requested that his daughter be ordered into his presence at once.

Wild-eyed and trembling, Wistaria was brought in. Gone from her face, pale and drawn with the intensity of her sufferings, was all the sun. During the three days preceding the arrival of her father she had been locked up alone in an interior room of the palace. No one had approached save her august aunt, who brought food with her own hands, and whose absolute silence inspired her with a great dread. She would speak no word, or even deign to look at the unhappy girl. Wistaria, rendered frantic by her fears for her lover, had ofttimes thrown herself at her aunt's feet, piteously beseeching that she would enlighten her as to the fate of her lover. But the Lady Evening Glory would shake her skirts icily and contemptuously from her grasp, to retire without a word of response.

Now Wistaria prostrated herself before the parent who had always inspired her with such incomprehensible fear. He motioned her to be seated, though he himself remained standing. Mutely, mechanically, she obeyed him.

For a moment there was silence. The deep-set eyes of the father looked out at the young girl, noting the piteous tremble of the hands, the small, bowed head, the down-drooped eyes which dared not meet his own, and all the other evidences of her sufferings. Whatever the thoughts of the father, whether merciful or cruel, his impassive face revealed not his inner feelings. In some strange way this samurai seemed steeled against the pain of the world itself. Suddenly he spoke, his hollow voice smiting with a shock the frail, highly strung girl.

"My daughter, had you a mother to love and guide you, you would not now be unhappy."

He paused to note the effect of his strange words—strange because of the lack of emotion and sympathy that should have accompanied them. Wistaria raised her head painfully, but she did not speak.

"Therefore," continued her father, "I wish to inform you that it is because of an enemy that you are now motherless, and therefore misguided."

"An enemy?" repeated Wistaria, dully.

"And it is to take my revenge upon this enemy that I am now about to impose a certain duty upon you which may at first seem repugnant. Before I do so, however, I wish to remind you that you come of a proud and heroic race, my daughter, no member of which has ever faltered in his duty. I would therefore, my daughter, much rather see you strong and fearless than weak and trembling, as you now appear."

Raising herself bravely, with a superhuman effort the girl grasped at her strength of will.

"My weakness, honorable father, is but physical. Speak your august will with me," she said.

"That is well," returned the samurai, briefly. "I have a few questions first of all to put to you. I need not say that I expect truthful answers, and will tolerate no prevarication."

The girl bowed her head with a certain dignity of submissiveness.

"Of what rank is your lover?"

Wistaria trembled.

"I do not know," she replied, in a low voice.

"He has not mentioned his rank to you?"

"Only that he was of honorably insignificant rank."

"Humph! Well, that is but a natural reply. What is his appearance?"

For a brief moment a gleam of strange pride came over her face. She pressed her little hands passionately together.

"Oh, my father, he is honorably noble, I do assure you. He possesses—"

"I did not ask for a rhapsody upon his merits," interrupted the samurai, coldly. "However, I am satisfied as to his rank."

A tear fell softly upon her little hand. Feeling, rather than seeing, her father's irritation, she brushed it away impatiently, trying vainly to appear brave.

"Now," resumed Shimadzu, half to himself, "if he is of noble rank it follows that he is close to the Mori family. Very good."

He turned to his daughter.

"He is a good Imperialist?"

"He is honorably loyal," she replied.

"Loyal to his prince, you mean, or his party?"

"Surely to both. He could not be otherwise. He is a brave and true gentleman, my father."

"Very well, I have no more questions to ask you. I shall now outline to you the duty I have prepared for you. You are ready to obey my will?"

"In all things, honored parent."

"That is well. I commend you for your filial words. First of all, I desire all possible information concerning the young heir of Mori."

"But—" she faltered, "how is it possible for me—?"

"Your lover," said her father, quickly, "is a Mori courtier. There is no doubt he will give you all the information I require."

"Oh, then, my father," she cried, clasping her hands together, "you will be lenient towards him, will you not? You will permit him to see me?"

"I have nothing against your lover," said her father, with slight irritation.

"Oh, father!" In a moment her face was aglow with hope and happiness.

"I advise you to listen to me," he rejoined, coldly.

"Speak! speak, august father! I will follow your commands faithfully, joyfully."

"I wish to know the nature of this prince, his habits, his mode of life, and the esteem in which he is held by his people. Once you have learned these facts, you must secure for me specific details concerning his political schemes against the Shogun."

Gradually Wistaria had risen to her feet. She had grown strangely pale. Her eyes were frightened and apprehensive.

"You desire," she repeated, slowly, as though she scarce comprehended the words—"you desire to know the secrets of—of his honorable party?"

"Exactly."

"You desire," she began to repeat, "to know the secrets—"

"More than that."

"More. You—you—my father, you would not injure his—his party?"

"Your apprehension, my lady, for a hostile party, is strange for one of your training. Are you, then, turned Imperialist?"

"No. I have no fear for myself, my lord. But he—he—You must understand, my lord, he believes in—loves his honorable party— whether right or wrong. I would not injure it because of his sake."

"I have had enough of this weakness, my daughter, and you must admit I have been patient. To relieve your mind, however, of one thing, I will inform you that I have no designs against either this young man or his party."

"Oh, you lift from my heart, my honored parent, a weight too heavy for me to bear."

"Pugh! It seems you are determined not to listen to my orders."

"Speak at once. I will not again interrupt you."

"Very good. While I have said I have nothing against this Imperialist party, I am, nevertheless, desirous of knowing all their plans and secrets. It will be your duty, therefore, to ascertain these for me. Do not interrupt—" as she made as if to speak. "You would say your lover is too loyal to betray his party secrets, even to you. Then you will use your wit to compel him to do so."

"I—I will do so," she replied, drearily.

"That is not all. I wish you to force your lover into betraying some scheme or intrigue of his prince which would, if brought to the attention of the Shogun, implicate him criminally. Now I have arrived at my chief desire—in other words, I wish to accomplish the ruin—the death of the Prince of Mori."

Wistaria's head swam in vertigo. She scarce could think or feel. Only one horrible thought hammered itself into her mind. By the cajolery and arts of a false woman she was to assist in the betrayal of the prince to whom her lover had sworn allegiance. It was revolting, cruel, horrible. The mere thought of it made her head whirl in dizziness.

When she attempted to speak, her words escaped her slowly in gasps.

"I can—not—do—that!"

A terrible expression came into her father's face.

"You dare defy my authority?" he shouted.

"Oh, my father, put upon me any other task but this. It is base, cruel, cruel. And I—I am only a weak woman—"

"That is true. Do not, then, I advise you, attempt to pit your weakness against my strength. If you are so lacking in all those qualities admirable in a woman and a daughter of a noble race, I shall take means to force you to do your duty."

A sudden wave of courage swept over her. She ceased to tremble, though the samurai was fierce and menacing. There sprang into her eyes a light of defiance.

"You have reminded me, my father, that I come of a race of proud and heroic men. Then let me tell you that I, too, am conscious of possessing the intrepid blood of my ancestors, and that you can force me to do nothing against my will."

As she spoke she had backed slowly across the room, away from her father, as though retreating from a blow. Now she stood against the wall, her arms spread out on either side, the hands clutching the partition.

"In ten minutes I shall show you, my lady," said her father, between angry, clenched teeth, "the fate of one who dares defy her honorable parent."

"Do so," was her astonishing response. "Kill me, break all my honorable bones, my lord. We all must suffer and die!"

"You are too quick to choose your method of punishment, my lady. I have a more subtle means of teaching you the duty of a child to its parent. Do not imagine that I shall kill your body. It is your mind and heart I shall crush."

"What do you mean, my lord?"

"You will understand, my lady, when your lover is paying with his life for—"

"Oh no, no, no, no!" she cried, wildly, her hands groping through blinding emotion as though she would push away from her some horror too awful for utterance. "No, no, no!"

She fell down at her father's feet, burying her face in the folds of his hakama, her hands clutched about it frantically. "Oh, my father—no, no, no!"

She could say no more.

"You will obey my commands?" inquired the father, bending over her.

"Yes, yes—oh, my lord—anything on earth you may command. Only spare him, I beseech you, I pray to you, as I would to a god!" She fell to moaning and crying with the weakness of hysteria, no longer brave, defiant.

He raised her not ungently. Holding her hands firmly, he looked sternly into her face.

"Listen to me, my daughter. The task may seem to you horrible. It should not be so. It is a righteous, holy cause you serve. I have sworn to the dead, pledged myself, to encompass a certain vengeance, which must not escape me now. I have lived for no other purpose. If I have seemed a cold, unfeeling father, stern, unsympathetic, and unloving, it is because I have a mission in life greater than that of a father. It is you who must help me to attain this ambition. Vengeance—honest, righteous vengeance—for a wrong done me and mine is a holy cause. No Japanese girl can regard it otherwise. The Prince of Mori is our bitter enemy. We must accomplish his undoing—his death!"

"Yes, yes," she said, between her chattering teeth; "and you will not harm *him*?"

"I repeat I have nothing against this man. It is his prince whose proud spirit I will break! Kill!"

"Yes, yes—only *his* prince—the old prince. You wish me to kill him? Yes, I will do so."

"No; it is the young prince who must die—the son of the Prince of Mori. Do you not understand that I accomplish a more complete revenge by compassing the death of him who is the salt of his life?"

"Yes, yes; I see it clear. I must kill the innocent. Ah-h! Oh, it is cruel, cruel!"

She was weeping brokenly, piteously at his feet again, her physical strength quite gone.

The samurai leaned over her.

"Soon, my daughter, you will have regained your strength and will. From your attitude of a little while ago I am made aware that you are possessed of such qualities as might impel you to attempt to betray your father. Be assured that you shall be given no opportunity for doing so. For your own good I would advise you to lay the honorable force of repression upon your disturbed spirits, and bring yourself to do that which I have set for you with completeness and swiftness. In this way you will render a service to your father and family, and save the life of this man you love."

IX

April danced lightly over the land. Merrily she flung her rainbow showers of sweetest water upon the earth, the trees, the fearsome grass which March had coaxed in vain to do more than peep its head above the soil. Now the land was covered with a mantle so soft and tender that its young life seemed a thing that it were wanton to crush beneath the foot.

Early, early in the morning, before the birds and flowers had cocked up their little heads to seize the first sun-kiss, a lover stood in a garden all made of gently sloping hillocks, crowned with trees whitened, as if frost-laden, with the full bloom of the cherry and plum. And the lover's voice called softly and tenderly to his lady's casement:

"Lady Wistaria! My sweetest Wistaria!"

At first there was no response. Moving nearer the casement, he called again:

"Sweetest, dearest one, will you not come to your window for a minute—but a fraction of a minute?"

Softly a hand slid back the shoji—a slender, small, expressive hand of perfect form and contour, and then a young girl's face appeared at the opening. Her eyes were very dark, and infinitely, intensely sad in expression. Indeed, one might almost wonder whether their very brightness was not caused by the dews of unshed tears. She was pale. There was no color in her face at all, save that of her red lips.

So pale and ethereal she seemed to her rapturous lover that, for a moment, he was filled with an eerie fear—was she mortal, or one of those fragile spirits who abide on the earth for a season only? Then, all in a moment, her eyes meeting those of her lover, the sadness of the night passed from her like a shadow which is vanquished by the sunlight. An instant later she was again pale.

"Speak to me at once," implored the lover, "for but a moment since I thought you a spirit. Dearest one, assure me that my passion is not in vain, and that my eyes deceive me when they fancy that yours are sad."

Her voice faltered and trembled at first. Gradually she steadied it.

"My honorable eyes," she said, "are not always faithful mirrors of my heart. Yes, indeed, you are deceived, my lord. Look again. Surely you will see that—that they do smile."

"Yes," he replied, regarding her somewhat wistfully, "it is true. They do smile, and yet—" He hesitated. "You do not appear happy, Fuji-wara."

A strange little laugh escaped her lips. But she made no reply. She had turned her eyes from his, staring out before her. As the trouble deepened in the lover's eyes, he reached up, touching very gently the small white hand on the sill. The light touch of his hand startled her. Before he could speak she had recovered herself, leaning farther over to him. Her words sounded strangely harsh.

"My lord, do let us resume our conversation concerning this brave cause to which you adhere."

He flushed warmly.

"It seems incongruous," he replied, after a moment, "that a tender maiden should be interested in political conflicts."

"That is very unkind, my lord. You do not credit me, then, with any other quality, apparently, than that of pale softness. Indeed, my vanity has saved me from the knowledge that the gods have been most unkind."

"Nay, do not speak so," he tenderly chid her. Of late he had chafed not a little at her persistent waiving aside of all tenderer subjects to discuss those of larger import to men alone.

"Well, then," she persisted, "say that I am capricious, whimsical, what you will. But do, pray, humor me, and if I find it necessary"—she stammered over her words—"if I find it interesting to discuss such matters, pray allow me to do so."

"Do so, then, at once, dear one! I am all ears to listen and all tongue to reply."

"Pray tell me, then, are you truly an Imperialist at heart, or merely so in name because you are a Mori?"

"Pray tell me where my insignificant sympathies should lie, and there I swear to you shall they be."

She protested that he but begged her question. Did he, then, consider, because she was but a weak maiden, that her interest in such a matter must needs be a slight thing? Was she not herself a daughter of a samurai, and did not the flame, the fire of patriotism glow unceasingly in her breast also?

"Dear Wistaria," entreated the lover, "I pray you do not disturb your gentle bosom with these questions which are meant for soldiers, not for maidens."

"Nay, then," she replied, and there were tears in her voice now, "why will you persist so? You are quite wrong, too. Let me repeat: I am the daughter of a family whose women have had their honorable share in the affairs of the nation."

"True, but your house has stood always on one side only. They have never deigned even to hear the argument, the pious, patriotic cry of the other side."

"My house! Well, my lord, and am I a house?"

He kissed the slender hand on the window ledge. It reached just to his lips.

"Nay, I swear you are a goddess. It could not be possible that one so good and fair would favor an evil cause."

"Evil? Ah, then, my lord, is the cause of my house an evil one?"

He looked up into her eyes earnestly.

"I should be a traitor, my lady, did I take advantage of the friendly hospitality your house has offered me to repay it by sowing seeds of mischief."

"But if the seeds were not mischievous, my lord? If they were worthy and good?"

He dropped her hand abruptly, and paced for a time up and down the small grass-grown walk beneath her window.

In the shadow of the room behind the Lady Wistaria another face appeared for the space of a moment only. Long, lean, cadaverous it was, wherein fierce eyes burned like living coals. With a shudder, Wistaria clutched her hand over her heart. Back to her casement came the lover.

"My sweetest girl, do not let us discuss so melancholy a subject."

Impatient to speak with her of other matters nearer his heart, the lover let full, passionate appeal shine in his eyes. Wistaria's paleness deepened, if that were possible. Her eyes grew humid with repressed sadness. Her voice trembled and broke in spite of her words.

"Melancholy, my lord? Nay, you would treat me as a child. You would turn my heart from a lofty subject with the graceless remark that it is too melancholy for me."

"Lady, I would turn your heart to the holiest of all subjects on earth."

"Ah, what is that, dear Keiki—No, no, no! Pray excuse my honorable rudeness. Do, pray, my lord, rather perceive my intense curiosity in the matter of which we have spoken. Then when you have enlightened me, speak whatever you will, my lord. I will listen."

"And concerning what am I to enlighten you?"

"The question which cuts our country into two bitter factions, each defiant and warlike towards the other."

Into the lover's face there crept vague, baffled perplexity mirroring the thought beyond. Coquetry, or desire for political truth—which swayed his mistress? If the former, there was no combating it; if the latter, then—why then he would speak her true. He said:

"Will you tell me, then, whom you have been taught to regard as the ruler of Japan?"

"Why, our good Shogun Iyesada," she returned, promptly.

"Yet he is not so regarded by every one in Japan."

"Why is that?"

"Because there are many who would see our rightful sovereign, our divine Emperor, upon the throne."

"But, my lord, his Imperial Majesty is, indeed, already upon the throne, is he not?"

"Only nominally. I fear, my lady, that you have not read the *Dai Nihon Shi* of the Prince of Mori?"

"No, but I am much interested in it."

"The history," continued the young man, with vehement bitterness, "was purged repeatedly by the Yedo censor of the Shogun. It dared to speak the truth to the people. I do assure you it was not destroyed, however, before it had done its work well."

"How? Pray do tell me all about it."

"Have you never heard that pious—fanatical, if you will—cry, a barely half-muffled war-cry now, 'Daigi Heibunor!'" (the King and the subject).

His voice rose with a growing passion. Into his eyes leaped the gleam of the patriot.

An exclamation escaped the lips of the young girl.

"Oh, my lord, do not speak so loudly. I would feign warn you. I—I—"

She broke off in her agitation. But her apparent fear for him only filled her lover with a great joy. His voice softened.

"Fuji-wara, will you suffer yourself to listen hereafter to a confessed traitor?"

"Dear lord, traitor to the wrong?"

"Oh, dearest girl, can it actually be that you sympathize with our noble cause?"

"I—I—Tell me, do, pray tell me, with whom does the young Prince of Mori sympathize?"

"Oh, the rascal is a descendant of the Mori of whom I spoke just now."

"And an adherent to his views?"

"Possibly."

"You do not know for a fact," she urged, tremulously, "just to what party the Prince does adhere?"

"My lady," replied the lover, with some constraint, "the Prince has his pride of caste. He is also not without the inherited germs of patriotism in his soul."

"And still they do say that he is as silly as a butterfly, and so given to frivolity that his head can hold no serious thought."

"I do assure you," replied the other, flushing warmly, "that our prince is not all he may seem."

"My lord, I have conceived the most overwhelming interest in this young Prince Mori."

"Indeed!" The young man started back in humorous dismay. The girl smiled now, a little, dreary smile.

"Be assured, my lord, that the interest is not of a sentimental nature. But it would seem that the young Prince was surely born for a great purpose."

"Yes?" inquired the other, eagerly.

"And that is, to follow in the steps of his honorable ancestor."

"Oh, dearest girl, you fill my soul with joy! I am ready to swear that your sweet heart beats for the right—the noble cause to which—"

"The Prince Mori is sworn?" she interrupted, quickly.

"Ay! and all the patriotic sons of Japan!"

"And what do these sons of Japan propose to do? What are the plans of the Prince Mori?"

"My lady!"

"Pray, why do you start so, Keiki-sama?"

"You ask a weighty question with the same lightness you would bestow if inquiring about the weather!"

"Then the tones of my voice do me injustice."

"Wistaria, I swear I will not speak another word on this subject. No—not even to you."

"But—"

"No, no. I swear I will not."

"My lord—"

"Did I arise an hour before the sun, think you, to preach politics to my mistress?"

"You recall the hour to me now. It seems I must bid you farewell. My maid even now is tapping on my door. Do, pray then, depart."

The young man appeared cut to the heart at the parting. He sighed so deeply that Wistaria could not bear to gaze upon him, and, conscious of the impatient presence within, she drew her windows back hastily and shut out the sight of her lover from her. Then she faced her father within.

"You have heard all, honored parent?"

"Everything."

"You are a witness of my continued efforts. I fear we have learned all there is to know."

"Your opinion was not asked," replied the father, coldly. "Your services are all I require. You will resume them to-morrow."

The Lady Wistaria prostrated herself before her parent with the utmost humility.

"I am prepared to obey your august will in all things," she murmured, in the most filial and submissive of voices.

X

The aged castle moat was darkly melancholy, though its banks on either side were beautiful with the damp grass and the meeting willow and wistaria. Cold, still, and deep were its waters. At night it seemed grewsome and uncanny, perhaps because of the tragedy of its history, which every Catzu courtier knew. Even in the bright sunlight its beauty was seductively sad, for its dark waters were covered with white lotus, mingled with red and purple, with golden hearts, whose little cups each held one drop of dew—a glistening tear.

Wandering dejectedly along the banks of the old moat, Keiki vainly sought in his mind for some clew to the phenomenal change in his mistress. Though at times her eyes seemed drowned in tears of tenderness, more often they were coldly glassy. Her conversation, too, was spasmodic, devoid of all endearment, and of a sort alien to lovers. When he had first seen her after the illness which had kept her from his sight for some days, he had lost all self-control in the joy of beholding her once more. In ardent imagination he revived the memory of those dream-days on the little rock island of the twenty geishas, but though she appeared to have recovered her health, she no longer accompanied him upon such excursions. Indeed, she was rarely seen in the Catzu palace, except on the formal occasions of the guest-room. Keiki had been forced to content himself with those early morning meetings at her casement, so brief, so unsatisfactory. For she no longer murmured shy words of love and happiness. She talked, instead, of ridiculous matters, the politics of the country!

Nevertheless, through her apparent sympathy for this cause so close to the heart of the young man, she had revivified those thrills of patriotism which, for the nonce, he had pushed aside to devote all his heart and mind to the sweeter employment of loving.

In a moment of enthusiasm, only two days before, he had confided to her the far-reaching plans of the Mori princes for their country. She had begged him with tears in her eyes to tell her of them; then, before he had half finished, she had entreated him wildly to tell her no more, and the next instant, piteously, tremblingly, begged him to continue. And then as he went on she had dropped her head upon her arms and buried her face from his sight. Her emotion had thrilled him. At the moment he could have fallen on his knees, beseeching her to do something to hasten their marriage so that he might return to Choshui to do his part in this noble cause. Before he could speak, however, she had raised her face and gazed for a moment upon him with such an expression of penetrating agony and appeal that he had sprung towards her, hastily crying out her name, "Wistaria! Wistaria!"

A moment later she was gone. The following morning he had waited in vain in the garden beneath her casement. Over and over again he had tapped upon her shutters and called her name, but there was no response. He had met with the same experience this morning. Keiki was very miserable. Since the change in her seemed inexplicable, his confidence was shaken—not his confidence in her faith or truthfulness, but in her love. He began to torture his mind with the possibility that she might not love him, that she had been but a girl, after all, who, flattered by his manner of wooing her, had thought she returned his affection. His faith in her purity of soul was so perfect that no slightest thought of any designs upon his political schemes ever occurred to him in connection with Wistaria.

Thus unhappy, worried, and very much in love, Keiki walked moodily along the bank of the old castle moat, his old assurance and egotism completely gone from him.

Suddenly as he strolled along something struck him sharply on the temple. Stooping, he raised from the ground what seemed to be a soft pebble. Examining it more closely, however, he perceived it to be a lady's fine paper handkerchief rolled into a little ball. Half wonderingly, half idly, Keiki undid it. A faint, familiar perfume exuded from it as he shook it out. In an instant he was pressing it rapturously to his face. It was from Wistaria. Tenderly turning it about and enjoying its sweetness, he found as he was smoothing it out a little word in the centre:

"Go."

The lover became pale as death. He read it again, then repeated it aloud—"Go!" Its meaning was plain. He did not doubt for an instant from whom it came. That one little word from her explained everything— the change in her, her realization that she did not love him, and this silent means of telling him the truth. He crumpled the handkerchief in his hand. A moment later he was pacing—almost running—up and down along the bank of the silent, mocking moat. He could not think. He could only feel. Then he threw himself prone upon the ground, his face buried in the long grasses. He was smothering and choking back

ONOTO WATANNA

the hoarse, terrible sobs of a man—one who had been trained in the inflexible school of the samurai.

The day passed over his head. The sky, ruddy with the setting sun, paled gradually, until it seemed as though a veil were drawn softly across it. Still Keiki gave himself up to his despair. For him it seemed that the sun had gone out, life had ceased.

As the shadows continued to spread their batlike wings over the heavens, darkening, darkening the skies, until only an impenetrable vault of darkness dotted with myriad magic lights was above and about him, he still lay there.

A rustle disturbed the grass. Possibly a hare running by. Keiki heeded it not. Something was stirring, moving near him. Mechanically, dully, he listened. Some one had lost his way among the willows and with his hands was feeling his way. From his own despair Keiki was recalled by the sudden acute knowledge of possible danger to this person who had evidently lost his way. One false step towards the boggy grass, and beyond was the treacherous moat, whose water-flowers and reeds hid its dark surface. Suddenly he sprang to his feet and called out hoarsely:

"Who is the honorable one?"

He fancied he heard a cry. He ran towards it, then stopped short. He had come upon her there in the willows. Her kimono shone out startlingly white with a stray moon-beam upon it, but her gown was not less white than her face, which stared into the darkness like that of a statue.

Slowly he went to her as though drawn by subtle, compelling hands. Close to her, almost touching her; he did not speak, because he could not. Bitter words had sprung to his lips only to die before birth. He perceived that she was trembling from head to foot. Her hands stood out from her sleeves, each finger apart, and they trembled, quivered, shook.

With an inarticulate cry he caught them in his own, inclosing them warmly, almost savagely, in his grasp. Then his voice came to him. It was very husky and strange.

"Speak!"

"Go!—Go!"

This was all she whisperingly cried. She kept repeating it over and over between her chattering teeth. As he wound his arms about her shivering form he found that she was dripping wet. Could it be that she had fallen into the moat? By what miracle of the gods, then, had she been saved? The dark waters were so deep—so deep!

"You are wet and cold! You have met with an accident?"

"No, no," she said. "It was the honorable grass—so wet—so cold, like a lake. I crawled through it, on my hands and knees, close to the moat."

"But why did you do it, why did you do it?" His voice was imploring.

"To come to you. To be with you—to—"

He clasped her closer, warmed to the soul by her words.

"Ah, then it is not true," he cried, "and you do still love me, Fujiwara?"

"Better than my soul. Better than my duty to the gods," she whispered.

The sound of her voice was muffled. Her words literally sighed through her lips. He could not comprehend; he knew only that she loved him, had come to him, and now she was all water-wet, pale-eyed, and trembling as one who sleeps with fear. And because that strange voice hurt his soul, he covered her lips with his hand. She made no remonstrance, but sank into his arms, almost as if she had fainted. But looking down he saw her eyes were wide open, shining like dark stars. They startled him. They were like those of a dead woman. He shook her almost roughly in his fright.

"Wistaria! Speak to me! What is it? Tell me your trouble."

"Trouble?" she repeated, dazedly. "Trouble!"

Then she remembered. She grasped his arm till her fingers almost pierced through the silk into his flesh.

"You must go—go! Go quickly—run all the way. Do not stop one moment—not one little moment."

"Go away? Run? What are you saying?"

"Listen! In a moment, perhaps, I may not have power to speak. My strength is failing me. I thought you would obey the word I sent you. But I saw you fall down among the grasses, and all day long I have watched from my window, waiting, waiting, waiting to see you depart. No, no—listen unto me—do not speak. I escaped the vigilance of my jailers—my executioners. Oh, will you not understand? I have come through perils you cannot imagine to warn you—to beg you on my knees to go away at once. Hasten to Choshui!"

Her breath failed her. She had been speaking quickly, in sharp gasps.

"But I do not understand," he said.

"Your prince—your august prince is in danger!"

"What?"

"The Prince of—the young Prince Keiki," she gasped.

"The young Prince Keiki!" he repeated, incredulously.

"Yes, yes; they have discovered his secrets—they will arrest him for treason and—"

He almost shouted.

"His secrets! The cause! Oh, all the gods!"

"You can save him. There may be time. They will take him and cast him into a dungeon and kill him!"

"I must set off at once," excitedly he muttered. "What could have happened in my absence?"

Her shivering, trembling presence recalled him. He was distracted at the thought of leaving her. He could think of nothing else. He tried to see her white face in the darkness, but could only trace the pale outlines. Suddenly he took it in his hands.

"Fuji-wara," he whispered, in a voice of mingled love and agony. "How can I leave you? How can I do so? And yet you would not have me act the part of a coward, the false traitor. You would be the first to bid me go."

"Go, go!" she cried, releasing herself from his hands feverishly.

"And you?"

"Lead me back into the path. I shall find my way from there."

Leading her, he questioned anxiously:

"There is danger for you here, Wistaria? Tell me, or I shall not depart."

She turned the question.

"Last night there was a slight earthquake in the province. There is always danger. But you and I have pledged each other. For the time of this life and the next, and as many after as may come, I will be your flower-wife and you my husband."

At parting he kissed the hem of her kimono and the little, water-soaked foot beneath.

XI

When the tender veil of the first hours of the morning was raised from the face of the sun, the early light revealed a small, still, white face at a window where the morningglory, rising from the midst of spring roses, mingled with the wild ivy of Japan, clambered up and encircled the casement, and nodded until the blossoms touched and caressed the small, dark head. The eyes, darkly overcast with ceaseless watching, stared out through the mist of the morning, across the musk-laden gardens and over the silent moat, trying to pierce with the vision of love the distance beyond the lines of the province.

Thus all night long had the delicate Lady Wistaria crouched at her casement. Did the night winds stir the long grasses or rattle the boughs of the trees and bushes, the young girl started and trembled with unspeakable fear. Did the steady beat, beat of the wooden sandals of the guards at the palace gates for a moment cease or increase their rhythmic, orderly tramp, her heart bounded up, then almost stopped its beating. The slightest sound or stir made her tremble and quiver. Only the nightingale, softly, piercingly, ceaselessly singing throughout the night, comforted and soothed her like the song of an angel. Under its soothing influence she had fallen asleep, with her little, tired head upon her arms. But even while she slept, she sighed and trembled. Awaking before daybreak, she heeded not the shivering breezes of the passing night, but waited for the sunlight.

An alert guard of the palace gates, after the night watch, was wending his way through one of the paths which led out of the grounds, when he thought he heard some one calling his name. It was very early. But for the chirping of a few waking birds, the gardens were very silent and still. He stopped short in his walk and listened. There it was again—a woman's or a child's voice, calling his name, softly, almost appealingly. Turning sharply, the guard retraced his steps down the path, looking about him anxiously as he neared the palace.

"O—Yone! Yone-yara!"

He turned in the direction of the voice.

"O—Yone! This way! It is I—your lady!"

Then the guard saw the Lady Wistaria leaning far out from her casement. He ran forward and dropped on his knees, touching the earth with his head.

ONOTO WATANNA

"Closer! Still closer!" she called, in a whisper.

"Yes, my lady!"

He knelt close under her casement, his head bent, and respectfully attentive.

She whispered.

"I wish you to do me a service; will you not, Yone?"

"Oh, my lady!" was all the young man could stammer, out of his eagerness to serve her.

"I know you are tired after your watch, and it was long—so long!" She sighed, as though she, too, had kept the watch with him.

"No, no!" cried the young guard, hastily. "Indeed I am honorably fresh, my lady. Do not spare me any service."

"Then do you please run as swiftly as your honorable feet will carry you to the home of Sir Takemoto Genji, and bid him hasten to me here at once, without one moment's delay. Now hasten—do not wait!"

Like a flash of wind the young soldier had sprung to his feet, had leaped across the small division to the bridge spanning the moat, and was speeding through the wooded park beyond.

In less than fifteen minutes the samurai Genji was bending the knee to the Lady Wistaria.

"Thy service, my lady!"

"Oh, Sir Genji," she cried out, throwing all caution to the winds, "I am in such dire trouble—such fearful, cruel trouble!"

"Why, my little lady?" The big samurai was on his feet, regarding her with amazed eyes.

"Yes, yes—I know it seems incredible to you that I should have trouble of any sort, but indeed it is so, and—"

"Aré moshi, moshi!" soothed the samurai, patting her hand reassuringly.

"You will be my very good friend, will you not, Sir Gen?"

"Friend! Command me to cut myself in half and I will do so at once!"

"Last night," she whispered, "he—"

He nodded comprehendingly, certain that only one "he" could exist in my lady's mind.

"—he escaped!" she gasped.

"Escaped?"

"Oh, you know—you know of whom I speak."

"Yes, yes—certainly; but how do you mean—escaped? He was our honored guest, was he not?"

"His prince is my father's mortal enemy. My father has been my jailer for many days now, and I—I have been forced to cause him to betray his prince. Oh, will you not understand!"

"Hah! It is all quite plain! But why did you not inform me sooner?"

"Because until yesterday my father kept so constant a watch over me that I could make no movement he would not have perceived. But do not ask useless questions now, Gen. Help me. Tell me what to do—what to do."

"You say he has escaped? When and how did he go?"

"Last night, Gen. I climbed down the vine of the casement here. See, it is strong. My father for the first time had not been near me all day, and I thought I was safe from observation, though indeed I could not be sure. But I went to him and warned him of the danger, and he has gone to Choshui."

"That is very well, then."

"But my father may know the truth and will track him through the woods. I cannot live for the fear, the august dread, of what may befall him."

"Do not tremble so, my lady. Things are not so dark as they seem. It is quite impossible for your father to have overheard you; he left Catzu at noon yesterday."

"Ah! Then if that is so, it will be too late to warn the young Prince Mori," she cried.

"But do not think of this prince, my lady. Be happy that your august lover is safe."

"Oh," she cried, despairingly, "but I cannot have the death of this innocent prince upon my hands. I should die if anything happened to him."

"Well, do take some comfort, my lady. You say your lover departed last night. Very good. The samurai Shimadzu left yesterday at noon. Yet the young man, I am ready to swear by my sword, will be the first to reach Choshui."

"Oh, but vengeance and hatred will lend wings to my parent's feet."

"And the wings of vengeance and hatred, my lady, are not so fleet as those of the wings of love. Be assured."

"Sir Gen, you do not know, you would not believe all I have suffered."

Sir Genji's brows contracted. Ever since he had followed her to the old Catzu palace, when she was a tiny, bewitching little creature of five, with laughing lips and shining eyes, a flower ornament tumbling down the side of her hair and a miniature kimono tied about with a purple obi, she had been his favorite. He could scarcely believe it possible

ONOTO WATANNA

that any one could be cruel to this beautiful young girl. His looks just then bode ill for any one who should cause her pain. Nevertheless, for many days now the young girl's chamber had been not unlike that of an inquisitorial prison. It was true there were no thumb-screws or neck-halters or burning-irons within, but there were instruments of torture more refined and excruciating in their torture, because they pierced the mind rather than the body.

If the girl awoke screaming in the night, one could be sure that some creeping, spying presence had entered her chamber and had grown upon the consciousness of her dreams, rudely awakening her to the fearful nightmare of an unseen presence. In the early morning she was awakened from her sleep and forced to carry on those nerve-shocking, heart-breaking interviews with her lover. She fell asleep at night with the intuitive knowledge that one watched unceasingly in her chamber. She might make no stir or movement unobserved.

This Sir Genji heard for the first time.

"And I may rely on you for the future?" she asked, in conclusion.

The samurai raised his sword.

"With this, gentle lady, I'll serve thee and him," he said.

Then with a quick movement he flung the sword to the ground.

Three days passed away. She seemed like one in a dream, under a spell, as she hung over her flowers. Under the fruit-trees she wandered. Their petals, odorous and dewy-laden, fell around and upon her like a cloud of summer snow-flakes. They made her quiver with memories that caused her pain. She ran through the grasses away from them, her little feet scattering the petals before her, seeking the banks of the moat far away from where he had been wont to stand at the dawning, pleading for her love.

But the lotus with the dew in its cups smiled but to weep. She threw herself down by the water's edge, and swept with her hand the lotus back from the surface of the water. The flowers at her touch left one little oval spot, out of which her small face shone up at her with its startled eyes of tragedy. She fancied it a magic mirror wherein the face of the divine goddess of mercy was reflected. So she prayed to the goddess very softly, and quite as one whose mind has been over-weighted with trouble, for peace and mercy for that wilful and foolish Lady Wistaria, whose lover had passed out of her life and gone the gods knew whither. And the lips of the goddess in the water moved in soundless response, but, "He is gone—gone!" said the hapless Lady Wistaria.

XII

The Lady Wistaria was carried to her father's home at night. There was no gorgeous cortège, no gayly bedecked attendants or retainers to bend the back and knee to her. She travelled alone, in a covered palanquin borne on the shoulders of hired runners, beside whom the tall, lank figure of her father strode. They set her down in the heart of the city, the rest of the journey being made on foot. When she had last visited her father's home he had carried her on his back, after he had dismissed the palanquin, for she was then but a small girl of ten. Now she walked silently, dumbly, by his side. As they reached and passed through the silent little village that had impressed her as a child, strange fancies flitted in and out of Wistaria's mind. There was none of that strange up-leaping of the heart, experienced on returning to a home not seen for years. The old mystic horror and fear of the place had taken possession of Wistaria, but now, with a woman's wide-open eyes, her wonder and fear began to form themselves into vague fancies.

Slowly passing along the silent, spiral streets, climbing up and around hillock after hillock, they came finally before the small, whitewashed house with its dark, empty, cold interior. The old, old woman who had fondled and sung to the child Wistaria came hobbling and mumbling to the door. She wept over Wistaria's hands, caressed them, and drew her head to her bosom with a crooning laugh that was almost a sob.

"I am very weary and would fain retire at once," said Wistaria, as she returned the old woman's caress.

Madame Mume attended Wistaria tenderly towards the stairway which led to the upper part of the house. But, as she did so, Shimadzu called to his daughter in his hollow voice of command.

"Stay," he said. "I have much to say to you to-night."

Bowing obediently, if wearily, to her father, Wistaria handed her cape to the old woman and mechanically followed him into the ozashiki.

"My daughter," began the father, "do you know where you now are?"

This strange question surprised Wistaria, but she replied, with a gentle smile:

"In my honorable father's house."

"That is true, but do you know where your father's house is situated?"

"No."

"Very well; I will tell you, then. My house, though seemingly apart, because of its situation on the hill, is built in the heart of an Eta settlement."

"Eta?" repeated Wistaria, mechanically. She had heard the word somewhere before, but just what it signified her mind at the moment could not recall. So she repeated the word again, as though it troubled yet fascinated her. "Eta!—Eta!"

"Eta," repeated her father. "In other words, the social outcast, the despised pariah class of Japan."

Then silence fell like a swift, blank darkness upon them. Wistaria trembled with a creeping horror she could not fathom or grasp.

Somewhere, somehow, vaguely, dimly, she had heard of this class of people. Perhaps it was at school. Perhaps her aunt had instructed her in their condition. One thing was certain, she was suddenly made aware of just what the one word Eta signified.

It described a class in Japan upon whom the ban of ostracism and isolation had been placed by an inviolate heritage and a cruel custom. So virulent and bitter was the prejudice against them and the contempt in which they were held, that in the enumerations of the population they were omitted from the count and numbered as cattle.

Herded in separate villages, their existence ignored by the communities, none but the most degraded tasks were assigned to them— that of burying criminals, slaughtering cattle, that of the hangman and public executioner.

Whence they had come, why they were held in the contempt of all other citizens, what their origin, none could tell. When had there been a time in the history of the nation that they did not exist? Some old histories aver that they were originally captives from the great Armada of the Tartar invaders who dreamed of conquering the sacred realm. Others declare that they were the descendants of the public executioners from time immemorial; and again, more recent students assert that they were descendants of the family and retainers of Taira-No-Masakado-Heishimo, the only man in Japan who ever seriously conspired to seize the imperial throne by armed force. Whatever their origin, they were the outcast people of the realm. They were not permitted to mingle with or marry outside of their own class, and any one who chose to marry among them must either suffer the penalty of death or become one of them.

The long silence which ensued after Shimadzu had spoken the word Eta was broken by the Lady Wistaria.

"And why," she asked, with a tremor she could not keep from her voice—"why does my honorable father make his home among this outcast people?"

"Because," quickly came the passionate response, "your honorable father is an Eta, as is also my lady his daughter."

Wistaria's eyes, wide with shocked surprise, stared mutely up into her father's face. What! she—the Lady Wistaria, the dainty, cultivated, carefully guarded and nurtured lady—an Eta girl! Her mind could not grasp, would not hold the thought.

"Listen," said her father, slowly. "I was born in a city of the south, the seat of a daimio of eight hundred thousand koku. My father's house stood within the outer fortifications surrounding this prince's castle. I was trained in the school of the samurai. I grew up, honoring and swearing by this prince. When I became of age I entered his service. No love of man for woman was more persistent than my loyalty to his cause. Devotion to him was my highest ideal.

"My prince had a bitter rival and enemy. He was a good and powerful lord, though a Shogun favorite. This lord loved my sister and was loved by her. In an evil moment I listened to her entreaties, and forgot my allegiance to my prince in so far as to assist his rival to win and wed my sister, now the Lady of Catzu. Immediately I brought down upon my head the bitterest detestation of my own prince. I was assigned to the poorest and most degrading of posts, that of the spy and the suppressor of petty broils, and finally detailed to live in and protect a certain Eta settlement. So much of my time was thus forcibly spent among these people that I came to study, to understand, and finally to sympathize with them.

"I was young, as I have said, impressionable, and I had been trained in the school of chivalry. It fell to my lot to be the protector of an Eta maiden of such beauty of person and purity of soul that—"

He broke off in his recital, and, to clear his husky voice, raised with a shaking hand a tumbler of sake to his lips and swallowed it at a gulp. He began again, with passionate fierceness. His eyes glittered with inward fire.

"I married the maiden!"

With a sudden little sob, Wistaria moved closer to him and drew his hands up to her lips.

"My mother?" The words passed her lips as a quick, burning question.

"Thy mother," he repeated, and then she saw in the dim light of the room the great, shining tears roll down the hard crevices in her father's face. She moaned and crept closer to him.

"For her I became an Eta—an outcast. Do not shudder, my daughter. Has the word, then, so evil a sound? Then I perceive you have been wrongly bred—in the school of prejudice. The Eta, though an outcast, is a human being—more human, indeed, than many of our disdainful lords who ride over their heads and trample them like insects beneath their feet."

"Tell me of my mother," she whispered.

"Of her antecedents I know naught and care less. Her honorable grandmother still abides here in my house."

"Old Madame Mume?"

"Yes."

"Continue. Pray do so."

"After my marriage I was cast off immediately by my prince, my titles and honors were taken from me, my property confiscated. For all this I cared nothing. I was content and happy to be left at peace with my wife."

His long, thin fingers unclenched. He moistened his lips, biting into them.

"Did I say that this prince under whom I served was arrogant and cruel? Did I tell you he had a heart of flint and a pride so indomitable that he would not brook one of his samurai being other than of noble birth? Six of his vassals, the most graceless and worthless in the province, to humor his pleasure, undertook to seek me out in my exiled happiness and engage to make life intolerable for me. Whether their actual intention was evil or not, I cannot say; that they wrought evil is all I know, and that they came with the express knowledge and consent of their prince."

Wistaria observed that her father was trembling so violently that he scarce could speak. She pressed his hands convulsively within her own.

"Speak quickly, my father," she implored.

"They murdered her," he whispered, hoarsely. "Curses and maledictions upon their souls!"

XIII

The he death of the mother of Wistaria had taken place the day after the girl's birth. Her father had left his young Eta wife to go to the village to purchase medicines and food. She was in the care of her grandmother, who was old and weak, and powerless to protect her.

The Mori samurai, all of them in a state of savage intoxication, had come to the house demanding and calling for Shimadzu. They had been drinking heavily all day, and swore they would have their final cup with their former comrade.

When Madame Mume assured them of his absence, they insisted upon entering the house, and, pushing past the old woman, straightway took possession of the place. One of their number suggested that in the absence of Shimadzu they must be entertained by his Eta wife, whereupon the others, taking up the cry, boisterously began to shout for the hostess of the house.

Meanwhile the young wife, very weak and ill from her recent confinement, listened with feverish excitement to the loud voices and the bedlam of noises now rattling through the little cottage. Fearful for the safety of her lord, in a moment of delirium she arose from her sick bed to go to them, staggering through the dividing rooms until she came to the ribald debauchees.

As she pushed aside the sliding doors and stood in the opening, her white bed-robes about her, she seemed like an apparition. A sudden silence fell upon the revellers. It was broken by a samurai whose sake cup dropped from his nerveless hand to the floor, where it shattered into fragments.

The next instant there was a general movement towards the figure between the shoji. That simultaneous, half-savage advance seemed to snap the last vital cord in the woman. When they reached her she no longer swayed between the shoji. They bent over her in various attitudes of horror, where she lay prone at their feet, a white, crushed thing whose delicate life had been brutally snuffed out forever.

With a loud cry of fear and dismay they rushed from the chamber, out from the house into the open air, where their befogged brains still seemed to behold a vision of an avenging, pursuing spirit.

Hearing the wailing cries of the old grandmother while he was yet afar off from the house, Shimadzu began to run at his utmost speed, a premonition of disaster forcing itself upon him. Up the hillocks he sped. A moment of fearful, striving effort and he was beside the old woman. Something froze in Shimadzu, paralyzing his faculties. Power of speech and movement was gone.

The old woman caught his arm, shook it, and gazed with her fading eyesight into his staring eyes.

"Master, master!" she cried.

He only stared at the figure upon the floor. The old woman rushed from the house, shrieking and calling aloud for help. Neighbors came rushing up from the little village below and began to fill the house. They tried to arouse the stricken samurai, but he heeded them not. But when they attempted to move the young wife, a strange guttural sound of savage protest escaped his lips, so that they dared not touch her.

Then the neighbors mingled their cries with those of the old woman, and the house of death was rendered hideous with their ceaseless moaning and the muffled beating of Shinto drums.

All night long the samurai crouched in that paralyzed attitude by the side of his wife. But in the morning strong and stout armed men from the village, disregarding his cries of protest, lifted the body of the wife upon the death-couch, drew the lids over the staring eyes, closed the frothed mouth, where the teeth shone out like small white fangs, and folded the frozen white hands across her breast. Then the samurai came back to life—vivid, horrible, insane life.

Some kindly woman brought in the little Wistaria and held her towards him with a pitying exclamation, knowing that this little life could not but comfort the bereft man. He seized the child wildly in his arms. Then holding his one-day-old babe over the dead body of his wife, he swore a fearful oath of vengeance.

From that day the samurai had but one purpose in life, but one hope and ambition: to encompass the ruin and death of those he deemed the murderers of his wife. It happened that he came of a powerful family, who, in all his troubles, had offered him their sympathy and would gladly have received him back among them in spite of his marriage to an Eta girl. They were in high favor at court, and now they carried his case to the Shogun himself. The exiled samurai was forthwith ordered to appear before the Shogun, who had been deeply impressed and touched by his sorrows, and who had cause for prejudice against his former lord.

The Shogun offered to force his lord to restore to the samurai his estates and rank, but Shimadzu fiercely refused to accept these favors, wildly declaring that he would rather be buried alive than enter the service of such a lord. The Shogun, still anxious to please his family, begged him to make some request which it would be in his power to grant, whether for service under another lord, or at court in attendance upon his own person.

"I have but one request to make, my lord," responded the samurai.

"That is?—"

"To be made the public executioner."

All these things the Lady Wistaria now learned for the first time. She was as one struck down by a sudden shock of grief. In one little hour she had fallen from a great height, and had learned of things that had caused her to quiver with anguish and shame. She could not at once share the thought of the father whose wrongs haunted him, demanding vengeance and justice. She thought, instead, of other things. She was the daughter of the public executioner, the hangman!—an Eta girl— an outcast! The odium of it all crushed her. In that hour of agony her imagination conjured up the noble, highborn face of her lover, torturing her soul with its infinite distance from her. She knew now that he was as far beyond her reach as the sun.

"Shrink not, my daughter," came her father's voice harshly upon her thoughts; "your father's hands are not stained in the blood of any of his fellow-men save those who were his by divine right. To underlings I gave the punishment of the public criminal, but to myself I kept the sacred task of seeking, tracking, ruining, and killing with my own hands the destroyers of my house."

"Then," said Wistaria, in a strangely pleading voice, "you have avenged my mother. All is done, all is finished. Oh, my father, let us forget all this past, and go away where we may not be known and pass our days in peace until the end."

"Nay, all is not done," replied the father. "You forget that while I have had the holy joy of executing the six murderers of my wife, their prince still lives."

"Ah!"

"Once I served under him, honored him above all men; now I desire nothing else on earth but to bow his head in the dust. He is a great prince, beyond my reach, but I have sought and found a better means of striking at him. For this purpose, my daughter, I need your aid."

"You mean—" she began.

"This Prince of Mori is the man. Now you understand. His heart, his whole life, is wrapped up in his son. But yesterday, my daughter, I caught that son in the trap which I set through you. To-morrow he pays the penalty of the sins of his father."

Wistaria tottered to her feet. Then she fell on her knees and crept upon them to her father.

"Father, dear, my father, I beg, I implore you to show mercy."

"For whom do you ask mercy, my lady?" asked the father.

"For the innocent—this young Prince of Mori."

"You—you ask mercy for this prince!—you, the daughter of a murdered woman!" In an instant she was sitting up stiff and rigid.

"My lord," she said, "I am, indeed, too insignificant and unworthy to be thy daughter, but for one small moment I did forget our wrongs and fain would have spared my soul the sacrifice of innocent blood."

XIV

Early in the morning the inhabitants of the little Eta village were startled by the unusual sound in the streets of the "clip-clop" of palanquin runners' sandals. The Eta were not used to being carried in gilded norimons, or of travelling in any other fashion than on foot. Consequently, the spectacle of an exquisitely finished norimon, carried on the shoulders of liveried attendants, created as much stir as it is possible for the placid Japanese to manifest. The bamboo curtains of the norimon were closely drawn. The runners sped swiftly along, paying no heed to the raised shutters or the curious eyes at the wall holes. On either side of the palanquin two couriers or personal samurai walked.

The runners stopped before the house of Shimadzu, and, having thrown aside the curtains, bowed low as they backed before a veiled lady, who stepped from the norimon. The lady, however, unmindful of her bending servitors, hurried up the gravelled pathway to beat upon the door with her delicate fists.

The early morning visitor entered the house before the Lady Wistaria had descended from her chamber. When she threw back the covering from her head, the proud face of the Lady Evening Glory appeared with all its cold beauty and strange pallor. Her lips trembled so that she could not keep them together.

She had travelled all night in the utmost haste to throw herself at the feet of her brother, praying his mercy for the young Prince of Mori. She did not wait for her brother to question her, but began at once a pitiful, disjointed tale concerning her son Toro.

The young man had involved himself in great trouble in the Choshui province, and was now held a prisoner by the Prince of Mori. Toro, the foolhardy, imitating the actions of the young courtier of the Mori clan, had fared badly. Caught scaling the walls surrounding the palace of the father of the Lady Hollyhock, he had been arrested and brought before the Prince of Mori. This nobleman had at first intended to return the young fellow to his neighbor courteously, with some satirical rebuke which would scorch the vanity of the boy's father, but just at this juncture had come the fearful intelligence of the arrest, secret trial for treason, and sentence to death of the young heir of Mori. The old Prince, rendered frantic with fear and anguish, despatched word immediately to Catzu that unless the Prince Keiki were spared, the same fate should be meted out to the young Catzu Toro.

So the Lady Evening Glory had come now to her brother to demand, to beg the pardon of their enemy, this young Prince of Mori, while her husband had hastened to Yedo to seek the aid of the Shogun. Nevertheless, both father and mother knew that the fate of their son depended not upon the august Shogun, but upon their brother, the samurai Shimadzu, for the Shogun would scarcely have time to send forces to compel Mori to release Toro before the execution of Keiki took place, which would be undoubtedly the signal for the immediate despatch of Toro.

The unexpected answer the lady received from her brother stunned her so completely that she was robbed of all hope. Now she suffered in turn all the pangs of frantic despair and agony that her niece had so lately undergone through her agency.

"What!" cried the samurai, with stern derision, "permit the consummation of the work of a lifetime of misery and torture to slip through my aching fingers now? Not for a thousand nephews!"

Yet he endeavored in his rough and stern way to comfort his sister with these strange words:

"Catzu Toro is of samurai blood. It behooves him, therefore, to give up fearlessly his life for the honor of his family. He ought to bless the gods for the opportunity."

The mother wept, prayed, threatened. All in vain. Shimadzu was inflexible. Meanwhile the hour which had been set for the execution of the young Prince of Mori approached with more than the natural speed of time, and the Lady Evening Glory's couriers, the samurai Genji and Matsue, waited in agonized impatience for word of truce to carry to the old Prince of Mori.

Finding all her efforts to move her brother unavailing, the Lady of Catzu sought desperately though impotently to bar his egress from the room. She clutched the dividing shoji which opened into the corridor, then placed her back against them. When Shimadzu turned to the doors on the opposite side she rushed before him, and again sought to prevent his departure. Firmly, but not ungently, Shimadzu put her aside, whereupon she fell down at his feet, clasping her arms about his legs, while her lips emitted strange and piteous outcries.

Yet what could the utmost strength of a delicate lady do against that of a samurai man? With one quick movement he freed himself from her clinging hands. The next moment the Lady Evening Glory was quite alone. She suddenly realized that the gods had denied her all succor, and crawled across the room until she stood in front of the small shrine in the place of the tokonona. There she prostrated herself, but her lips could not frame themselves in petition to the gods.

How long she lay thus she could not have told. Gradually she became conscious that some one was kneeling beside her, and that a soft and tender hand was smoothing back the wild hair that escaped about her face. A gentle voice whispered:

"The gods are good—good! Take heart! They will not desert us! The gods are good!"

Then the proud Lady of Catzu, raising herself to a kneeling posture, gazing up into the bending, pitying face above her, saw her niece, whom she had so vindictively persecuted. Before she could speak one word, Wistaria drew her hand to her breast. Then the bereaved mother gave way to a passion of tears of weakness and despair.

"You are calmer now, dear aunt," said the Lady Wistaria after a while. "Weep no more, I pray you. But try rather to bring your mind to think clearly with mine. We must conceive some way by which we can outwit my honorable parent. We have yet two hours before the time when my father will depart for—for his prisoner."

But the after-effects of weeping, great sighs, rendered the Lady Evening Glory speechless. She could only shake her head hopelessly, helplessly.

"All night long," said Wistaria, "I have kept a vigil. I have thought and thought and thought, until my brain has seemed ready to burst. I, too, my lady, have yielded myself to such despair as you now feel. I suffer more than the pain of one who loses a beloved, for I am tortured with the knowledge that I am guilty. Oh, lady, was it not I who betrayed this prince, and would I not be the indirect cause of dear Toro's death also? Therefore it is my task to save the life of this prince, if that can be done."

"But it cannot—cannot," moaned the Lady Evening Glory. "Thou knowest not thy father!"

"And yet," said Wistaria, slowly, "I have thought of one way."

"Anata!"

"Tell me first, my lady, is it not so—that one who marries an Eta is forever after disgraced—branded?"

"Yes, yes, that is true—but—"

"It is of importance that I know all this. Now is it not also true that my father's chief ambition is to break the pride and spirit of the old Lord Mori?"

"Yes, it is so, it is so."

"Then, my lady, be comforted. Mayhap I shall find a solution to all our troubles."

Arising, gently she took her arms from about her aunt to hasten into the adjoining chamber. Her voice addressing the Madame Mume came to the Lady Evening Glory.

"Tell my honorable father," she said, "that I beg for just one minute of his honorable time."

When she returned to her aunt her face had a wan little smile of hope on it. The samurai Shimadzu followed her into the room. Wistaria prostrated herself before him with the utmost humility.

"You have asked for an audience, my lady. Speak quickly, for I have work to do ere long."

"Honored parent," said Wistaria, with her eyes upon his, "I have thought much upon what thou wert pleased to tell me last night."

"Indeed."

"And, my father, the more I have thought of the matter the greater have the wrongs of my father and mine, those of our house, appeared to me to be."

"Thou speakest now," said the samurai, quietly, "as becomes an honorable daughter."

"Oh, my father, so deeply do I feel the wrongs of our house that I have felt that even the very death of this young prince would not be a sufficient vengeance."

She was speaking slowly and distinctly, so that each sentence should take effect upon her father.

"Having broken the heart and spirit of my enemy," said Shimadzu, "I shall have accomplished all. It will be sufficient, and my work, my duty, will then be consummated."

"But think you, my father, that by the killing of this prince you will indeed have broken the heart and spirit of your enemy?"

"Ay! For I shall have robbed him of that thing which he prizes above all else on earth—his son!"

"But has he not seven other sons who would quickly fill the place of this one?"

"That is so. Were it possible for me to have seven instead of one Mori prince for execution this day, I would be seven times the happier."

"August father, you have taught me, and I have learned, that death is not the greatest of sorrows that can befall us. Execute this prince and he will quickly pass into another world, where the fates may befriend him. He will be beyond our reach. In the eyes of his parent he will have died an heroic and exalted death, since he gives up his life for what he deems a noble cause. Oh, my father, in all the empire of Japan, what Imperialist would not envy him such a death? No, the death of this prince would be inadequate revenge for the wrongs we have suffered. Far better if he could be forced to live so that he might suffer the devils of pain to gnaw at his heart all the rest of his life."

"Thou wouldst have him spared for purposes of torture?"

"Yes, honored father."

"Thou art indeed a woman," said the samurai. "Yet a samurai's sword has never been turned to such a purpose."

"That is right, for your honorable sword is not sufficiently sharp, my father."

"Thou speakest darkly, my daughter."

"I have thought darkly of our wrongs, my father. I have found a more refined revenge to inflict upon this prince, one which would wound him more deeply than the death of one of his eight sons."

"Well, and what is your revenge?"

"First answer me this: What would be the feelings of this proud and arrogant prince if his idolized heir were to be guilty of that very fault for which he exiled his samurai?"

"What fault?"

"The fault of marrying into a degraded and outcast class."

The samurai started. Then a strange smile flitted across his thin face.

"His pride would fall. Such a calamity would crush—bend—kill him!"

"True. Then if his pride is such, let us strike at it before his heart. I think I see a way by which this can be accomplished."

"How?"

"Bring this young prince hither. Leave him to me!"

"To you!"

She went very close to her father and raised her face upward so that he might see it perfectly.

"Look upon me, honorable parent. Am I not fair? Bring hither this son of an evil prince, and in twenty-four hours he will be ready to wed an Eta maiden."

"An Eta maiden!" suddenly shrieked her aunt. "Who? Not—" She made an indescribable gesture towards the girl.

"I," said Wistaria, throwing back her head—"I am an Eta maiden, my lady." She bowed very low, then moved towards the door. Before passing out she turned.

"I go," she said, "to garb myself in the dress of an Eta maiden. But do not believe, my lady aunt, that I shall have lost that beauty with which the gods have blessed me, and with which I shall win and wed this Mori prince to the disaster of his household and the triumph of my father's."

With that she was gone from the room. They heard her light feet flying up to her chamber above.

"It will crush—bend—kill the father!" muttered the samurai, softly. "It is well!"

"It is well!" repeated his sister, but in a different tone.

XV

The young Prince of Mori, no longer the Shining Prince Keiki, lay huddled in a corner of his dungeon. Vainly he had thrown his weight against the stone doors, only to rebound, baffled and bruised. Vainly he had called in piercing accents for help. There came no response from man or gods. Only his frantic voice, fleeing like the wind through the passage-ways of the empty prison, dark, damp, and for long unused, seemed to call back to him in the mocking tones of a demoniac.

A prisoner! A prisoner! He, the heir of Mori, the hope, the idol of the brave Imperialists, the son of the most powerful prince in all Japan, barring not even the Shogun himself! A prisoner! Penned like a common criminal within the stone walls of a loathsome dungeon! It could not be true. It was a hideous nightmare, caused by that terrible, ceaseless, excruciating pain in his head, and the mad turmoil in his brain.

He had been captured on the outskirts of his father's province. He was alone, with not one vassal or retainer in attendance upon him. He had made the wildest resistance. More than one samurai paid with his life for the capture of the Shining Prince. Overpowered by such numbers that it seemed madness not to yield, Keiki could not be taken while a spark of life remained in him with which to resist. Only when he was beaten quite senseless were the Shogun's officers and the Catzu samurai able to capture the Prince. Even then many of the samurai refused the inglorious task of carrying away the young Prince, who had fought against them with such desperate bravery. To drag his unconscious, bleeding, helpless body before his judges would be beneath the dignity of a samurai. So the office was assigned to some of the Shogun's spies.

When Keiki had returned to consciousness he was as one in a dull dream, a nightmare, wherein painful events wove a net about him from which he could not stir or move to save himself.

The trial had been a brief one. A few questions, a multitude of proofs, irrefutable evidence, the testimony of some false samurai now become a ronin, a private statement by the samurai Shimadzu—that was all. No word or question whatever was addressed to the prisoner, nor was he given the opportunity to speak in his own defence, had he been in a condition to do so. He stood between two guards, one on either side, while four others stood before him and a score at his back.

ONOTO WATANNA

Keiki was quite beyond understanding the proceedings, and only the Spartan will of the samurai lent to him that almost unnatural strength by which he stood stoutly upon his feet while his head swam. Out of a multitude of surging words and sentences only one word reached his ears and penetrated to his consciousness—

"Treason!"

And the word called up a haunting memory of a dark and stagnant moat wherein the sacred lotus blossoms, symbolic of the purity of woman, hid the treacherous waters beneath, of a sloping bank where the grasses grew high over his head, and the willows at the bottom waved in a foot of water. A young girl's face shone out of this strangely mixed background. It was very long ago, it seemed to Keiki, and though her face was quite dim to his vision now, he remembered that it was like unto the lotus, perfectly pure and peerlessly beautiful, only behind her beauty, unlike that of the lotus, there were no treacherous deeps of darkling waters. Keiki remembered vaguely now that she had crawled through the willows, through the moat, perhaps, to come to him to warn him of this treason. Treason? Whose?

Thus Keiki's tangled mind followed not the mockery of the trial, nor heeded the sonorous voice of the crier, who echoed the words of the Lord Judge, and shouted mechanically:

"Guilty! Death!"

A small company of armed men led him from the judgment-hall. They made a long journey, marching by night. Passive, stupidly indifferent to everything, Keiki was led to prison.

Only when they had locked him within the empty stone cell, did the old, passionate rebellion that had swayed him so savagely when he had resisted capture break out with renewed fury, driving in a flash his apathetic dulness from him.

His captors had taken his two swords from him, the two proud swords from which a samurai must never part. The Prince was to become lord over the samurai, yet he had been trained in the same school, and with as severe a discipline as that of the simple soldier. Had they left him these, his samurai swords, in all probability the Prince would have ended his misery. As it was, he spent the night in fruitless, impotent raving. Morning found him exhausted. Even the samurai's great power of will over the physical body could avail him no longer.

When the samurai Shimadzu unlocked the door of the cell no desperate, wild-eyed prince leaped at his throat. The young Prince of

Mori lay stretched across the floor of the dungeon. The glittering cords of his coat, the golden hip-cape, with its billowings and embroiderings of dragons and falcons, all the late luxurious finery which had earned for him the sobriquet of "The Shining Prince," and which were also the insignia of his high rank, were now torn and stained with the cruellest of colors. The dark hair fell back, clotted with the perspiration on his noble brow, from which the blue veins started through the fine skin. The long lashes covered the eyes and swept the almost boyish curves of the death-white cheeks. His lips were parted, and he was still raving, but in the babbling, weak, piteous fashion of one delirious from loss of blood.

After feeling the Prince's hands and head, Shimadzu was satisfied with his condition. Roughly binding up a bad wound upon the shoulder, he called for a stretcher. Borne upon this temporary couch, straightway the Prince was carried to the home of the executioner.

Meanwhile Wistaria had made ready for the reception of their expected guest. Having taken off her silken omeshi and removed the jewelled ornaments from her hair, she appeared in a rough cotton kimono, of a bright red-and-yellow pattern, such a garment as a laboring woman or one of the heimin would have worn. But she had taken especial pains with her hair and face. The shining, dark locks, which formed such a charming frame for her beautiful face, were spread wide and folded back, so that their beauty might be exaggerated. Because she was pale, as one about to die rather than to wed, she had rubbed upon her cheeks, chin, and brow brazen red paint, something previously she would have scorned to touch. Instead of brightening the pallor of her face, however, it only heightened its haggardness.

Wistaria sat in the centre of the chill, empty guest-room. She was smiling. She had been smiling ever since she had descended from her chamber. Her eyes were glassy, and shared not in that forced, blighting smile which she wore upon her lips. Very still, like an automatic puppet with the works unwound within it, she sat.

The Lady Evening Glory, on the other hand, flitted back and forth like a restless spirit. Sometimes she paused by the little, waiting figure, stroking the shining head. But in her heart the proud Lady of Catzu had little sympathy for the one who was to be sacrificed to the vengeance of a samurai. When she recalled that her niece was renouncing her lover to whom she had pledged herself to all eternity, she thought, with the selfish egotism of one who has outgrown her own heart, that in

ONOTO WATANNA

marrying a prince, even though she won him by trickery, certainly her niece would be faring better than if she had bestowed herself on one of his vassals.

Then, too, Wistaria, after all, was merely a female—an Eta maiden. So the lady's selfish mind fed itself upon one thought, mingled hope and suspense for the fate of her son.

When the sound of tramping feet were heard without, the Lady Wistaria did not stir, but the cold and stately Lady of Catzu went rushing across the room to fling herself against the window. The tramp of feet grew louder, deeper, heavier. They smote upon Wistaria's ears like the beat of Shinto drums at a funeral. Still she did not stir, not even when the doors of the house were pushed wide apart and the tramping feet entered, passed through the outer room, and then into the guest-room. The set smile upon her face deepened. Wistaria laid her head to the mats, prostrated herself in exquisite, humble greeting.

Thus, for some time, she courtesied low.

Some one pulled her sleeve. She sat up and stared at the figure on the stretcher. They had set it down beside her on the floor. Somewhere in another part of the house she heard dim voices, above them all her father's deep, hollow voice, sounding strange—clear.

A sort of awe and horrible reverence fell upon her as she clutched her aunt's hand. Then the two half crept, half crawled, close to the stretcher. Wistaria looked at the face, looked, and looked, and looked again. A heart-rending shriek burst from her lips. She fell across her lover's body, spreading the wings of her sleeve over and about him, as though to shield and protect him from all harm.

XVI

B rother, you were surely blind that you did not recognize your prisoner," said the Lady Evening Glory, after the lovers had been carried from the room.

"His appearance, my lady, had no interest for me."

"Now that you are aware he is her lover, what then?"

"All that is very fortunate. Whatever doubt I may have felt as to my daughter's ability to ensnare this Mori prince into marrying her is now set at rest. She already possesses his affection. Nothing remains, therefore, to be done save to bring about their early union. This shall be effected just as soon as the young man regains sufficient strength. Meanwhile—"

"Meanwhile?"

"You have permission to despatch word to Choshui that a delay has been granted to the Prince. This will keep them for a time from attacking Catzu Toro. Also, the shogunate, availing itself of the time to march upon Choshui, will rescue your son."

"But will not the Mori immediately retaliate by sending troops here to attempt the rescue of their own prince?"

"Not so, since the whereabouts of their prince is entirely unknown to them. As you are aware, his trial was in secret. Only the shogunate is acquainted with his present abode. The secret will be guarded, rest assured. In fact, for the very purpose of forestalling any such attempt on the part of the Mori, they have placed at my service a company of soldiers and a large number of spies."

"What are your intentions with regard to this Mori prince?"

"He shall marry, as you already know, the Lady Wistaria, and in that way will become an outcast, both legally and morally."

"And after their marriage?"

"Immediate notification of the fact to his father."

"And after that? What of the order from the shogunate touching his execution?"

"It shall be destroyed. I have given my promise to my daughter."

"But when this fact reaches the shogunate people they will resent it, and will never permit so valuable a prisoner to escape them. They will send troops, if necessary, to take him from you. In the event of your refusing to execute him, they will find another who will do so."

"Very well, let them do so. I have no doubt, however, that the Prince Keiki will escape them. But having become an outcast, he will be useless as an Imperialist leader."

"Which does not alter the fact that the Shogun's men will continue to fear him. Even now, you say, their spies and soldiers are lurking about on all sides. I tell you it is quite impossible for him to escape them now."

"Well, all that is his affair, my lady. So far as I am concerned, on the day of his Eta marriage I shall destroy the order of execution."

"Which would be a criminal act, and one that would place you under the ban of the law."

"That is true, but I shall answer, I assure you, for whatever unlawful acts I have committed during my lifetime to a higher tribunal than any that could be formed by the august shogunate."

"Brother, what do your words imply?"

"Sister, I cannot answer that question yet. When my purpose in life is accomplished you shall have the answer. And after that, will you perform a favor for me?"

"Certainly."

"The Lady Wistaria will be alone."

"Alone? She will have a husband."

"She will be alone, I repeat. Do you suppose I should rest peacefully in my grave with the knowledge that the blood of Mori was mingling with my own? I repeat once more, my daughter will be quite alone, sister. Be gentle with her, and as tender and kind as it is possible for one woman to be to another. She will not lack for worldly wealth, for I shall leave her a fortune. I do not wish her to return to Catzu. I desire that a small temple shall be built for her somewhere in a quiet and remote region. There I wish her to become a high priestess, to devote the remainder of her life to works of holiness and charity. In this way she will atone for the many sins of her father, and the gods will listen to her prayers and show charity to his soul."

"Oh, brother, from your words I begin to have lamentable fears that you contemplate committing some frightful harm to yourself."

"We are children of the same father, my lady. Your words surprise me. Surely they are unbefitting one of your blood and rank. Do you see any disgrace in my contemplations? I would rather wish that you would urge me to that deed you appear to dread, for otherwise my life would be without honor. Therefore lay aside your unworthy fears and assure me that you will carry out my wishes."

"I shall do so, ani-san" (elder brother), she replied, somewhat brokenly.

"That is all, then. Why do you wait?"

"For a letter signed by you as executioner, stating that the execution has been postponed indefinitely. We must put Toro's safety for the next few days beyond a doubt."

Hastily writing a few words upon paper, the samurai handed it to his sister, who seized it eagerly. Then, having examined the scroll carefully, she murmured a few words of thanks and prepared to leave the room. The samurai stayed her.

"One moment. By whom do you send this paper to Choshui?"

"I have two couriers."

"Well, but one of these samurai must attend you to Catzu."

"Certainly."

"Then only one can be sent to Choshui."

"But why so? I shall not leave here until my couriers return with intelligence as to the fate of my son."

"I can assure you, my lady, that your couriers will not return, and I should advise you to part with but one of the two samurai attending you."

"Why—?"

"The Mori people will not let this courier depart, rest assured, unless he divulge the hiding-place of their prince. This no samurai would ever do. If your courier has not the wit, therefore, to deceive the Mori, I am very much afraid his life will be endangered by this undertaking."

"And what samurai," inquired the lady, quickly, "would not welcome the chance of thus giving up his life in the service of his lord? What I have to decide now is, which of the two samurai to send, for each will claim the privilege of the undertaking."

"What are their names?"

"Sir Nishimua Matsue and Sir Takemoto Genji. The former has been in my lord's service for twenty years, and is so trusted by him that whenever I am forced to travel alone, as at the present time, my lord intrusts me to his especial care. You are already acquainted with the history of the other, Sir Genji. He was one of your own comrades in Choshui, but after your exile he deserted the Mori and became a ronin. Afterwards my lord pressed him into our service, and he became attached personally to Lady Wistaria. You will see, therefore, that it is a difficult matter for me to choose between these two brave gentlemen."

"Not at all. There is not the slightest doubt in my mind as to which is the most fit for the service. Bid the samurai Genji come hither, if you please."

A few minutes later the big samurai Genji and Shimadzu were bowing deeply to each other. From their low bows of silent courtesy it was hard to believe that these two men had once been the closest of friends and comrades in arms. Now they met again after many years of separation, yet neither exhibited that emotion which lay at the bottom of their hearts. Shimadzu did not even allow opportunity for the usual exchange of compliments, but went straight to the point.

"My good friend, your lady, my honorable sister," said he, "has an august mission for you to perform, but one fraught with exceeding great danger, and of a delicate and diplomatic nature withal."

The samurai bowed calmly, as though the fact of the danger were as indifferent a matter to him as the mission itself.

"In fact, she wishes you to carry word to Choshui of the postponement of Prince Keiki's execution. I need not point out to you the dangers of such a mission. The Mori will insist upon your revealing the place of imprisonment of their prince, and upon your refusing to do so will take drastic measures to compel you. These perils, however, will be to your liking, I am sure."

"To my liking, that is so," said Genji, "but—"

"What?" interrupted the Lady Evening Glory. "You hesitate! You do not set off at once!"

"I do not hesitate, my lady," replied the samurai, bowing respectfully. "I refuse. I do not set off at once because I am not going."

The Lady Evening Glory could scarcely believe her ears. Never in her memory had a samurai refused to do the bidding of his lord or lady. That Genji, of all samurai, should do so, astounded her. Nevertheless she brought herself to listen to his amazing words.

"My lady, long before I entered the service of my Lord of Catzu I was a ronin, an independent samurai who owed allegiance to no lord or prince. I was induced to enter your service not for love of your lord or desire to ingratiate myself with the Shogun powers, for, though a deserter for personal reasons, I was of the clan of Choshui, and an Imperialist at heart!"

"Such insolence," said the lady, furiously, "shall be punished with thy insignificant head."

"Tsh!" interposed her brother, angrily. "Permit our good friend to speak. I have a liking and understanding for his words."

"As I have said," repeated Genji, "it was neither for love of thy lord nor his cause that I entered his service, but because I desired to be near to, and to serve with my life, if necessary, the orphaned daughter of my old friend and comrade, the Lady Wistaria."

"It is well," said the Lady Evening Glory, sharply, "that you did not acquaint my Lord Catzu with all this. If my memory serves me correctly, you came to Catzu with great protestations and promises of allegiance and loyalty to his lordship."

"And," said Genji, "during the time that I have served the Lord Catzu, there has been no samurai whose allegiance has been more unswerving than mine."

"And yet," said the lady, scornfully, "at the first test the allegiance you boast of is found wanting."

"I respectfully beg to call your attention, my lady, to the error and injustice you commit in making such a remark. In following my inclination at this present time I expect to be discharged by his lordship, or I shall submit my resignation to him. Under the circumstances, I am once more a free samurai, and, being out of service, I am at perfect liberty to serve whom I please. Nevertheless I shall take delight in obeying any commands you may be pleased to bestow when I am at liberty to do so. At present I am not at liberty."

"May I inquire," she asked, with her cold eyes disdainfully fixed above his head, "why you condescended to accompany me?"

"Certainly. I had a fancy that you were about to set off for the place where the Lady Wistaria might be residing. Consequently I besought you to permit me to attend you. What is more, I had reason to believe that the Lady Wistaria would be in need of me. Hence, here I am, and here I remain, the gods permitting."

"If you suppose, Sir Genji, that by pretending zeal in behalf of my honorable niece you can excuse your conduct towards those in whose service you rightfully belong, you will soon discover your error, I assure you."

"There I disagree with you," interrupted Shimadzu, suddenly. "It is my opinion that my old friend's loyal zeal for the insignificant Lady Wistaria excuses him from any seeming lapses in his service to his lord, and in this I believe the Lord of Catzu will agree with me. Therefore, sister, let us call a truce to this harsh and useless exchange of bitter words. Instead, let us beg that Sir Genji will condescend to accept our gratitude for his loyalty to one who, though insignificant, is yet of our family."

Again the two samurai bowed deeply to each other. The Lady of Catzu shrugged angry shoulders.

"What is to be done?" she inquired, after a moment.

"Despatch the samurai Matsue at once with the paper," said her brother. "Meanwhile"—he turned to Genji—"deign to permit me to lead you to my Lady Wistaria."

XVII

The pain was quite gone from the brain and head. The fever had abated. A strange sense of coolness and rest pervaded the whole being of Keiki. The Shining Prince fell to dreaming, this time without a hideous nightmare being wrought upon his mind.

Once more he was standing in a royal garden, where the little winds blew about him laden with the faint, subtle odor of early spring; where the birds clattered and cried out indignantly at him for disturbing them so early; where the sun arose from behind the mountains veiled in a golden cloud and travelled over the heavens, pausing to tint the waters of a slender river to the magic glow of blood and gold. The soft, glad winds caressed as they called to him now. Moved to bend the knee in greeting and homage, he had become a sun-worshipper. He stood waiting beneath a flowered casement, waiting in a silence pregnant with inward feeling. Not a sound stirred about him; the birds had dropped to sleep again; but the glory of the sun had deepened and spread its full radiance upon the casement. Then very slowly a maiden's face, like a picture of the sun-goddess with the halo of the sun about it, grew into the vision, until gradually the dream-eyes of the Prince Keiki saw naught else save that haunting spiritual face, with its eyes laden with love and still suffused with unutterable sadness.

As suddenly as it had come, the vision faded away. Darkness passed between him and the face of his dreams. He sat upon his couch, stretching out imploring, beseeching hands as he called aloud, with a cry of piercing pleading:

"Fuji—Fuji-wara!"

Then he became dreamily conscious that soft hands were gently pushing him backward. He knew that her arms were pressed about him, that she had put her face against his own. He tried to speak, but she closed his lips with her own upon them, and answered, in that sighing voice of hers:

"It is I, Wistaria! Pray thee to sleep!"

Keiki fell into a delicious, dreamless slumber. Beside him, her arms supporting against her bosom the weight of his head, Wistaria knelt, unmoving, for the space of an hour. Her eyes had that strange, brooding, guarding expression of the mother.

Some one tapped with the lightness of a child upon the fusuma.

Wistaria tightened her arms about her lover. Her face became strained and rigid. Her eyes enlarged with mingled terror and savage defiance.

The tapping was repeated. Still she made no response. There was an interval of silence. Then the sliding door was softly pushed aside. Some one entered the room, and stood against the wall looking down at the little, silent figure with its face of appealing, helpless agony. The next moment the samurai Genji was kneeling beside Wistaria.

For a moment she could not speak, so intense were her mingled emotions. She had thought herself bereft of all friends on earth. In her father and aunt she could see nothing but menacing enemies who had assumed the dark guise of fiends. Yet here was Genji—Genji, her own, big samurai—whose very presence brought a sense of safety and repose. A strange little laugh, half a strangled sob, struggled through her lips.

In one glance Genji saw that the weight of the Prince in her slender arms was benumbing them. Without a word he lifted the sleeping Prince in his own arms and put him gently back upon the padded robe which served as his couch. Then turning to his mistress he half assisted her, half lifted her, to her feet. For a moment she leaned against him, dizzy with weakness.

In a broken, piteous, helpless fashion she began to cry against his breast, the pent-up anguish of many days finding its outlet.

Genji gently led her across the room, beyond the possible awakening of the Prince. His big voice, hushed to a whisper despite its huskiness, was as soothing as a mother's.

"Aré moshi! See, the big Gen is here. All is well! Very well!"

"Oh, Gen!" she sobbed, "I do not know what to do!"

"Do? Why, we must cease to weep, so we may have the strength to minister to the sick."

"Y-yes—I will cease to weep," she whispered, brokenly. "I—I will do so."

"That is right."

"And you will not let them harm him, will you, Gen?"

"No! I swear by my sword I will not!"

"You are so good and strong, Gen!"

Placing his hands upon her shoulders he held her back, then gently wiped the tears from her face.

"Hah!" he cried. "Now she is once again the brave girl. That is right. She is the daughter of a samurai, and cannot weep for long."

She tried to smile through her tears, but it was a very pitiful little smile which struggled through the mist.

"Now," said he, "tell me everything."

"Do you not know all?" she asked.

"No, I do not. I am in darkness as to how your lover comes to be here, wounded and ill; but I surmise that he was captured while on his way to Choshui and prevented from warning his prince."

"You do not know," cried Wistaria, looking up into his face with startled eyes, "that he is the prince himself?"

"The prince! Who is the prince? What prince?"

"The young Prince of Mori. He"—she indicated Keiki—"he is the same person."

It was Genji's turn to start. He made a movement towards the Prince, but Wistaria grasped his arm and stayed him.

"Nay, do not go to him. He is so tired, Gen. He has been awake, though unconscious, all night long, and he needs the honorable rest the gods have denied him so long."

"But you do not mean to tell me that your lover is the young Mori prince?"

"Yes, even so, Gen, though I knew it not until—until they brought him here."

"Brought him here! Why—but this man—the Prince Mori is condemned to death! He was found guilty of treason—he—oh, it is quite impossible!"

"Alas! but it is true."

"You do not mean that your father brought him here under penalty of death?"

Her head was bent forward. She covered her face with her sleeve.

"Shaka!" exclaimed Genji. "We must do something at once."

"Yes, oh yes! You, Gen, you will take him away—will you not, Gen?—and protect him, for if you do not they will kill him, or force me to marry with him."

"Force you to marry with him!"

"Yes. Do you not understand? I am only an Eta girl."

"I know that."

"And my father believes that if he were to marry me to the Prince he would legally become an outcast, and it would break his father's heart."

"That is very true."

"Then you see, Gen, how imperative it is that he should be taken away at once."

"Why, no, I do not so regard it."

"You do not? Then what am I to do?"

"Marry him at once."

"But, indeed, I cannot do so."

"Why not?"

"Oh, Gen, it would be too humiliating for him to debase himself. I could not be so false as to deceive him and drag him down from his high estate. I could not do it."

"Pugh! You overrate the ignominy of the Eta. In the old days when your father married among them the prejudice was at its bitterest. He is not aware of the changes which are rapidly taking place in the thought of the people of Japan to-day, nor does he know that this very prince represents to the people that new era which is about to dawn wherein all men will have equal rights and privileges. Your honorable father has lived only in his own sorrows, knowing little of what is taking place in his country. Take advantage of his ignorance, I advise you."

"But he would never forgive me," she said.

"Who? Your prince? Never forgive you for marrying him! Why, I thought he had wooed you for that purpose!"

"Yes," she sighed, "but he did not know the truth then. Perhaps if he had known of my lowly station—"

"It would have made no difference. I tell you I am well acquainted with this family of Mori. They are a proud but not ignoble race, and this new scion has shown a braver and better blood than all of his august ancestors."

"I cannot do it," she said, shaking her head despairingly. "So do you, pray, Sir Gen, assist me to put him in hiding somewhere."

"Tsh! That is impossible. Why, see, he is a big fellow. We could not carry him far, and the place here is surrounded by spies. He would meet a worse fate than if—"

She became paler and shivered visibly.

"I do not like to hear you speak so," she said.

"I do not like to see you act so, my lady," said Gen. "What! You would desert your lover when he most needs you!"

"Oh, Gen, no! I did not say that."

"When there is a way by which you can save his life, you refuse to do so? Very well, then; better deliver him up at once to his executioners."

"Oh-h!"

She interrupted him with a sharp cry of fright. The sound of her voice reaching the Prince as he slept, he turned uneasily on his couch, sighing heavily. Genji and Wistaria listened to him in breathless silence. Then, with her face turned towards the Prince, Wistaria moved close to his couch, whispering tremulously:

"Yes, yes, I must do it. It is the only way—the only way!"

"That is right," said Genji, patting her hand reassuringly.

She walked unsteadily back to her lover. Once more she sank down on her knees beside him. Her face wore an expression the big samurai could not bear to look upon. He moved very silently and stood against the door of the chamber, straight and immovable as a statue, and strong and invincible as a war god on guard.

XVIII

Prince Keiki was pacing restlessly and impatiently up and down the chamber wherein he had lain ill. It was the month of June. From the small opening of the doors Keiki could see that the uneven hillocks which appeared on all sides were blazing with the gorgeous flowers colored by the yellow sun above them.

At the door of the chamber, his arms folded across his breast, his eyes quietly following the glance of the plainly irritated Prince, the samurai Genji stood, still in the attitude of a guard.

"Why," inquired the Prince, frowning savagely, "may not the shoji be pushed completely to one side? I suppose this honorable house is fashioned like any other Japanese abode. Since I am not permitted to venture out of this honorable interior, at least I might be allowed to look upon more of the outside world than is to be seen through such a narrow space."

He indicated the screens, only partially opened, which half discovered, half concealed, a sloping balcony.

Very deep and respectful was Genji's bow.

"It is my distasteful duty to be forced to disagree with your excellency," he said. "Your highness's august health is such that your chamber must be sheltered even from the summer breezes."

The Prince stopped sharply in his walk.

"Spare yourself such imaginative effort, Sir Genji," he said. "That, you are well aware, is not the true reason why I am deprived of sufficient air, and am forced to remain in a room with my shutters closed so that not even the breath of summer may enter."

At Genji's second obeisance, the Prince, with an impatient motion, commanded him to cease, and to give his undivided attention to his remarks.

"Now will you do me the kindness to inform me what all these mysterious precautions mean? Wait a moment. Do not speak, for I perceive you are about to utter some further prevarication. Think before you speak, and try to see that it is useless to attempt to deceive me."

"Well, my lord," said Genji, "knowing as you do the peril in which your life will be placed if—"

"Oh yes, I perceive all you would say. I have recently been rescued from a blood-thirsty executioner; I must remain in hiding for some time, and so on; but what I wish to understand is why is it necessary for me to continue imprisoned?"

"Well, my lord, you would not wish a Shogun spy to catch a glimpse of you by chance?"

"I fear no spy," said the Prince, with contempt. "If I were permitted my own way" he added, savagely, "I would not linger here, but would start out alone, and cut my way through such worms and vipers."

"If you wish to do so," said Genji, with some asperity, "I shall take no measures to prevent you; but I had thought your highness desired to remain here at all events until after your wedding."

The young Prince sighed, and, seating himself on a small lacquer stool by the parted doors, he rested his chin upon his hands and stared out gloomily at the landscape.

After a moment, in a gentler voice he rejoined:

"Is it not yet time for her to come?" without turning his head.

"No, my lord."

The Prince sighed again.

"I once prided myself upon my habit of early rising," he said. "Now it has become a nuisance."

Silence again, and then:

"Sir Genji, what has become of the Lady Evening Glory? She has not returned to Catzu?"

"No. She still condescends to accept my humble hospitality."

"I have not seen her lately—a fortunate circumstance, by-the-way. The lady oppresses me."

"She has been much engaged with the marriage garments of the Lady Wistaria."

The Prince's face softened at the mere mention of Wistaria's name, and the look of impatience passed from his face. For a time he seemed plunged in a pleasing reverie. Again he questioned the samurai.

"Do you not think it a strange fancy for my lady to wish to be married here at your house instead of at Catzu?"

"Not at all. Your health is such that an ordinary wedding would be harmful; besides, think of the danger!"

"Well, it is my opinion that the state of my health is exaggerated. All I need to drive away my paleness quickly is the open air and the golden sunlight. As for the danger, I was not thinking of a wedding in Catzu, but one in my own province. I should be perfectly safe there with my own samurai to protect me, and a half-dozen other southern clans ready to come to my assistance."

"I cannot conceive of your excellency's impatience and dissatisfaction," said Genji, "when I recall that you are about to be wedded soon, and to one for whom any prince would be only too glad to sacrifice everything."

"You are right, Sir Genji. Yet is it not strange that, despite all this, I feel melancholy. I cannot understand it." He paused, and turned on his seat to look back at the samurai. "Sometimes it appears to me that I have caught this sadness of spirit from my lady herself."

"What, the Lady Wistaria? Impossible."

"It is true," said the Prince, thoughtfully.

"Why, she sings half the day like a bird—"

"Whose heart is broken," quickly ended the Prince.

"She plays like a child—"

"Who is commanded to rejoice."

"Her soul is as gay—"

"As a priestess whom the black temple shuts from life."

"Pugh! She laughs—"

"With tears in her throat"; again the Prince finished the sentence. "Yes, it is so, I tell you. I am not deceived."

"Your affection, my lord, causes you to imagine things that do not exist."

"No, my affection but increases the acuteness of my perceptions."

"If you will permit an unworthy vassal to venture an opinion, I would say, my lord, that for one about to wed in a day, your excellency wears a most funereal countenance."

The Prince arose abruptly, as though he would shake off some oppression that beset him.

"Let me tell you, my good fellow," he said, approaching Genji more closely, "when one we love appears to us to be cloaking behind a mask of painful gayety some secret sadness, the world is apt to wear a haggard aspect which one's own self must reflect. If you repeat that my imagination but conjures up such fancies, then I will say that I must be insane."

Silently, for the space of a few moments, the two men remained looking into each other's faces. They started simultaneously at the soft patting of approaching footsteps.

"One request, Sir Genji," whispered Keiki, as the footsteps drew nearer. "Will you for once relax your guard and permit me to be alone with—"

"But—"

"You can guard my person just as well outside, and should any one attempt to attack me you will certainly be made aware of the fact by whatever noise a pair of lungs can force."

"Her aunt would consider it unseemly," said the samurai, with some hesitation.

"I do not make it a request," said the Prince, patiently, "but merely beg the favor."

A light tap on the door, and the next moment Wistaria had entered the room. Her arms were full of flowers, flaming red and yellow blossoms that grew wild on the hills, while about her garments clung the odors of the fields and the mountain. She was damp and sweet with the morning dew shining on her hair, clinging even to her face and arms.

"What!" cried Gen. "You have been out already?"

She nodded, smiling wistfully over the flowers, which the Prince silently took from her arms and set upon the floor. His eyes never relaxed their gaze from her sweet face.

"My lord's chamber," she said, as she shook the dew and a few clinging leaves from her kimono, "is so barren of the beauty of summer that I thought the fields might spare something of their wealth."

Keiki turned an imploring glance to Genji. The samurai turned hastily to the door.

"Well, then," said Genji, "I shall go and bring you some honorable water for the flowers."

The moment Genji had left the room the Prince seized Wistaria's hands impulsively.

"Wistaria," he cried, "now I have some questions to put to you."

One startled, upward glance at him she gave. He took her face in his hands, compelling her eyes to meet his own.

"Why are your eyes so dark?" he asked.

She attempted to smile.

"The gods—" she began.

"No," he interrupted, knowing in advance what she was about to say, "but here, and here." He passed his fingers gently over the dark shadows that framed the pitiful eyes.

"Have they not always been so?" she asked, with a pathetic attempt at lightness which did not deceive him.

"No," he replied, almost vehemently. "When first the gods blessed me with the joy of beholding you, they were not so."

"Well," she murmured, tremulously, "I am becoming honorably older. That is all."

"No, that is not the reason," he cried, passionately. "A few months could not have wrought the difference, nor the other changes I perceive in your face. The rose is gone. You are pale and too frail. Your lips—ah, I cannot bear it!"

With an exclamation of pain he broke off.

An expression of fright appeared in her face. Her hands clutched about his.

"My lord," she cried, "you—you do not think that I—that I have ceased to be beautiful?"

"No, no. You are more beautiful than ever. You could not be otherwise than beautiful, my beloved, but you appear to me so frail that I am beginning to believe you are some spirit. Tell me, do tell me, what has wrought this change in you?"

For a moment she remained silent. Then she laughed. Her hands, with a little, childish motion of delight, she clapped.

"Wait," she cried, breaking from his arm. "I will show you the cause."

She ran across the room and brought a little mirror, which she polished with her sleeve as she returned to him. Then leaning against him, she held it before his face, while she put her own cheek against his.

"Look within, Keiki-sama. Said the gods: 'Such a pale and wan Keiki will need a companion, so we will make the Lady Wistaria's face to match his!' So they did so."

With a gesture of despair, he pushed the glass away.

"No," he said, hoarsely, "for mine is pale and thin from much illness, while yours—"

"From love," she said, in a breath.

XIX

W istaria" said the Prince Keiki, with a very firm clasp of her hand, "just now I insisted that the samurai Genji should cease his futile deception by useless prevarication. And now I ask you, I beg you, not to hide under a cloak of levity any secret trouble which you may have, and which I, as your future husband, am entitled to know."

The mirror slipped from the girl's hand. She stared at it hopelessly.

"Now answer me," continued her lover, insistently. "Is it not true that you are in trouble?"

"Yes," she said, in a low voice; "yes, but—" Her voice broke, and she turned her face from his gaze. "But, alas, I cannot tell it to you, my lord."

"Nay, do so," he entreated, with such pleading in his voice that she came back to his arms and nestled against his breast with a little wounded cry.

"I am waiting," he said, softly.

"I cannot tell you," she murmured against his breast.

"Why not?" he inquired, quietly.

In her nervous restlessness she broke away from his arms again. Her hands noiselessly clapped each other repeatedly. She could not remain still.

"Why not?" repeated the Prince.

"There are many reasons," she said, in a low voice, still maintaining the distance between them.

"Nay, think a little while, and see whether your heart will not suggest to you that the mere telling of your troubles to me may be their solution. Remember I shall be your honorable husband very soon"—he smiled a trifle sadly—"and then I shall command you to tell me the truth, you know."

Wistaria sat very still now. Ever since Genji had come upon her that first day with the wounded Prince in her arms Wistaria had been a prey to the utmost despair and anguish. The infinite faith and trust of her lover filled her continually with a greater horror of her deceit, for she could not forget, not for one moment, the part she had been forced to play in the undoing of the Prince. How could she add to her other iniquities by inveigling this noble and generous-hearted Prince into a marriage which would not fail to debase him? And yet she had no alternative, for otherwise his life would be the forfeit. Was it possible for her to tell him all this? Would it be, as he had said, a solution of her misery to confess her own deceit and warn him of the danger in which he stood, that of marrying into an outcast family?

As she thought thus sadly, the gentle voice of her lover brought the tears to her eyes. But she held them back, almost feverishly placing a greater distance between herself and the Prince. In that moment when his tender eyes held hers in their gaze, while he trustfully waited for her to speak, she was ready to tell him everything.

"You are about to tell me all," he said, as though he understood her unspoken volition. "Do not mistrust me. Believe in my adoration for you. Give me thy heart completely."

A sudden shivering took possession of Wistaria. Instead of speaking, she drew her sleeve across her face, a characteristic habit with her when in despair. Gradually her head sank forward, until she knelt at his feet in an attitude of humility.

"Nay, do not kneel," he cried, "nor hide thy face from me. Do not so, I beseech thee."

Having permitted his assistance in rising, she freed herself from his encircling arm.

"Look at me, my lord," she cried. "Tell me, what do you see?"

"A maiden as beautiful as the sun-goddess and as good—"

"Nay, then, do not speak so. Look at me again, my lord. Have you then found such pleasure in my beauty that you have not even remarked my garments?"

"Your garments?"

Bewilderment was in his face.

"Yes. Are these the silks, my lord, worn by the ladies of your rank?"

"Nay, but though I cannot conceive why you should be garbed in cotton, yet I see no disgrace in the fact. Perchance the samurai Genji is honorably poor, and you are so courteous as to dress in homely garments while a guest of his honorable household."

"I am not a guest of his household, my lord."

"But—"

"I know it has been told you so. Nevertheless, this is the house of my father."

"I do not understand," he exclaimed.

He added immediately, "If it is that your honorable father is poor—"

"You are wrong, my lord. My father is in the service of the government. His remuneration is ample."

"Then do explain to me the reason why you are so garbed and situated."

"Because it is so enacted by the law," she said.

"The law!"

"I am an Eta woman."

"An Eta! Impossible!"

"That was the offence for which my father was banished—because of his marriage to an Eta maiden."

The Prince stared at her aghast. She stood as still as if made of stone. Her lover's silence was due to his repugnance at this revelation, she thought. Seeing his effort to speak, she prayed a little prayer to the gods that he would spare her. The Prince found his voice.

"Then by the royal blood of my ancestors, I swear," he cried, "that I shall be guilty of the same offence as thy honorable parent, and for thy sweet sake I, too, shall become an Eta."

With a little, trembling cry she started towards him.

"But thy cause! Oh, my lord, thy noble cause!"

"The cause!" He threw back his head and laughed with buoyant joyousness.

"Fuji-wara," he said, "do you not perceive that a new life is about to dawn for this Japan of ours?"

"A new life," she repeated, breathlessly, hanging upon the words that escaped his lips.

"A new life," he said, "with our country no longer broken up into factions, when men shall have equal rights and privileges."

He smiled at her rapt face, and possessed himself of both her little hands.

"Dearest and sweetest of maidens," he said, tenderly, "in marrying me you do not wed a prince. I am pledged to the welfare of the people. Know you not that the great cause of the Imperialist will bring about that Restoration which will overturn all these crushing tyrannies and injustices which press our people to the earth? Repeat with me, then: 'Daigi Meibunor! Banzai the Imperialist!'"

Suddenly she remembered the blow she had dealt the cause. Her head fell upon their clasped hands.

But over her fallen head the voice of the Prince Keiki was full of joy.

"And now I have heard the great trouble, and have I not burst it like a bubble? Henceforward, then, let there be only happiness and joy in these eyes and these lips." Reverently he pressed her eyes and lips.

ONOTO WATANNA

Genji was heard outside the door. His face was very grave and his whole appearance perturbed when he entered.

Bowing deeply to the Prince, he addressed him hastily:

"Your excellency, the Lord of Catzu has arrived at my insignificant house and is below. It is his wish that the marriage of his niece should be celebrated without further delay. I come to you, therefore, to beg that you will consent to its immediate consummation."

"I comply with gladness," replied the Prince, "but may I inquire the reason for this haste?"

"The Lord Catzu Toro is in critical peril in your august father's province."

"Enough!" interrupted the Prince, impulsively. "You desire my immediate mediation in his behalf?"

He turned to Wistaria with an exclamation of delight. "Now," said he, "we shall see all our troubles melt into thin air like mist before the sun."

"But I have not told you all—there is more still to tell. I pray you—" Wistaria began.

"There is no time," interrupted Genji, severely, "and I beg your highness will convince the Lady Wistaria of the necessity for haste."

"That is right," said the Prince. "There is a whole lifetime before us yet in which thou canst tell me thy heart. Come. Let us descend to the wedding-chamber."

XX

No Prince of Japan had ever been wedded in so strange and lowly a fashion. There was not a sign or sound of the gratulation, rejoicing, or pomp which usually attend such ceremonies. When the Prince Keiki and the Lady Wistaria, attended by the samurai Genji, entered the homely wedding apartment, they found a small group, pale and solemn, awaiting them. It consisted of the Lord and Lady Catzu and one who was a stranger to Keiki, but whom he knew to be the father of the Lady Wistaria.

The waiting party bowed very low and solemnly to those who had just entered. Their greeting was returned with an equal gravity and grace. There was a pause—a hush. Keiki looked about him inquiringly, and then he shivered. The true solemnity of the occasion dawned upon him so that even the near joy of possessing Wistaria at last passed from his mind. He was about to join through marriage two families who hitherto had had for each other nothing save hatred and detestation.

Timid and pale as his glance was, he scarcely dared to look at the Lady Wistaria, though he knew she was so weak and faint that the samurai Genji had to support her.

Somewhat sharply, the voice of the Lady Evening Glory broke the silence.

"Why do we wait?"

The Lord Catzu stirred uneasily, glancing from the bridal couple to his wife, and then to the inscrutable face of Shimadzu.

"If I may be permitted to remark," he said, apologetically, "the Lady Wistaria is certainly garbed unbefitting her rank and race."

"Chut!" said his wife, angrily, "you would delay matters for such a trifle? Every moment counts now against our son. Will you let such an insignificant matter as the dress of your unworthy niece hasten the possible death of our beloved?"

"When it is her wedding-dress, yes," said Catzu, stubbornly. "May I be stricken blind before I witness such a disgrace brought upon my honorable niece's dignity. She must be married as befits her rank, I repeat."

A sour smile played over the features of the Lady Evening Glory.

"That is true. Well, her rank is that of the Eta," she said, tartly.

Having found the courage to disagree with his lady, Catzu now set her at complete defiance. He marched towards the door.

"Very well, then. I refuse to witness such an outrageous ceremony. The lady may have Eta kindred, but do not forget that she has also the blood of royalty in her veins."

His consort could hardly suppress her fury.

"I appeal to you, honored brother," she said. "How shall it be?"

"And I," exploded Catzu, who was in an evil and contrary temper, "appeal to you, my Lord of Mori," and he bowed profoundly to the Prince.

Shimadzu made no response. His glance met that of the troubled Prince. Keiki flushed under his penetrating eyes. Then he spoke with graceful dignity, bowing meanwhile to the trembling Wistaria.

"Let her be garbed," he said, "as befits the daughter of her father and the bride of a Prince of Mori."

There was silence for a space. Then Shimadzu made an imperative gesture to Genji, who gently led the girl from the chamber, followed by the angrily resigned Lady Evening Glory.

The three men, now alone, waited in strained silence for Wistaria's return. Straight and stiff, with heads somewhat bent to the floor, they remained standing in almost identical attitudes. Gradually, however, Catzu broke the tension by an attempt to relieve his excessive nervousness. Resting first on one foot and then on the other, he shifted about. His eyes lingered in painful sympathy upon the Prince, and then irresolutely turned to the samurai. Perspiration stood out on the lord's brow. He was suffering physically from the strain.

After a long interval of this intolerable silence, the doors of the chamber were again pushed aside. The samurai Genji entered. Bowing deeply, he announced:

"The Lady Wistaria and her august aunt enter the honorable chamber!"

The two ladies, close behind Genji, now followed him into the room. Immediately all prostrated themselves. When they had regained their feet, it was found that Wistaria was still kneeling. Then Genji perceived that she had not risen because she was unable to do so. Without a word, he lifted her to her feet. One moment she leaned against his strong arm, then seemed to gather strength. Stepping apart from him, she stood alone there in the middle of the floor.

Despite her waxen whiteness, she was more than beautiful—ethereal. Her lacquer hair was no more dark than her strange, long eyes, both set off by an exquisite robe of ancient style, as befitted a lady of noble blood.

When her hand touched that of the Prince he felt cold as ice. Involuntarily his own palm enclosed hers warmly. He did not let it go, but drawing her closer to him, unmindful of the assembled company, he tried to fathom the tragedy that seemed to lurk behind her impenetrable eyes. But, her head drooping above their hands, he beheld only the sheen of her glossy hair. Then she passed from his side to her uncle and her father.

Almost mechanically, his eyes never once relaxing their gaze from the face of his bride, the Prince went through the ceremony. After the service he tried to break the uncomfortable restraint. He proposed the health of the two noble though previously misguided families, whose union had now been so happily consummated. But his own cup was the only one held high. Gradually his hand fell from its elevation. He set the untasted sake down among the marriage-cups and sprang to his feet.

"Let us diffuse some merriment among us," he cried, "for the sake of the gods and for our future peace and happiness. Such undue solemnity bodes ill for our honorable future."

The samurai Shimadzu stepped forward, facing him fairly.

"My lord and prince," he said, "I have this moment given the signal for a courier to hasten immediately to Choshui to acquaint my bitterest enemy with the tidings of the marriage of his heir to my insignificant daughter."

The Prince smiled, despite his uneasiness.

"Surely, my lord," he said, "you make a goodly new and honorable custom. What! an announcement, perchance an invitation for one's enemy! That is well, for we have overturned all false maxims relating to vengeance against an enemy. We have buried our wrongs in a union of love, and embrace our enemies as friends."

"With august humility," said the samurai, coldly, "I would suggest that your highness's assurance of our embrace is premature."

"Premature! What, and this my marriage day!"

"Your marriage day may be a source of woe to your proud house."

"Well, that is so," agreed the Prince, thoughtfully. "Nevertheless," he added, cheerfully, "my honorable father becomes more lenient with the years. Moreover, he has but to behold his new daughter to forget all else save the fortune the gods have bestowed upon us."

"Be assured your father shall never behold her," said the samurai, with incisive fierceness.

ONOTO WATANNA

"What is that?"

"You have heard."

"But I do assure you that my marriage, though it may provoke the momentary anger of my father, will never debar my lady wife from her position in our household. You forget that my honored parent is very old, and I shall soon have the honor of becoming Prince of Mori in my own right. I shall then have no lord to deprive me of my rights, even if I had disregarded the law."

"You may as well be made aware of the fact at once," said Shimadzu, "that no blood of mine shall ever mingle with that of the Mori!"

"I do not understand your honorable speech. Has not our august bloods just now become united?"

"Only by the law, my lord."

"Well—?"

"My daughter, your highness, shall never accompany her Mori husband to his home."

"Very well, then. I will remain here with her. I am quite satisfied to renounce all my worldly ambitions and possessions for her sake, if such is the command of her august father," and the Prince bowed to his father-in-law in the most filial and affable manner.

"If you remain here you will not be permitted to live."

A low cry, half moan, came from the new Princess of Mori, who lay against her uncle's breast. Keiki turned to her at that cry. He was seized with a foreboding of events to come. Again he turned to the samurai.

"Will it please you, honored father-in-law, to speak more plainly to me?"

"Very well. This marriage, your highness, has been consummated not for the purpose of uniting a pair of lovers, but to fulfil a pledge which was made to one who was murdered by your parent—a pledge of vengeance."

"But I cannot perceive how this is accomplished," said the Prince, now pale as Wistaria.

"You have married an Eta girl."

"I am aware of that," said the Prince, somewhat proudly.

"I have not finished," said Shimadzu. "Are you aware that you are at present under sentence of death?"

The Prince made a contemptuous motion.

"By order of the bakufu (shogunate). Yes, I am aware of the fact."

"Very well. I am the executioner!"

"You!"

"It was I who caused your arrest, and afterwards brought you hither with the intention of executing you."

A flood of horrible thoughts rushed across the Prince's mind, bewildering him. As if to press them back, he clasped his hands to his head. Shimadzu continued in his cold and monotonous voice:

"After your arrest, it was brought to my attention that a more subtle revenge against your parent could be gained by marrying you into that very class of people so despised by your father, and forcing you to become guilty of the same offence for which I was exiled."

Stirred as he now was, Keiki's faith in Wistaria still remained unshaken. That her father had had a hand in betraying him he was assured, but he could not yet recognize in the deed the delicate hand of the woman he loved.

"Through the agency of my daughter," went on the samurai, "I was soon able to learn sufficient concerning the workings of the Imperialist party of which you are the head—"

"The Imperialist party!" repeated the Prince, and he bounded towards the samurai with the cry of a wounded animal. His hand sprang to his hip, where his sword had been restored to its sheath.

"You—you!" he shouted. "It was you who betrayed me—who—"

"You are augustly wrong," said the samurai, moving not an inch, despite the close proximity and menacing attitude of the Prince. "You honorably betrayed yourself!"

"I!"

"Certainly. To her." He indicated, without naming, the Lady Wistaria.

Slowly, painfully, driven by the goading words of the father, the blazing, burning eyes of the husband sought Wistaria, there to rest upon her while infinite horror found mirror in his countenance. Motionless thus he stood.

Wistaria, braced for a shock she could not meet, leaned against her uncle, whose head bent over her. The Lady Evening Glory smiled, as one who delights in the soul of a cat. Calm, satisfied, unmoved, remained Shimadzu. Keiki's eyes bulged from their sockets, his mouth gaped open. At last one word burst from his lips, but it was as eloquent as though he had uttered a thousand.

"Thou!"

Her head sank low. He recoiled a step. But with entranced horror he continued to gaze at her. Her face was like marble, out of which her dark eyes stared as though made of polished, glazed china. And as he gazed, terrible thoughts and remembrances rushed upon Keiki, overpowering, weakening, paralyzing him. After a long, immovable silence he leaned slowly forward until their faces, close together, were on a level.

"It is true?" he whispered, hoarsely. "Speak! Speak!"

"It is true," she replied, in a voice so small and faint that it seemed far away.

His sword leaped out of his scabbard. He raised it as if to strike her down. But his hand fell to his side. Then he spoke, in a hoarse, fearful voice:

"The gods may forgive thee. I, never!"

With that he was gone from the chamber. They heard the clash of his sword as it touched the stone pavement, then the sound of his flying feet, loud at first, and then dying away into the silence.

XXI

Having fulfilled his purpose in life, the Shimadzu was ready, eager, for his own self-immolation. He had prepared for this event with strict observance of an elaborate etiquette, just as he, a samurai, would have prepared for any event of importance in his life.

The little house had been thoroughly cleansed and whitewashed. Fresh mats of straw had been laid upon the floor, and the walls were recovered. To admit the sunshine, and the air of the out-door world, the windows were thrown wide apart.

Shimadzu produced an ancient chest, from which he brought forth rare and costly old garments, emblazoned with the crests of a proud family, and a pair of very long swords. The hilts were of black lacquer. The guard, ferule, cleats, and rivets were richly inlaid and embossed in rare metals. But the beautiful blades were the parts which shone out in their noble, classic beauty. They were extremely narrow, glossy, and brittle as icicles. The very sight of them would have awakened a feeling of heroism and awe in the bosom of one less alive to what they signified than Shimadzu. They were, in fact, two swords which, belonging to a hundred ancestors of Shimadzu, had been used only in the most glorious service.

"The girded sword is the soul of the samurai," and Shimadzu muttered an ancient saying. It had been long since he lost the right to wear them through his marriage into the Eta class, and now he regarded them with such intense emotion that fierce tears blinded his eyesight.

Reverently, tenderly, he lifted them to a place upon a white table before a shrine in his own chamber. Then with a low groan he prostrated himself before them, rather than the figure of the Daibutsu, which placidly rested upon the small throne.

In his inmost soul, this samurai felt he had done a good and righteous thing in achieving his vengeance, even though the innocent were sacrificed. Trained as he had been in the harsh school of the samurai, in which self-denial, contempt for pleasure and gain, scorn of death or physical hurt, and the righteous vengeance upon an enemy were esteemed virtues, he was steeled against all fear and pain. His conscience was satisfied with itself.

After his silent prayer, he rose to his feet very calmly and with a degree of solemnity. He had gathered fresh strength from his prayer.

The ceremony of hari-kari he performed with grave dignity and punctiliousness.

First of all, he gently lifted the two swords and held them in the sun, their knightly significance strong in his mind. One was to use against all enemies of his lord, the other held ever in readiness to turn upon himself in atonement for fault or faintest suspicion of dishonor, or, as in his case, when a duty has been fulfilled and honorable death is desired as a crowning end.

The samurai Shimadzu was without a lord, or, rather, he disdained and cursed the one under whom he should have served. Hence he broke into a dozen pieces one of the two swords, spurning the glittering pieces with his foot.

Then silently he disrobed to the waist. Very slowly and precisely he pressed the sword into his body so that he might lose none of the pain, which he would have scorned to resist. No moan escaped his lips. No muscle of his face quivered.

As the sword sank deeper his brain whirled with the dizziness of nausea, but, still stiff and relentless, his arm obeyed the will of his soul, even continuing mechanically to do so when his head had fallen backward into semi-unconsciousness. He was one hour and a half in dying. No words could describe the excruciating nature of such pains. Certainly, as a samurai, his was a fitting end.

Such was the nature of this people that to his friends and relatives his act was regarded as an honorable and admirable thing. Had he faltered in its accomplishment they would have urged him to the deed, entreating him to save himself from the stigma of dishonor which would otherwise smirch his good name.

The following day a large number of Catzu samurai and vassals marched through the Eta settlement and ascended the small hill upon which stood the house of the public executioner. The body of the samurai was carried with the utmost respect and reverence from the Eta house, whence a train, bearing it in due state, departed for Catzu.

From the Eta house the Lady Wistaria, too, was carried. Her train was even more like a funeral procession than that of her father; for those who carried her norimon and who followed in its wake had long been her personal attendants and servitors. Now, because of their love for her, they wept at almost every step of the journey.

The two mournful processions left the Eta settlement side by side, but their different destinations led to their parting company at the base of the hill. The one carrying the dead samurai turned in the direction of Catzu. There, fitting ceremonies were to be given to the departed soul of Shimadzu, after which he would be interred in the mortuary hall of his ancestors.

The train of the Lady Wistaria turned to the south, travelling many miles over bare and uninhabited regions, over plains, past hamlets and small towns and villages, on towards the mountains of the south.

While the last rays of the setting sun were still illumining the west, the cortege of the new Princess of Mori entered a forest of evergreen pines. When it emerged, the darkening sky had deepened its colors until a melancholy calm wrapped the land in an effulgent glow. The moon had risen on high and was shimmering out its holy light. The earth, reflecting its gleam, seemed a tableau of silent silver.

They had reached a beautiful and tranquil hill. At the top, above the pines and cedars enclosing it in nature's own sacred wall, the amber peaks of a celestial temple, with its myriad slanting lights, pointed upward in the sky. Their journey was ended.

Very still now stood the cortège. Low and deeply bent stood the silent attendants, as with streaming eyes they gazed longingly upon the slight young figure which the samurai Genji, almost bowed over with personal grief, assisted to alight from the norimon. In her white robes the Lady Wistaria seemed a spirit as she stood there under the moonbeams. Mutely she looked about her. As the muffled sobs of her servitors reached her ears, she wrung her hands with an unconscious gesture of anguish greater than their own.

As if in sympathy with the intense sadness over all who were there, nature herself seemed to show signs of her own distress. Clouds rolled over the skies above the mountains, veiling the moon and the star beams. A little river that flowed at the foot of the hill was heard sobbing as it rolled with a mournful sound over its rapids.

But the lights twinkled out warmly from the temple beyond, and a white-robed priestess was descending to welcome the novitiate. An odor of sweet incense, such as of umegaku or tambo, was wafted to the watchers on the hill from the temple doors. Wistaria turned her face towards it. Then back again she directed her glance to her kneeling servitors. Her voice was as soft and gentle as a benediction.

"Pray thee" she said, "to take care of your honorable healths. Sayonara!"

She hesitated on the threshold of the temple. Then silently she entered the place of tranquil rest amid the shadows of the mountains.

ONOTO WATANNA

XXII

The Prince Keiki had been on the highway three days before he became again something more than an unconscious automaton. After the first great shock of Wistaria's revelation had passed from him, there had come a desperate terror and horror which seemed to numb his faculties. For several days he was not conscious of anything either within or without him. There was no anguish in his heart or intelligence in his brain. His memory of events succeeding Wistaria's unmasking, as he believed it, was as vague as the tangled threads of a dream. He had fallen into that apathetic lethargy with which he had been afflicted upon his arrest.

He had, it is true, uncertain recollections of a place passed on the way, or of a halt here and refreshment there, but he could not assert that they were real. He might have dreamed them. He could not tell.

Then Keiki returned to his normal being. He awoke as from a troubled sleep to a world of torment. Could he have slept, and, sleeping, have imagined the events with which the name Wistaria was repulsively associated? No! It was, alas, all too true. He must bear it. As the first sharp anguish of his awakening passed away, there came visions to comfort Keiki.

When what he termed in after years his great awakening burst upon him, he found himself walking down a muddy road which led, his sense of locality told him, south to his province of Choshui. It was raining, fiercely, sullenly. Almost with a feeling of relief, Keiki found that he was wet. It gave him new life and new courage to do some simple elemental thing, such as drawing his cape tighter, closer about him. Then, as he battled against the wind and the driving rain, a fierce joy came to him. He was wise in the wisdom of suffering. His life should be devoted to the cause. No woman should destroy the significance life held for him.

Too long had he tarried with inclination. He had pictured to himself a beautiful highway through life, upon which Wistaria should tread by his side. She was lost forever. The rough path, the developing path of struggle, should be his. He would not falter. He would be true first to himself, his higher self, and then to the holy cause of his country. Patriotism and the restoration of rightful rule to the Mikado should guide him in every act. The events through which he had passed had consecrated him anew. His life could not be taken; he could not fail, until all had been accomplished.

In the new life which he was about to enter his course would not always be plain; he would not always be understood. For that he must be prepared.

When the Prince Keiki had thus settled the past and ordered the future, he began to take cognizance of outward conditions, as became him now. It was wet, and growing dark. He must seek shelter for the night. Turning aside from the highway, Keiki asked the simple hospitality of the country-side from a little house hard by the path of travel. Although it was long past the hour of their evening meal, the good dwellers in the cottage sent their daughter to the rear of the house to prepare food for the hungry Prince.

Sitting alone in a corner, Keiki, waited upon by the little maiden, found a quiet and comfort that three days ago he would have thought impossible. A strange comfort exhales from a perfectly appointed meal after the heart has been tried. It is the acme of despair, the realization of one's duty to one's self. Keiki, absorbed in these fantastic reflections, suddenly became conscious of the fact that for several minutes past the little maid had been making strange signals to him. Seeing this, he signed to her to advance. She did so, but in a faltering and almost fearful fashion. When near enough to him to speak without being overheard, she glanced in terror at his face and slipped to the ground, where she prostrated herself at his feet, her head nodding in frantic motions of servility.

"Why, what is this?" exclaimed the Prince, displeased.

"Y—your highness!" she gasped.

"Speak," said Keiki, sternly. "You appear desirous of serving me. What is it?"

She rose tremblingly.

"You must not tarry here long," she whispered. "The spies of the Shogun are about."

"Ha!"

"It is broadly reported that the Shining Prince Keiki has escaped his fate. The roads are beset. They are tracking his footsteps. Even now some of them are before the house. Oh, my lord, I know you to resemble too closely the Shining Prince for you to linger here. We—the whole country—are in sympathy with thee and would befriend thee, but the shogunate—" She broke off, her fear and distress completely overpowering her.

ONOTO WATANNA

Keiki laid an alert hand upon his sword.

"None may take me now," he said, defiantly, "for I am become invincible."

"Come!" urged the little maid.

"Whither?" inquired the Prince.

Pushing aside the doors at the rear, she led Keiki into the garden. Passing through it, they came to a wall. The maid spoke.

"Climb this, turn to the west. Go along the road a bit until you come to a cross-path. Take that, and you will come out upon your southern route below the danger point. I—"

There was a movement in the bushes behind.

"Oh, all the gods!" she cried. "It is too late, I fear!"

"What do you there?" a voice, stern with threatening, demanded from the bushes. The maid responded:

"Peace to thee! I do but bid farewell to my lover."

A laugh answered.

"Do not fear, maiden. We do not disturb cooing birds," came from the bushes, and a drawn sword was shifted from hand to hand, carelessly.

The warm blood surged about the temples of Keiki. Because of the perfidy of Wistaria, he would accept no service from her sex.

"I did not need thy lie, maiden," he said.

Then to those in the bushes he shouted:

"I am he whom you seek, the Prince Keiki. Come, take me!"

As he spoke, he hurled his cape to the ground and rested his sword with its point upon his sandalled foot. Quick as was his action, it was met by those lurking in hiding. Three forms glided out from the bushes. Three blades flashed towards him. Keiki's quick eye perceived that those attacking him wore but one sword. They were evidently merely Shogun spies or common soldiery. Their clumsy handling of their swords filled his soul with a wild elation. He would have some play with these vassals—he, Keiki, the most exquisite swordsman in Japan, and the most finished Jiujutsu student.

"Come hither—hither!" he taunted. "Without dishonor ye may yield yourselves to me, Keiki, the invincible!"

A savage yell replied. In imagination, perhaps, the Shogun spies saw the glittering price of the Prince's head within their hands. They closed with him.

The hand of Keiki instantly snatched the second sword from his belt. With a sword in each hand he met the advance. The sword in his right hand met and parried the initial blows and thrusts of his two adversaries; the sword in his left met the blade of the third, and, though it could not attack, maintained an effective defence.

The attacking swordsmen were startled. Such a thing was beyond the traditions of the samurai, and a feat wellnigh impossible.

Of a sudden the blade of the first of Keiki's adversaries dealt a vicious blow. Keiki met it with his left-hand sword, and before the blade could be recovered by his enemy the sword in his right hand had turned to the second adversary. This one, unprepared for Keiki's sudden onslaught, fell back, with his sword-arm severed at the wrist. Again the first antagonist thrust; Keiki met him. He now had an antagonist on either side of him, at points nearly opposite. He answered the blow of the one with the first of his two swords, while the other recovered his blade. There could be only one issue to such unequal combat. The position of his adversaries would not permit Keiki to fight them with one sword alone. Alive to the necessities of his position, Keiki kept slowly turning as his opponents tried to take him from behind. Suddenly Keiki fell upon his left knee, as though overcome, while with his right-hand sword he kept up a vigorous attack. The sword in his left hand became feebler, weaker in its movements. Thinking Keiki affected by some of the numerous small wounds with which he was covered despite his defence, the soldier on Keiki's left rushed in to despatch him, leaving himself but poorly guarded. The sword opposed to him became swiftly active. It passed into the breast of the samurai, where Keiki, glad that its necessity was over, allowed it to remain.

Quickly regaining his feet, the Prince devoted himself to his remaining enemy, who was a better swordsman than the others.

"Yield!" threatened Keiki, as he dealt a furious blow at the other's head.

His antagonist laughed. Immediately Keiki thrust in quick succession at the other's breast, head, and throat. His first blow was parried. The second at the head was a feint. As the soldier raised his sword to meet it, Keiki unopposed, thrust through his throat. He fell.

Breathing heavily from his exertion, Keiki looked about him for the maid, and the spy whose hand he had severed. He found the maiden bending over the lifeless body of his antagonist. From her hand a small dagger slipped to the ground. Satisfied as to her safety, Keiki quickly drew out his left sword from the breast of his opponent. Then without a word he climbed the wall and took the southern route again, disdaining to follow the directions of his late hostess.

In a rice-field farther down the road he bound up his wounds with the torn lining of his haori. Through the larger part of the following day he slept.

Alarmed by the recent occurrences at the little house by the highway, Keiki, who believed that the Shogun had put a price upon his head, now travelled only at night. The days he spent in sleep, and in locating, without exposing himself too much, the scenes of foraging expeditions made at night through which he managed to secure the means of sustenance.

The vigorous and unnatural fight through which he had just passed had a further invigorating effect upon him. Before that he had been near to death in his thoughts—death for the cause. Now he resolved in fresh and vigorous determination to live—and to live gloriously for the greatest cause that had ever made a pulse to leap in Japan.

At dusk on the fifth day after the fight, Keiki set forth upon the last stage of his journey. He was now near to the borders of the Choshui province. A few hours later he reckoned that he had crossed the boundary and was well within the limits of his father's country, when there came to him the sound of swords clashing beyond a turn in the road. Keiki, now grown cautious, skirted the spot through a field, and then crept within sight of the place.

Five men were pitted against three, while on the road lay the bodies of two more. Keiki had made up his mind to aid the lesser party, when an exclamation in well-remembered tones came to him. It was from one of the lesser party, old Hashimoto, a trusted follower of his father.

In a moment Keiki was in the road. Before either party were aware of his presence, he had killed two of the larger number.

"I aid thee!" he shouted, as with his father's men he engaged the despised Shogun followers. Speedily another of their number fell. The four obtained the easy surrender of the others.

Hashimoto approached the Prince.

"We thank thee for thy aid—" he began. Then, recognizing Keiki, he started back a pace and fell upon his knees.

"My noble prince! My master!" he cried, as he caught his robe and reverently pressed it to his lips.

"Thy master?" repeated Keiki. "My father, what of him?"

"Taken, your highness."

"Taken?"

"After the rumors of your capture, your highness, we at once determined to raise the Imperial standard against the Shogun, and your father—"

"But we were not ready. None of our plans had been carried out!" cried the Prince.

Hashimoto answered:

"True, your highness, but your father was promised the assistance of most of the southern clans. Consequently he seized a number of Buddhist monasteries and cast their huge bronze bells into cannon. His undertaking was revealed to the Shogun before our allies could join us, and he was surprised and taken captive."

"He serves a sentence?"

"He was sentenced, your highness. But the gods have anticipated—he is dead."

Keiki threw off his cape, which Hashimoto respectfully lifted.

"Attend me to the fortress," he commanded.

The followers bowed deeply. Suddenly Keiki raised his voice.

"Daigi Meibunor! The Shogun shall die!" he cried.

The followers answered with a cheer.

With head bowed in deep thought, Keiki led the way towards the principal fortress and castle of the Mori.

XXIII

Upon his return to the fortress, Keiki, as the capable and devoted leader of the cause of Imperialism, was deferred to by his brothers. He at once assumed in his own right the command of the resources of the clan.

The household was put upon a footing even more military than before. Regular watch was kept at all points of the estate and at the boundaries of the province. Reports of all crossing the boundaries of the province in either direction were made to Keiki each morning.

An army of laborers impressed into service from the Mori as well as the friendly southern provinces were put to work strengthening the defences of the Mori fortress, now become the war headquarters of the Imperial party.

The castle itself, situated within the centre of the province, approach to which on all sides must be made through friendly provinces, with the exception of the Catzu, because of its natural defensive properties, became the nucleus for a host of outworks sheltering the activities of Keiki. Within the line of fortifications surrounding the immediate vicinity of the fortress were the factories and foundries now built by those who acknowledged Keiki as their leader. For while all this owed its inception to the Shining Prince, it could not be carried out with his resources alone. The neighboring clans, whose lords in the past had held equal and superior rank to the Shogun, sent of their best to the Prince of Mori. The clans of Satsuma, Ozumi, Hinga, Nagate, Suwo, the Liu Kiu Islands, and others ordered their artisans and mariners to Keiki's headquarters.

The old Prince of Satsuma, more learned in European civilization than Keiki (although Choshui was the home in Japan of Dutch sciences), was the Prince's preceptor. Under his direction the cannon foundries, whose weapons of war were to oust the Shogun, were built. A sort of light rifle designed by Satsuma was manufactured under his direction near Keiki's fortress. The castle, which in time of war would afford protection to all these works and foundries, was reduced in the number of its living apartments. These were situated within the inmost recesses. All about the old portions of the house were built broad platforms. Upon their edges were set stone walls with openings for cannon. These, as fast as they came from the foundry, were set in tiers so arranged that they could command the approaches to the large circle, within which were set the factories and works of the Imperialists.

In the midst of these activities Keiki found relief from the flood of memories that otherwise might have overwhelmed him. He felt that now he was rising to true greatness. For him personally, selfishly, life held nothing. It was for his country he labored. So austere and unbending was his demeanor, that for months after his return his brothers forebore to speak of the message that had come during his absence.

But one evening as he sat in his chamber alone, within the centre of the fortress, his brother, Komozawa, came to him and held out in silence the letter which had disturbed them. Keiki read sufficient to ascertain its tenor. Then gently he laid it aside. There was no passion to his tones or manner as he said, coldly:

"Brother, whatever truth or falsity may lie in this epistle is of the past, and concerns me alone. It cannot affect the future. Speak to me no more of the leaves of last autumn."

"But—" began the brother, timidly.

Keiki sprang to his feet. There was a cloud upon his brow, dark and threatening. His sword showed half its bare length.

"Not a word," he said, "or, dearly as I love you, this blade shall give you explanation."

Komozawa bowed submissively and retired.

In the thoughts that the words of his brother had called into being Keiki was led to remember the imprisoned Toro, whose existence he had forgotten. Immediately he ordered the youth before him.

To his surprise he found that Toro, instead of appearing sullen or dejected, was quite cheerful and optimistic. He greeted the Prince with so much bonhomie and frankness that Keiki was puzzled at first to know how to treat him.

"Toro," he said, "I have come to a decision regarding you."

"That is good," said Toro, at once, "for I really am becoming interested in my prospects."

"And what are your prospects?" said Keiki.

Toro fingered his sash buoyantly, and assumed the attitude of a gay spark.

"Well, if it please you, my lord, I should wish to remain in Choshui, but at peace and liberty, pray understand."

Keiki frowned impatiently, but Toro remained apparently unconcerned.

ONOTO WATANNA

"In fact," he added, ingenuously, "I would very much like to remain in Choshui as a guest—such as your excellency was in my own province. I do assure you, my lord, that I have not been treated with the equal hospitality and courtesy offered to your highness in Catzu."

"It is impossible for you to remain here," said Keiki; "matters have changed."

"Then let me recall a certain promise made to me by your excellency. For my services in your behalf with my lady cousin in Catzu, you in return—"

He stopped abruptly, held by the expression on the other's face. For the first time he perceived that the Prince was in an unnatural state of mind.

"Wistaria, my lord—what of her? You do not mean to tell me that you failed in your suit!"

With a sob in which no tears intermingled, Keiki raised his sword, only to drop it, groaning inwardly.

"Return to your father, Toro. Be warned by me that this is best."

"But I wish to repeat that your highness promised—"

"Listen. If you remain here, your life will not be safe. Do not further protest. I will say this, that if your lordship does not care to follow my suggestion, I shall be forced to eject you or allow my officers to deal with you."

Toro shrugged angry shoulders, a gesture to Keiki reminiscent of his mother. The action displeased him. Sharply he clapped his hands. To the officers answering his summons he said, briefly:

"Be good enough to have my Lord of Catzu taken to Catzu under such escort as he may require." To Toro he bowed perfunctorily: "Good-day, my lord."

The preparations and activities of the past few months had brought all within the domination of Keiki to active readiness for war. Keiki himself was now of greater value to his cause, since old Satsuma had taught him all he knew—the result of years of European study and reading—of the making of the munitions of war. The lingering disease which threatened Satsuma need carry no fear to the Imperialists. Keiki, the disciple and heir in knowledge to Satsuma, could well cope with any man in the world in the utilization of the war resources at his hand.

Only a pretext, a happening that should afford the opening wedge for war, was wanting to the Imperialists. The public mind must be quieted by the outbreak of hostilities as the logical outcome of some event, not as a sudden, uncaused outburst.

It was during these days of waiting that the old Lord Satsuma sought Keiki out in the interior of the fortress. There was an evident perturbation and embarrassment manifest in his bearing. Keiki, alarmed lest some accident should have endangered one of the projects of the labor of years, started upon sight of his hereditary friend.

"My Lord Satsuma, is it ill with you?" he inquired with solicitude.

He noted that the face of Satsuma showed as never before that its master would never live to see the Restoration. This thought saddened him.

Satsuma, though in some pain, smiled gently.

"Ill indeed it is with me," he said.

Keiki reached out and impulsively seized the hand of the old warrior, pressing it with sympathy that words could not have expressed.

"I may not be with you," continued Satsuma, "on the day of the bakufu's undoing."

"Nay, do not say so."

"It is so, nevertheless," said Satsuma. "I must go before—"

"My lord, it is but the common lot—the common happiness of life to give up, to cease to struggle. Your achievements have been many. This rifle by my hand, that cannon in the embrasure, all these will speak for you with terrible effect after you yourself are long silent."

"Prince Keiki, it is not for myself I think thus sadly of life and death. I have a daughter. We are on the eve of war, the country is unsettled. I cannot leave her unprotected to share its uncertain fate."

"But surely," said Keiki, with a mild surprise, "your daughter will be well cared for among her many honorable relations."

"Alas, no, that is not possible. Her stepmother is ill disposed towards her, and all of her brothers are pressed into the Imperialist service."

"This is very sad," said Keiki, "and if it were in my power to aid you I would beseech you to command me immediately."

"It is possible for your highness to aid me," said Satsuma, slowly.

"How? Let me know at once how I can do so."

"By permitting my insignificant daughter to have the personal protection of so chivalrous a prince as your excellency."

"My personal protection!" exclaimed Keiki; "but I am engaged in the work of warfare."

"True, but my lady would not distract you from these tasks. Her presence in the fortress need scarcely be felt."

ONOTO WATANNA

Keiki sprang to his feet and began to pace the apartment in a perturbed manner. Under his thick brows old Satsuma regarded him keenly.

"My lord," said Keiki, stopping suddenly in his walk, "your suggestion gives me much pain, because I am unable to grant your request. It is quite impossible. This is not the place for a woman."

Drawing himself up proudly, Satsuma replied, in a ruffled voice:

"Very well, your excellency. You refuse me."

After a moment, as Keiki averted his face and did not reply, he continued:

"I am an old man, travelling over the last stage of the journey of life. I had a natural longing to have with me in these my last days my beloved child. Hence, feeling assured that you would not deny the wish of a dying father, I took the liberty of bringing her hither with me."

"You brought her here!" cried Keiki, in amazement.

"She is within," said the old Prince, quietly, as he indicated the interior apartment.

With difficulty Keiki curbed his temper. Satsuma had not long to live. He would tell him his secret: he would bare to him the source of his buried grief. Thus his old friend would recognize the impossibility of his being brought into contact with any woman, and perceive how unfitted he was for the task of protecting her.

So it happened that while without a storm raged, and rainy blasts struck sharply into the faces of the sentinels about the fortress, Keiki related his story to his aged friend. Once during the recital the shoji moved, then there appeared in it two tiny holes. Once there crept into the room, mingled with the tempest and the sentinels' sharp cries without, a muffled sob.

"You have passed through the heart's narrowest straits to the mind's broadest realm," said old Satsuma; "but permit me to still insist that while your highness's story has touched me deeply, I cannot agree with you that it should be permitted to affect the fate of my daughter."

"You are right," said Keiki, gently. "It must not do so."

"You will allow her to remain here?"

"Yes."

Satsuma bowed deeply and gratefully.

"The camp," said Keiki, thoughtfully, "is no place for a woman, but here in my fortress she will be safe."

"Your highness," said Satsuma, with much emotion in his voice, "no words of mine can express the thanks of a grateful heart. Goodnight, my brave boy; the gods comfort and bless you."

In the adjoining apartment a small figure, half crouching by the dividing doors, sprang to its feet. A girl ran to him with a little cry and threw her arms about his neck, pressing a little, wet face gratefully against the heavily limned one of the old Prince.

"It is well," said Satsuma, patting her head.

"How can I thank thee?" she breathed.

"By endeavoring to feel as if thou wert indeed my own daughter instead of a distant relative. But come, thou art pale, and your garments are soiled and torn with travel."

"The journey was long," she sighed, glancing at the frayed ends of her kimono, "and do you know, my Lord Satsuma," she added, "I could scarcely hire a runner to carry me, because of my unworldly attire, and so I was compelled to make much of the journey on foot."

Meanwhile Keiki sat alone, his hands clasped before his eyes. All the bitterness of a lifetime welled within his bosom. He was trusted above men; at young years the idol of a brave nation; fate was bearing him upon a wave of the highest destiny that could not fail to beat down the rotten dikes of oppression. Yet all this brought no peace, no happiness. He realized in a moment the futility of all his efforts to put the soul of the Lady Wistaria out of his heart. Only in fierce action and strain that should engross all his faculties could he even find a temporary easement. After that, the gods pity him! After that, he could not live. There should no longer be any delay. There should be war, and that speedily, perhaps on the morrow.

XXIV

However fiercely the Prince Keiki desired and sought for instant action, there were excellent reasons in the delayed march of some of the clans journeying to the Mori fortress for the temporary postponement of hostilities.

Keiki at first was bitterly opposed to any further delay, but the reasonable arguments of the older daimios and the insistence of Satsuma, the practical leader of the movement, won him over. It was their logic, not their authority, which restrained him. He would be compelled to wait no longer than a few days more, certainly not more than a week.

One morning shortly after Keiki's interview with the Lord Satsuma concerning his reputed daughter, who so far had kept apart in strict retirement in her apartments in the castle, Keiki found in his morning reports a reference to the youth Toro. He was riding post-haste in the direction of the Choshui province with the evident intention of crossing its frontier. What was the will of his excellency respecting him?

So this, then, was the way in which the rash youth repaid his consideration, mused Keiki. Or perhaps he came because of the Princess Hollyhock. If that were so, he would send him back to Catzu again, with a friendly warning against the perfidious sex.

"He approaches the frontier?" he asked the soldier who brought the reports.

"Yes, your highness."

"Well then, let him ride unmolested towards our fortress. So long as he advances do not touch him, but at the first sign of his return seize him and bring him to me."

The soldier bowed.

"It shall be as your highness commands."

So it was that Toro, to his surprise, was allowed to proceed unharmed through the hostile country of the Mori. His journey was without incident until his arrival before the fortress. There a guard barred farther progress with his sword. Toro flung himself from his panting charger.

"The Prince Mori?" he questioned.

"Expects you and will give you audience shortly," returned the guard.

The young heir of Catzu was conducted to a chamber within the outer circle of the fortress's defensive works. While this chamber was not within the inmost area of the edifice devoted to the living apartments, yet it was sufficiently near for the occasional passage of some peaceable member of the household through the grimmer servants of war to occasion no comment. Moreover, it adjoined the apartments set aside for the Prince of Satsuma.

Thus when the daughter of Satsuma chanced to pass through the chamber, none showed surprise until the youthful Toro came. His astonishment, however, was such that instantly his mouth gaped wide. Before sound could add its audible testimony to his visible astonishment, the girl had clapped her hand upon his lips. A quick glance about the chamber told her that they were unobserved. She took Toro gently by the shoulder.

"Come," she said.

Half an hour later the old Lord Satsuma stood before Keiki in alarm.

"My daughter is not to be found," he cried.

"Not to be found!"

"No, my lord. I committed her to thy care. Thou didst promise to guard her."

Keiki was troubled. His conscience smote him, for he had painfully put off making the acquaintance of Satsuma's daughter and had left her to the care of his underlings.

"My lord," he said, "I will have search made at once. Your honorable daughter must be found."

Satsuma, in deep agitation and concern, left his pupil's apartment to make further inquiry of the guard. He had advanced but a little way into one of the armed outer chambers of the fortress when a note was slipped into his hand. He tore it open and read it through in amazement. After a second reading a broad smile overspread his face. He sought no more for his daughter. Instead, he despatched a hurried note to Keiki, briefly informing him that his insignificant and unworthy daughter had become ill with longing for her home, and had departed thence on her own account. As she was very efficiently attended, he had no fears for her safety.

Meanwhile Keiki was holding audience with Catzu Toro.

"This, then," he said, severely, "is the gratitude of the Catzu for me. I have spared your life, twice forfeit to me by every law of lord and samurai. You have come back, it seems, and are determined to make fresh trouble for yourself."

Keiki paused. Toro answered, quickly:

"I have come back to you, your highness, to offer my allegiance and my service."

"Your allegiance!"

"My poor aid, rather, to a cause of whose nobility I learned during my stay in your province. Sovereignty is not with the Shogun, but the Emperor. Place the rightful ruler upon the throne, oust the usurper and tyrant, and the rights of the people will be listened to."

"Who taught you these counsels?"

"My own conscience, my lord."

Keiki smiled.

"Are you quite certain, Toro, you did not read your new principles in a lady's eyes?" he asked, dryly.

Toro blushed.

"The Princess Hollyhock appears to have been a teacher of some weight," said Keiki.

Toro cried, warmly:

"My lord, you do me injustice. I love the Princess Hollyhock, it is true—I confess it. But what my honor dictates, what my conscience has seen, has naught to do with the Princess." Ingenuously: "'Tis, my lord, I do protest, but a happy coincidence that her views are mine. Were it otherwise, though tears did blind my eyes, I should perceive the right way; though sorrow choked my voice, I still would cry, 'Daigi Meibunor!'"

Toro dropped to his knees, his extravagance of expression seeming not to have affected his sincerity. Keiki put out a quick hand to raise him. In a voice of deep emotion he cried, impulsively:

"Toro, my brother, I wronged you. Now I make amend and receive you into our service. My heart was bitter because of my own sorrow, but it still has generosity left for you, friend of my hopes. You are of the days of flowers. Now, after the flowers have withered, I still receive you."

"The flowers have not withered," said Toro, impulsively. "Do listen to me. Perchance—" He broke off in some confusion, as by some sudden remembrance.

"Speak no more, I pray thee," said Keiki, commandingly.

"Forgive me. I would speak of my gratitude to you."

"Toro, I will place you in command of a small company. At first I could not do more without antagonizing some of my people. They would say that your adherence was too recent."

Toro replied:

"I do not seek that honor. I ask a humbler station."

"You shall be upon my personal staff for the present," was Keiki's response. "Later, as occasion offers, I will honorably advance you."

Keiki now rose. Bowing to Toro, he signified that the interview was at an end. Still Toro hesitated.

"You wish to have further talk with me?" inquired Keiki.

"I crave pardon," said Toro, somewhat embarrassed, "but—"

He went towards the doors into the adjoining apartment and signalled to some one within. A youth entered quietly. He was slight, yet of a grace that owed its being equally to his exquisite proportions and to his entire command of his physical being and comportment. A youth's fringe hid his forehead. His eyes, cast down, were veiled from Keiki. He did not wear the armor of Toro or Keiki, but carried under his arm a small encased sword, which he handled easily.

"My lord," said Toro, "I have, as you see, been able to make a recruit. He was to be my personal follower, but since I am to serve on your staff I have no need of him."

"I am not an exquisite. I do not need a little man to follow at my heels," said Keiki, surveying with disapproval the dainty lines of the little warrior.

The unwelcome visitor flushed to his ears. Toro glanced at him with what seemed a suspicion of humor. The youth, seemingly infuriated, whipped out his sword.

A sudden suspicion of treachery came to Keiki as he brought his hand to his own heavy blade and put it at guard. But the thought of the youth attacking him seemed to amuse him also, so that he took no trouble to defend himself.

Perhaps, too, it was because of his astonishment, and the heaviness of his blade, and not because of lack of skill, that the tiny blade of the youth slipped down Keiki's guard, and, leaving the line of defence, sought, cut, and carried away a rosette from the cuirass of the Prince. Plucking it from his blade, the youth thrust the rosette into his breast, while on his knees he offered his sword to Keiki with its point directed towards his own breast.

Keiki made a motion of surprise. The youth had answered, and worthily, his taunt. But his life hung upon the generosity of the Prince. Toro saw that here was a test of the soul of Keiki.

The Shining Prince laughed loud and long.

"Good! I receive thee at once into my service. Thy name?"

"Jiro, my lord," half whispered the youth from his kneeling position.

"Well, Jiro, just now you held my life in your hands. For the sake of a worthy cause I thank you for sparing me. A thrust in the loosened corsage below that rosette would have done for me."

Jiro rose to his feet, but remained with his head respectfully bowed before the Prince.

Toro clapped him on his slight shoulder.

"In the days soon to come, when your life is sought by the foes of the cause, my lord, Jiro and I will protect you."

When Toro, flushed with his strange success, sought the Lady Hollyhock, he found her wholly unresponsive.

"In faith, my lord," she said, mockingly, "it was not right for you, a Catzu lord, to ride through the outposts of your hereditary enemy, simply for a glimpse of an unworthy and insignificant maiden."

"Nay—" remonstrated Toro.

"To abandon your father's house and hopes for a girl—that is not what the daughters of Nipon are taught."

"My dearest lady—"

"To follow one's conscience were an honor, but to forget all blindly, to betray your cause, to betray your house to win a wife. Think you she would have you after such perfidy? She would not be worth possessing did she favor you then."

One little, unfeeling hand Toro carried to his heart.

"Dear lady," he said, "I did not do it for thee."

The Lady Hollyhock frowned, and withdrew her hand immediately.

"You did not?" she exclaimed.

"Nay, dear lady. I did it because of my conscience, because I believe in the Emperor, and not the Shogun."

The Princess turned her back upon him.

"You are angry, sweet lady?" interrogated the agitated Toro.

No reply.

"Lady, you were angry with me when you thought I did it for you, and now when you know I did not you are still angry."

"A princess must have her brave knight," said the Lady Hollyhock, haughtily.

"You know why I did it," said Toro, ready to forswear everything at her demand.

Again he sought her hand, but still she denied him.

"Oh, not so fast, my lord. Let me whisper to you a report I have heard."

"A report—concerning me?" said Toro, in bewilderment.

"Concerning a certain Catzu gentleman who recently awaited an audience with the Prince Mori. He was placed in a certain interior chamber, which happened to adjoin the apartments of the daughter of a certain prince of prominence. This Catzu gentleman, it is said, disappeared into this lady's private apartments. Since which time the lady has been banished to Satsuma by her own father."

"Lady," said Toro, in a great state of mingled fear and bewilderment, "I pray thee repeat not such a story, even to the flowers."

With a scornful and angry little laugh, the Lady Hollyhock, who had inwardly hoped for a denial by her lover, stepped away.

"I am not likely," she said, "to tell of my own supplanting."

She drew the doors sharply between them.

Toro, alone, mused upon the imputation of her words.

"She is mine if I tell her a secret," he said, "but that secret is not my own; I cannot tell it!" He added, with a naïve wisdom: "Nor can I trust her. A woman is like unto a volcano, which, even when inactive, is palpitating to spit forth its fire, and which, when it does vent its fury, bursts the bounds of its late enforced suppression."

XXV

A SMALL portion of the night had been spent by the Prince in that sleep, troubled by nervous starts and awakenings, which was now his only repose, when there was a sound of disorder in the great enclosure without the fortress. The challenging of sentinels, the rattle of arms, the gallop of a considerable body of horse, came to him plainly within the palace interior.

Hastily Keiki passed through the castle apartments to a parapet high above the area of the enclosure. Leaning against a cannon, he sought among the shadows for the cause of the disturbance. If he had any fears as to the state of his defences, none appeared in his face, now grown impassive almost to the point of apathy.

Gradually, as his eyes became accustomed to the semi-darkness of the enclosure, he saw that his followers were receiving an accession of fresh troops, many of whom were mounted. Quarters for the rest of the night were being made ready for the new-comers. Plainly, it was the arrival of some of the long-expected clans.

With the knowledge that a report would be made presently, for such was his standing order by day or by night, Keiki returned to his apartments, seeking, after a few further preparations, the chamber in which he was accustomed to receive guests.

Soon a number of his people, among them Toro and the boy Jiro, ushered in his cousin, the cadet Lord of Nagato. Scarcely had he announced the number and strength of the clans he had gathered about him, when he burst out:

"Strange news, your highness!"

"Speak," said Keiki, briefly.

"With these eyes have I seen it. Ill augurs it for our land and cause."

"Speak," said Keiki, impatiently.

"My lord, I have just come from Yedo, whither I went alone in disguise, joining my men only yester morn."

"My lord," said the impatient Keiki, "pray remember that the hour is late. All things wait upon your utterance. Tell me in a breath what is your news. What did you see in Yedo?"

"Foreign ships-of-war sailing up the harbor."

"What was their purpose?"

"They demand the opening of our ports, closed for two hundred years, to the trade of the world."

Keiki reflected.

"It is evil—this complication with foreign peoples at this time," he said. "But proceed, my lord."

The other continued:

"Four foreign ships-of-war are now in Yedo Bay. They are American. They are in much doubt as to who is the ruler of the country. The Shogun Iyesada has assured them that he reigns supreme. Treaties are now being negotiated. The Shogun has taken it upon himself to change the policy of our country without reference to the Son of Heaven" (the Mikado).

"This is treason," cried Keiki. "We must march against the Shogun at once."

"Nay, my lord, permit an insignificant vassal to suggest that our country must present at this critical juncture an undivided front against the foreigner. It may be that the Shogun in his weakness before the foreigner but temporizes in his presence. The foreigner must be expelled, and, after that, the Shogun dealt with."

"You are right, my lord. I congratulate you upon your wisdom and foresight, and beg that you will now retire to rest."

"May I inquire whether you purpose taking any action, your highness?" inquired Nagato.

"I am decided," said Keiki. "In the morning I shall set out for Yedo, whatever the peril. I must make observations."

Long after the others had retired, Keiki tried to review clearly the train of events that had led up to this occurrence. He must decide upon his course. In spite of the European knowledge transferred to him by the Lord of Satsuma, the very term "foreigner" sent a vague thrill of unknown terror to his soul. He had been told of their arms and other methods of warfare; many of their secrets were his. He had, if not their armaments, at least fair imitations—gunpowder, cannon, and rifles. Yet in spite of all this, an emotion that was not fear, not cowardice, made its way subtly to his heart. These foreigners stood for a strange civilization which, despite his vaguely derived knowledge, might yet include greater destructive agencies.

Then who could clearly see beyond their diplomacy? They might come simply, as they said, to demand open ports. But their own history showed that such things had been the forerunners of wars of aggression, wars for the acquisition of territory. No man might know what the extent of the latter demanded. They were a distinct peril to the whole

ONOTO WATANNA

of Dai Nippon. Yet what was to be done with regard to the shogunate? Iyesada was dealing with these foreigners, making treaties, without the sanction of his imperial master, the Mikado. If, on the other hand, Keiki should move with all his forces against the Shogun, would not the foreigners, taking advantage of civil war, better their mysterious position and gain whatever object they might have in view?

No, it seemed clear to Keiki that, unless something unforeseen intervened, every energy must be made by a united country to keep out the foreign powers. When this was definitely accomplished the Mikado's reign would be established with little delay before the foreigners could recover.

This was the final and definite conclusion reached by Keiki. He saw a certain advantage in the arrival of the foreign ships-of-war, provided they came in good faith. They would serve to distract attention from the aroused and armed state in which the southern provinces now were, to which they had been brought under his direction.

"I will go to Yedo at sunrise," he told himself.

His temples were throbbing painfully, the result of long nights without sleep, of long days of thought and care. He sighed and drew his hand across his brow.

"My lord is ill?"

He started at the voice. It had a vaguely familiar sound. The young boy, Jiro, had started towards him a pace, and then had retreated backward, as though overcome by his temerity.

"My lord is ill?"

"An insignificant pain in the brow," said the Prince.

The boy slipped behind the Prince softly and fell upon one knee.

"Dear lord, will you not permit me to relieve the pain of your august brow?"

The Prince stirred uneasily. Again the strange quality of the boy's voice touched some hidden spring of memory. Taking his silence as consent, the boy laid a soft, cool hand on either side of Keiki's temples, pressing them with his finger-tips. The action, the touch, recalled in an instant a memory that was better than sleeping. It was thus the Lady Wistaria had been wont to woo away the pain that beset his brow when he had lain ill in her father's house.

Suddenly the Prince clasped his hands over those on his brow. Gradually he was drawing Jiro to a position facing him, when, eluding the Prince's grasp, Jiro sank to the floor and laid his head at Keiki's feet.

"Oh, my lord, I beseech you not to be angry with me for my forwardness. It was my solicitude for your pain—"

"Nay, rise," said the Prince, gently. "Pray do not confound me with apologies."

With his head still drooping, the boy retreated towards the door.

The Prince smiled at the fear apparent in Jiro's demeanor.

"You have done me no ill," he said, kindly; "you have actually soothed away the pain. I thank you."

XXVI

Upon his arrival in Yedo, Keiki made use of every precaution his ingenuity could devise, that the Imperialists might not discover his presence in the capital of the Shogun's government. His approach to the city had been attended only by Toro and Jiro, but during the last stage of the journey the three had separated, entering the city from opposite directions to meet in an isolated quarter near the water-front. Here the Imperialist party found it advantageous to maintain a small establishment whose squalid exterior gave no promise of the comparative comfort to be enjoyed beyond the threshold by those in possession of the pass-word.

From this house the movements and plans, the thoughts even, of the shogunate government in its own Yedo capital were observed and reported to those seeking the return of rightful sovereignty to the Mikado in his Kioto capital. Here at all hours of the night came men in mean dress, whose bearing, though consciously abased to that of merchants or laborers, was unmistakably that of the noble; here came strange, imperious young men who might pose as water-carriers, but whose hands sought an imaginary sword-belt at the least obstacle, and slight youths whose loose garments too poorly hid the curves of feminine figures. Of late the activity and the going to and fro of these persons had increased, but apparently without exciting the attention of the municipal authorities.

Although the young Prince of Mori had employed all artifice in gaining the Yedo headquarters of his party, yet he was surprised to note that his person attracted scarcely any attention. His position of peril, and his naturally observant mind, on guard to catch the slightest suspicious augury, would have led him to exaggerate any apparently hostile glance. Everywhere, the sole topic was of the foreigners, their strange behavior, their stated purposes, their mysterious ways, and their utter indifference to all Japanese usage.

When Keiki had been greeted by his fellow-Imperialists, and he had described to them the state of his southern resources, they in turn gave him such information as they had concerning the foreigners, whose arrival had obscured the future of their operations against the shogunate. The Prince of Echizen, temporarily in charge of the headquarters, reported in detail to his military superior the events which he had not yet described in his regular despatches to the head of the Mori family.

"I was unable, my lord, to send you further news," he said, "beyond the mere verbal report communicated by the Lord of Nagato before your departure."

The foreigners, he went on to say, had been on the coast some days now. They had first appeared in the bay of Yedo.

"Why were they not sent to Nagasaki?" demanded Keiki. "They should have been told that all foreign affairs are administered from that port."

"Ah," returned Echizen, "they are dealing with the bakufu, not the Emperor."

"Proceed, I beg you."

"When first they came upon the coast they announced to the Governor of Niaga that they bore letters and presents from the President of the United States of America; that they must deliver them to the Emperor in person, or to a high official appointed for that purpose. They were told by the shogunate, which took upon itself the right of dealing with matters intended for our Emperor, to go to Nagasaki. They replied by moving nearer up the bay to Yedo, which they took to be the Emperor's capital.

"They have sent out parties in boats to take soundings in the bay, despite the Governor's protests, and each hour brings them nearer to Yedo. This frightened the shogunate, which finally set a day for landing. To-morrow, near the fishing village of Yokohama, they are to land and present their letters to commissioners appointed by the Shogun to receive them. They will await a reply."

"What is their nature and strength?" demanded Keiki.

"They are four ships-of-war. They are Americans, and in command of a high Lord Perry."

"But why do they deal with the Shogun?"

The Prince of Echizen replied:

"They are ignorant of our true internal condition. They do not know that we have one true Emperor, a shadow of power, and a war lord, a Shogun, who rules for himself. These Americans are of the opinion that they are treating with the Mikado, with the Emperor of Japan. Their letters and credentials are inscribed to the Emperor of Japan."

Keiki reflected upon what Echizen had told him. The national situation was rapidly becoming strained. If the foreigners should be driven from the country, well and good; but it was now no time to attack the shogunate, which must be as embarrassed as its opponent over the advent of the Americans. In all events, the only present policy was delay. The shogunate might be destroyed by the foreigners, yet—

A sudden determination came to Keiki. He must know the attitude of the Shogun, even at risk to himself. He turned to the future premier.

"Your highness," he asked, "can you procure for me a uniform of the household of Iyesada?"

"What! the Shogun?"

"Yes."

"Certainly. In fact, one of our clan, who is secretly in sympathy with us, is a member of the Shogun's household and stands close to his august person. You may pass for the Lord Sakura."

Keiki, wrapped in a long cloak, stood near the entrance of the house awaiting some favorable moment, when the street should be clear of passers-by, to slip out into the night. As he was about to make a sudden spring to gain the street a hand clutched the hem of his cloak. The boy Jiro was restraining him.

"Go not out alone, my lord," he entreated.

Keiki frowned impatiently.

"One would think I were about to encounter danger. I go but to observe. There is no danger," he said, sharply.

The trembling hand of the boy Jiro tore wide the cloak.

"This uniform, my lord. It is of the Sho—"

Keiki, feeling a pang of sorrow at hurting the boy, but determined upon his mission, did not defer action long. At any moment, the street comparatively quiet, might be filled with wayfarers. He pushed Jiro gently but insistently from him and went out into the city.

At first he kept to the side streets, traversing much useless distance, but directing his general course towards the palace of the Shogun. Once or twice he thought himself followed, but, retracing his steps, came upon no pursuer. Finally he came to the avenues, where further concealment were fruitless and would only invite suspicion. In these thoroughfares, therefore, he flung back his cloak, permitting liberal glimpses of his bakufu uniform.

He found still the utmost indifference pervading the city concerning the movements of mere individuals, be they of the court of the Shogun or the court of thieves. In the storytellers' halls and the theatres, on the street corner and in all public places, groups speculated upon the presence of the foreigners in Japan. There was abroad a subtle, indefinable fear that in some way the coming of the foreigners was to change the destiny of the empire. The more ignorant could not see clearly in what way this was to come about, but there was present in their consciousness fear of an impending evil.

Nobles of both parties were unsettled. The foreign visitation might mean annihilation to either party. Ruin it did mean to one, but which? The shogunate seemed in the ascendant, since it had been recognized, blindly, but still recognized, by the foreigners. Thus among all classes there was manifest a great unrest, none the less threatening and fearful because its import was hidden. Plainly the shadow of events to come had darkened the nation's mind.

The tradesman in his shop, showing his wares to a purchaser, stated their price uncertainly.

"Just now, honorable sir, the price is three yen, but the gods alone know what it will be to-morrow, whether more, less, priceless beyond measure, or smaller than nothing at all. The barbarians—"

"Ah yes, these barbarians." His purchaser would nod understandingly.

At a street corner a woman approached a strolling samurai in the Shogun's uniform.

"Honorable samurai," she said, "what of the foreigners who have come?"

The samurai shrugged his shoulders.

"I'll tell you all I know of them," he murmured, without enthusiasm.

A group formed about him.

"What do you know of them?" pressed one.

"Tell us all," said another.

The samurai shifted one of the swords.

"Of a certainty I'll tell you all."

"Yes?"

"Of a truth they have come," he answered, as with a movement of disclaimer he passed up the street.

In the story-tellers' halls the reciter was besieged with requests for stories and information concerning the Americans. In some cases he frankly avowed his ignorance, and in others regaled his hearers with the weirdest tales of a resourceful imagination.

Witnessing incidents of this kind upon every side, Keiki continued on his way to the palace. Of one thing he was now fully assured. Whatever policy for the future might be decided on by him and his associates could not be put into immediate effect. The popular impulse, the popular mind was dazed, and was not ready for action. Meanwhile he would learn all he could of the intentions of both foreigners and Shogun.

Keiki was now quite near the palace of the Shogun. His cloak he threw carelessly about him in such wise that while his uniform was exposed his features were muffled. The gate before which stood the samurai on guard at the outer post was open. Without a word Keiki strode haughtily past the guards. They gave no challenge.

Within the grounds enclosed by the stone walls there was no reflection of the disquiet manifest throughout the city. From the broad, elevated balconies of the palace, shining in the soft light diffused through the fusuma, there floated down to the strained ears of Keiki the sound of women's laughter and the harsher tone of men's voices. Music mingled with other sounds that indicated the quiet enjoyment of the night. The very guards at the doors were careless in the performance of their duties, looking with the eye of artistic appreciation upon the night's gentle festivities.

Still undisturbed, Keiki passed through the palace entrances. An officer of the guard stared curiously for a moment after him once, then turned in forgetfulness to answer a woman's jest. Keiki ascended a stairway. In an upper ante-room he met an undermenial.

"The chamber of the Shogun," he said, coldly.

"Honorable lord," began the menial.

Prince Mori thrust a parchment before his eyes.

"The chamber of the Shogun at once," he said, sternly; "these despatches admit of no delay."

"His august excellency is very ill and has retired," said the servant.

Keiki turned upon him shortly.

"I know. Go!"

The attendant preceded him.

"One minute," said Keiki; "understand, my mission is secret. But pronounce the name Sakura to his augustness."

The man bent low. Then he entered a chamber. He reappeared shortly, and having signed to Keiki to enter, disappeared down a stairway. Keiki waited until his footsteps had passed away. Then he crossed the threshold, hesitating in the fashion of one who enters a strange apartment for the first time, conscious that its occupant has an advantage of prior acquaintance.

XXVII

For a moment Keiki was blinded by the profusion of light that blazed near the door of entrance, leaving the rest of the chamber in shadow. It was a large room, its walls tapestried in silk, wrought with embossed figures telling the history of the early Tokugawa wars. At irregular intervals about the room were set screens bearing the same gold-embroidered, symbolic figures. There were a few low tables, against which were thrown the implements and paraphernalia of war—swords, helmets, cuirass, armor, all richly wrought.

"Who are you?"

Keiki became conscious of a presence in the room. Stretched upon a low divan in a shadowed recess lay an indistinct figure, at whose elbow a low table, piled high with parchment and writing materials, stood.

"Who are you?" repeated the voice.

Keiki approached nearer, bowing courteously, though somewhat stiffly.

"Sakura," he said, to gain time, while he held out a roll of paper in his hand. He drew nearer to the figure on the divan. The cold eyes of the other scanned him without fear.

"You are not Sakura. You are—I know you. Be good enough to bring me that cabinet."

Keiki crossed the apartment to the spot indicated by the other's gesture. He brought a small, inlaid, lacquer box to the side of the divan.

The one upon the divan, without a trace of nervousness, opened the box and held up to the Prince of Mori a picture of himself.

"See," he said, "I have your portrait, with an interesting description attached of certain cannon foundries and works I believe you maintain in the south. Ah, there is something else written beneath the picture." He held it to the light. "Mori, head of the rebel cause, to be followed and beheaded. What is it you want with me?" he finished, replacing the portrait in the box.

Mori laid his hand upon his sword.

"What do you want with Iyesada? I am he, as you are well aware. It is less than a year, I believe, since your lordship was at my court."

Mori winced. The memory of that last visit recalled his first meeting with Wistaria. He became very pale.

"What do you want with me?" inquired the other, quietly watching him.

"To know your intentions towards the foreigners."

"Are you aware," returned the Shogun, "that a single sign from me would bring down a thousand guards upon your head?"

Mori smiled coldly, grimly.

"Ah, but your highness will not make that sign," he said.

"Why will I not?"

"Because your highness loves life."

"You would murder me?"

"I would cut off your head and show it to the people as the head of a traitor and an enemy to the Son of Heaven."

The Shogun appeared rather amused than alarmed. He regarded Mori with a peculiar and penetrating glance. Then he sighed.

"I was young and venturesome once," he said. "I, too, at one time, secretly believed as you do. Now—" He shrugged his shoulders.

"What are your intentions regarding these foreigners?"

"Are you here to treat with me, young Mori?"

"If you wish, yes. I represent a considerable party in the empire. I ask with right, for one day I shall unthrone your excellency."

Iyesada turned himself quickly upon his elbow, while his eyes continued to scrutinize the other keenly.

"What would you do in my place?" he asked.

"Refuse their every demand and drive them into the sea," returned Mori, as the blood tinged his cheek.

"No, you would not; that is, not if you are as far-sighted as I take you to be. Japan has been sealed to the foreigners for two hundred years, during which time she has grown strong in the development of her resources and her civilization. That period is at an end. It can never return. Foreign nations will demand trade with us. They will not depart at our refusal. They will use force, if necessary, holding that every nation must share in the comity of nations. If a nation refuse, they will divide her."

"Pah!" said Mori, impatiently. "Is the policy, then, of our Imperial realm to be dictated by a hoard of barbarous peoples concerning whom we know naught, save what our history in the past has taught us? When in the years long past they were admitted to our lands and we opened our arms in hospitality towards them, what was our reward? Foreign disease, insolent demands, a fanatical religion, intolerant and exacting. Finally we came to be treated as dogs by these our inferiors until we were forced to expel them, since which time has not our land been the happier for our seclusion?"

"It would seem," said Iyesada, "that you are not, in spite of the reports I have heard concerning you, keeping abreast of the times. You are not a son of the dawning new Japan; you would retard the progression which is pressing upon us from all sides."

"I would not have this progression come from the outside. I would have my country advance from within. That is the reason I am an Imperialist. You are right, my lord; a new Japan is about to dawn, but not through the invasion of yonder barbarians, but because the rightful ruler of our country will be restored to his throne."

Iyesada frowned.

"Again I ask," continued Mori, flushed with his feeling, "do you intend to treat with these foreigners?"

"I will treat with them. I will yield, but combating every step."

"I could declare a truce with you," said Mori, "and I possess the power to enforce it, if you will assume your rightful function of war lord and expel the foreigners."

Iyesada looked him through. There was in his glance the patient scorn of the man who sees beyond his life.

"You appear, Prince of Mori, to appreciate European civilization, you who have fashioned rifles. I have looked to you as one who might think with me. I thought you represented progress, in spite of the fact that your activities were directed against myself. I have left you to yourself for a time. I thought you saw, as I see, the new Japan, the Japan that in self-defence must assimilate European civilization to beat back these Europeans. I could offer you much."

"I belong to the Emperor, who rules by the right of the gods."

To his feet the Shogun leaped. Into his disease-deadened eyes there came the fire of strong will. He raised his arm.

"Sovereignty belongs to—"

"The Emperor," finished Mori, passionately.

"To the strongest," said the Shogun; "to that one who, seizing it, by his ability and wisdom uses it for the good of all. I am strong—he is weak. The strong—"

The Shogun ceased. Across his face there shot a spasm of acute pain. His breath came in gasps. Mori helped him to regain his couch. He smiled gently, sorrowfully.

"I said I was strong, yet I am indeed weak. I cannot live to see the new Japan. You may; but go, go! I have tried to save you from the folly of blind enthusiasm. You disappoint me—"

ONOTO WATANNA

"My lord!"

"I will allow you to go in peace. Until now I have thought well of you. Now I give you up to your fate. Your life is in danger."

Mori's hands clutched his sword-hilt. The Shogun shook his hand weakly.

"Not now. You may leave the place safely, but I warn you that henceforth you will be hunted. You will be killed the moment you show yourself. I give you twelve hours!"

Keiki bowed profoundly but coldly.

"As you please, my lord," he said, in leave-taking.

As Mori retraced his steps through cross-streets he heard hesitating footsteps behind him.

His sword flashed out. Running around an angle in the street, he came upon a slight figure.

"Who goes there?" he shouted.

"It is I, my lord," said a strangely sweet voice.

"Jiro! Well, my boy, so you followed me?"

"To protect you, my lord."

Mori's amused eyes scanned the slim figure of the stripling. He laughed tenderly.

"There was no need. I have twelve hours yet," he said, reflectively.

XXVIII

As Jiro followed closely behind his master on their return to the little house by the water-front, he noticed signs of intense preoccupation and irritation in Mori. The boy attempted to walk beside him, gazing into his face with that wistful appeal of the eye which Mori had been unable to fathom whenever his attention was caught by it. Now he was too much occupied with his thoughts to be more than disturbed by it. With a gesture of impatience he exclaimed, abruptly:

"Thou, Jiro, walk a space behind me."

Jiro fell back. In this wise they proceeded for some minutes until Jiro perceived that Mori was making signals to him. Jiro, quickening his step, came nearer to the Prince.

"Jiro, thou sluggard, hasten," called the Prince.

Jiro made trembling haste.

"Call a norimon at once," ordered his master.

Jiro ran into an adjacent street, returning shortly with the vehicle, at whose curtains he stood waiting for his lord to enter. Keiki's absent glance fell upon the face of Jiro. It was tear-stained. The eyes wore that strange expression of appeal which always touched certain emotions in the heart of Mori, so that even in his harshest mood he could never be otherwise than gentle with the lad. Entering the palanquin, he drew Jiro in after him.

For a time they travelled in silence. Jiro broke it to inquire very timidly:

"Whither do we go, my lord?"

If Mori heard him he made no sign. The journey was continued in silence. At the end of what seemed to Jiro two full hours, Mori dismounted from the carriage and bade the runners wait for him. Jiro saw that they were upon the ridge of a headland overlooking the bay at whose head stood the Shogun's city of Yedo.

At a sign from Keiki the boy followed the Prince down a path leading to the shore below. As they made their rough way along, Jiro saw lights flashing out in the bay, and occasionally he thought he heard the sound of oars.

A great distance up the shore he saw men at work upon a little building facing the bay. They were busily engaged by the light of abundant torches. The speed of Mori, however, permitted the boy to take few observations. Already his breathing was heavy and labored in his attempt to keep up with his master.

As they neared the water the curvature of the shore hid the torch-lighted spot from view. With sullen glance directed ahead of him, Mori kept on until he stood almost at the edge of the water, which in lapping, inky darkness glided and twisted at his feet. Then with his chin resting upon his arm, half reclining against a giant bowlder which, torn from the headland above, had ploughed a grudging way hither, Keiki looked out across the water.

It was silent—a silence made impressive and accentuated by elemental sounds, the lapping of the water below, the bursting of a crested wave, the swirl of pebbles and sand thrust insistently up the beach by the drive of the water. The darkness seemed a thing alive, which, taking on fiendish, malign personality, sought to blind the mind, the heart, the emotions, as it did the eyes.

There was an all-pervading suggestion of fate, of adversity, of other propagated influences through the night. Subtle spirits hovered, circled through the air, met, clashed their wings, turned, trembled down, down. Jiro could have shrieked aloud, could he have found voice.

Gradually, faintly, as the monotony of the natural sounds numbed his physical sense of hearing, Jiro found that a new sense of appeal to his ear was being made, off in the darkness. As they reached his consciousness, with their unmistakable human origin strongly impressed, his fright gave way. In its place came the calm of nerves raised to a higher tension. It was now the creaking of chains, the wooden friction of oars, the movements of men on board ship. All at once lights gleamed forth. They defined by their frequency and position the outlines of a vessel not unlike the smaller native boats plying in the bay. Other lights appeared in quick succession. Soon the forms of four giant vessels were indicated rather than revealed.

"The foreigner!" said Jiro, under his breath.

Then high up in the air, above the leading of the four defined vessels, flashed a variety of colored lights. These were instantly answered from the others. There was the rhythmic sound of men at work upon some machine, the clatter of chains at the bows, and the vessels moved nearer to the shore.

These manœuvres were partially understood by Keiki. The lord of that fleet, hitherto unseen by any Japanese, was getting up his anchors and drawing nearer to the shore, having sent out his boats first to take proper soundings.

Every light below the deck line revealed an open port, and every open, lighted port showed a gun slung shoreward. The squadron's people were to land the next day, but they were all vigilance in the mean time.

One by one the vessels moved to their new positions. After an interval, the noise and movement seemed to cease about them. A light was hoisted aloft on board the leading vessel. Instantly every light disappeared from the ports, and the blackness of the night again enveloped their movements.

Mori turned towards the boy, noting curiously the spasmodic working of his features.

"What is it, Jiro?" he asked, kindly.

"It is a strange civilization," said Jiro, in a choking voice.

"Civilization!" repeated Keiki—"civilization! I seem to hear that word everywhere to-night."

XXIX

All through the night, while Mori and other Imperialists looked interrogatively to the forces within and without the country, and while the dreaded foreigners kept careful watch upon their ships, native artisans reared the structure afterwards known in the memories of the strangers as the "Treaty House."

Simple as was the building, its erection was attended with certain outward signs which would have led the observer to identify in them the same spirit pervading the market-place, the open public gathering space, the theatres, the shops.

Those who labored under torch-light, an unusual proceeding in itself, were impressed with a misshapen, grotesque, wholly undefined fear. Artisans as they were, they realized, if subconsciously, that their act had in it the germs of a future—dark and ominous, their instincts asserted. The Japanese officials—of a minor grade—who directed the work, being higher in the scale of intelligence, were by no means so vague in their minds. They believed firmly that the raising of this simple building meant the downfall of their country, its government, its institutions. Rapacious foreigners for two centuries had insulted them and flouted at Japan, had returned to accept no delay or parley.

Indeed, certain *sub-rosa* expressions of opinion and declarations of purpose among officers of the fleet, translated to them by visitors to the foreign ships of that alien nation alone tolerated in Japan at this period—the Dutch—had deepened the alarm. The strangers had said in effect: "No nation has a right to withdraw herself from the comity and commerce of other nations. Japan must come to this view; amicably, if possible, but through cannoned arguments if not otherwise."

Every act of the strangers thus far had been in accord with this secret expression of policy. The reserve and punctilious etiquette of the Japanese had been met with a bold advance by Commodore Perry's squadron. At each pretext for delay advanced by the Japanese the ships had moved nearer to Yedo, believed by the officers of the squadron, knowing nothing of the Shogun-Emperor relationship, to be the capital of the Emperor of Japan.

When Perry had been told that he might deliver his letters and credentials to minor officials, he had replied that first they must send to him commissioners second in rank only to the Emperor. Perry himself, imitating the seclusion of those whom he sought to reach, took care to be seen or approached by no Japanese, delegating inferior officers to the task. Now for the first time he was to show himself to the people, and the nobles, the princes Aidzu and Catzu, in their capacity of high commissioners were to meet him.

Thus it was that all watched the work upon the Treaty House in sullen emotion. The workmen themselves moved in complete silence, which was broken not by word, but only by the noise of their operations. Their superiors gave their instructions by gesture or brief word.

The building itself was not pretentious, although its situation on a slight elevation near the water was central, in full view of the fleet out in the bay, and was overlooked by the surrounding heights and bluffs. It consisted of an ante-chamber and a long audience-hall, around whose side a sort of divan had been built. At the head of this apartment a number of chairs were placed for the comfort of the foreigners. In the centre of the space, upon a raised platform, whose tapestries and hangings suggested the altar of some semi-barbarian church, stood an immense, red-lacquered box, destined for the reception of the papers brought by the foreigners for transmittal to the "Emperor."

In the distance were the encampments containing the retinues of the princes Aidzu and Catzu, to which the artisans withdrew when, as a final touch of preparation, they had secluded the entire surrounding of the Treaty House by the erection of huge bamboo and silken screens.

All were now awaiting the hour of eleven in the morning, the hour set for the ceremonial. The departure of a boat from the *Susquehanna* was observed. In addition to its rowing crew, it contained a single officer in the stern.

Those about the Treaty House watched the dancing course of the boat over the waves, until, having discharged its officer at the coastline, it withdrew into stiller water; watched with seeming apprehension his landward course up the heights.

The officer was young; he knew a few words of Japanese, and went at once to the point upon his arrival before the Treaty House.

"What do these screens mean?" he demanded.

The minor officials looked from one to another. One official, a determined expression passing for an instant over his face, stepped forward. He bowed politely.

"We—insignificant and unworthy brained men that we are—cannot understand that honorable language that you speak. It is not Japanese, nor yet Dutch, which alone we know."

Enough of this speech was understood by the lieutenant. Plainly, they pretended not to understand his Japanese.

"Wherefore these hidings of the light of the honorable sun from our insignificant eyes?" he continued in Japanese, changing his idiom.

Again came the answer of the Japanese official.

"Your excellency, we cannot understand."

The lieutenant uttered an oath. These heathen were trying, he told himself.

"Any one here speak English?" he demanded.

Instantly a figure sprang forward out of the crowd of sightseers beyond the military lines. Having advanced boldly, the volunteer hesitated an instant, as if he had acted upon an impulse, regretted a moment too late. It was Mori, but Mori still in disguise.

The American lieutenant saw his hesitation.

"Do you speak English?"

Keiki summoned such knowledge of the language as Satsuma had taught him. He answered briefly:

"Yes."

"Then ask what these screens have been put up for."

Keiki repeated the question to the Japanese officer, who, angered at his penetration of their evasion, cast surly glances upon him. They answered readily, however. Mori translated their reply into English a moment later.

"They say," he reported, "that in Nippon all great gatherings are private. These screens keep off the common, low people."

"Tell them these things must come down," ordered the officer, in what the Japanese considered an impolite, not to say insolent, tone.

Mori translated.

"What do they say?" asked the lieutenant.

There was a pause.

"Nothing yet," said Mori, stiffly.

While the officials still stared, the officer turned to the offending screens. With his own hands he began their demolition. Slowly, one by one, the Japanese joined him. Soon the space once enclosed by the screens was bare to the view of all on the American vessels. The officer moved towards his boat.

"I wish to speak some more words with you," said Mori, following him.

"Oh, certainly. What is it?"

"Not here, if you please. Down by the boat."

"Come."

Followed by the angry looks of the whole group of Japanese sub-officials, in which there was distinct hostility towards himself, Mori went with the lieutenant to a spot towards which the boat was approaching.

"Now what can I do for you?" inquired the officer, more affably.

"You think you treat with the Emperor?" inquired Mori, his face flushed by the other's lack of courtesy.

"Certainly."

"You do not."

"What?"

The officer started, regarding Mori sceptically.

"No, you do not. You but treat with his war lord—the Shogun."

"What's the Shogun?"

"There are two emperors in Japan; one the rightful emperor, the Mikado; the other his vassal, his war lord, who is without authority to deal with you. He makes seeming submission to the Emperor."

"Is this true?"

"Tell it to your master, that Lord Perry. Ask that he demand the truth from those sent to meet him, in the public gathering."

"Why, this is astounding! It must be looked into. Will you come on board with me and report it in person?"

Mori shook his head.

"No, I cannot," he replied, "but let him seek the truth where it must be told unto him."

They had been speaking in Japanese, with an occasional word of English, when one was unable to understand the other's rendering of its equivalent. The officer returned to English.

"Your name?" he asked.

Mori replied in Japanese.

"Your master is honorably ignorant of my name and rank. The truth from any source is sufficient. Ask at the proper place, and you will know that I speak truth."

The officer paused, with one leg lifted over the gunwale of the boat. He made a sudden movement towards his men, sitting with raised oars.

"Seize him!" he ordered.

Before the sailors could drop their oars and obey, Keiki, who divined the significance of the words, ran rapidly along the sandy beach, disappearing beyond a headland.

"Damned awkward, this," commented the lieutenant, "but it must be reported to the old man." Then to his crew:

"Give way, men!"

XXX

Whatever speculation the sudden friendly interposition of a Japanese into the American officer's dilemma caused among the sub-officials in charge of the Treaty House, it did not run a lengthy course. News that was whispered about, first among the multitude of unofficial visitors crowding all the surrounding points of vantage not occupied by the Shogun's troops, penetrated gradually to the focal spot of the greatest curiosity, the Treaty House. It was an event of secondary importance to the expected visit from the men-of-war. The princes Aidzu and Catzu had arrived from Yedo, and were now awaiting the foreigners in the quarters prepared for them.

Many of those present had never seen these powerful princes. So, crowding past the common soldiers, they pressed upon their headquarters, until stopped by the chosen guard of samurai surrounding the princely pavilions.

About the tent of Catzu the press of the mob was heaviest. The huge Sir Genji, toying with his glittering blade significantly whenever a curious citizen came too near the entrance, remarked grimly to a fellow-samurai:

"Of a truth, all the dogs of Nippon invade our ranks to-day. I have only to extend my sword to split a dozen fat merchants."

"Extend it, then," growled the other, as with the flat of his blade he dealt a gentle blow upon the pate of a vender of wines.

The treatment accorded to the crowd by the samurai engendered no bitterness. The mercantile classes, awed at all times by the sight of one in samurai orders, shrank back at the first sign of displeasure brought upon themselves from the proudest grade in Japan.

Nor, indeed, was the real displeasure of the samurai at any time in evidence. They, too, like the common people, were engrossed in the expectation of events. Although their impassive faces did not permit the revelation of their real feeling, there was among them the same subtle curiosity and foreboding.

From across the bay, rolling and reverberating, striking the rocky angles of the highlands and driven back repulsed, came the long roar of the foreigners' saluting guns. Instantly the populace became silent, riveted to whatever locality they occupied.

Among the ships there was bustle and movement. The foreigners

ONOTO WATANNA

were lowering boats from every vessel in their squadron. With their crews and officers sitting in them, the boats swung from the davits into the water. Plainly the squadron was sending every man and officer to be spared.

While the guns were still vomiting forth their salute to the occasion, the Lord Catzu came forth from his tent. With a wave of his hand he turned to Genji.

"Drive me back this rabble," he ordered.

Instantly the samurai, joining with the common troop, beat back the mass of citizens, forcing open a wide lane, that extended but a short distance towards the Treaty House. Where no guards were, there the people obstructed the passage.

Genji quickly remedied this by despatching guards to clear a pathway to a point where a similar line from the Prince of Aidzu's pavilion should join. Into the two paths opened by the Shogun's troops the cortege of the two prince-commissioners passed. That of the Lord Catzu was headed by a troop of the young sons of samurai, boys small in stature, bearing aloft a silken banner whose gold embroideries were the crests of the Shogun and his feudal vassal Catzu. Next rode a troop of inferior samurai, heavily armed, on black horses. After them came the chief vassal of the Lord Catzu, mounted on a white horse, with three of his own vassals, each with his train of attendants. Finally, at the head of a brilliant and sparkling train of warriors and courtiers, came the imposing and portly Lord of Catzu, carried in a gilded norimon. A company of samurai, whose chief upon all ordinary occasions was Sir Genji, brought up the rear.

The train of the Prince of Aidzu was, in general order and arrangement, similar to that of the Lord Catzu.

The two cortèges moved in lines slightly converging until they met. Then the heads of each side column or division rode side by side. Throughout the whole company, in perfect order, this arrangement held, the left train of the Lord Catzu being nearer the bay than that of Aidzu. So completely was the symmetry of the parallel movement carried out that the Prince of Catzu had on his left the Prince of Aidzu.

At the moment of complete juncture, a word of command sped back among the allied ranks. In a moment Genji, at the head of a large body of mounted samurai, passed to the right of his lord on his way to the van. A similar body passed along the left.

These samurai, arrived at the front, rapidly drove the crowds back from the line of march, leaving a passage, which they lined at intervals, clear to the Treaty House. Each samurai rode back and forth in the side space he had kept free to himself.

The gorgeous pageant advanced rapidly through the short passage until its head rested upon the entrance of the Treaty House. Instantly the lines of the two princes divided as before, falling back on either side until the two norimons of the princes were reached. These advanced as before until the chief vassal of each prince stood before the Treaty House. Then the vassals assisted their lords to dismount from their norimons, bowing deeply and profoundly as they did so.

Side by side the two commissioners marched to the door of entrance, whose threshold they crossed alone. After a respectful interval the chief vassals and functionaries, with a number of samurai, followed their lords. The military force and other attendants still stood with their ranks open outside. Genji gave a quick command, and, the double ranks closing, faced about so as to present a solid armed front to any one moving against the Treaty House.

Inside, the princes with their chief commissioners were ranged at the head of the Treaty House, in silent waiting on the foreigners.

Meanwhile the fleet of small boats from the squadron were nearing the shore. Splendid as was the retinue of the commissioners, and outnumbering as it did that of the Americans, yet it was apparent at a glance that Perry had stripped his ships of all but a small force. The boats, crowded to the gunwales, moved slowly to the landing-place, built over-night.

First, the bodies of sailor-soldiers were disembarked. They wore the dress of sailors, but each carried a musket. Then a band came ashore. Finally the officers of the squadron and Perry's staff itself mingled with the others. A small guard was left with the boats before the march was taken up to the Treaty House. Then, in quick step to the music of the band, the company set off, travelling at twice the pace of the Japanese retinues.

The band marched first. Then came the marines with their officers. In the centre was the Commodore Perry, with his staff. Following were more marines and officers.

As this array proceeded in the quick, sharp, uniform step peculiar to disciplined bodies, there were no shouts of applause, no encouraging cheers, no uncovering of heads, no clapping of hands. The silent multitudes regarded them sullenly, expectantly, fearfully.

"Gad!" exclaimed a young lieutenant, "they don't take to us. This is no Fifth Avenue parade."

"No, it is not. More like action," mumbled his companion.

When the officers came within sight of the entrance and saw the columns hostilely arranged, there was a movement of alarm. But quickly the dual force of Catzu and Aidzu spread out to permit a passage through itself.

The Americans gave an order. Their band went suddenly to the rear, its place taken by a body of marines, who moved until their head rested upon the door of entrance. They in turn opened a way for the division at whose head marched the chief officer. With arms at "present," they stood awaiting its approach.

At the head of the division now advancing, under the colors and backed by minor officers, strode a commanding figure. It was that of a full-bodied, ruddy, stern-featured man, in whose every poise of body and head was command. He was bareheaded. About his temples the breeze from the bay scattered his short, slightly gray hair.

The sight of the Japanese army in its menacing position, facing the multitudes, may have carried alarm to his soul. It had been instantly met by his counter arraying of marines; but there was no fear manifest in face, gait, or manner. Without pause he entered quickly the audience-hall, followed by his officers. Turning his head to neither side, he seated himself in a chair similar in respect and position to those occupied by the commissioners.

There was a pause, a momentary embarrassment was felt by all present. Then the American commodore summoned the Dutch interpreter, through whom the conversation was to take place.

"Inform them," he said, "that I have some questions to ask."

XXXI

When the company of foreigners had passed into the Treaty House, the few moments intervening before the beginning of the ceremonies within were employed by the samurai still on guard outside in scrutinizing the cards of those citizens whose rank permitted them to fill the vacant rear of the hall.

At first the samurai, exacting in their task, examined carefully the invitation of each applicant. When, however, those in charge warned them that the time was short, they crowded ceremoniously within their lines into the hall, while those without, whether card-holders or not, were driven back roughly.

The movement had been noted in its first stages by Mori, who with Toro and Jiro had been forcing his way steadily towards the guarding samurai. When the first press of the rejected smote him on all sides, he turned to Jiro.

"If we are separated in this turmoil, I would charge you, Jiro—" he began.

The sudden interposition of a double rank of samurai drove him back, while it swept his companions within the circle of those being forced into the Treaty House. Turning, Jiro watched Mori struggle under the disadvantage the crowd imposed upon him. Then, with a resigned smile and a shrug of the shoulders, Mori made to Jiro a sign of writing. A moment more and Toro and Jiro found themselves within the audience-chamber. They gained places beside an opening through which the samurai preserving order outside could be seen.

When the American commodore addressed his first words to the interpreter, the Lord of Catzu arose. Toro and Jiro whispered together as they caught sight of the gorgeous figure. The interpreter translated to him the words of the American. Then through the interpreter the Lord of Catzu made reply:

"August sir, Lord Admiral of the unknown fleet, we will have joy in answering your honorable questions—any and all—in good time," he said. "But first allow us to offer our apologies. We were unable to provide you with arm-chairs such as your excellency is accustomed to occupy on board your honorable ships; for that reason we are greatly pained, and trust you will overlook our impoliteness. But that chair which you now fill and whose brothers we humbly occupy, out of compliment to your excellency, resembles it so far as our abilities have been able to copy it."

The American commodore looked at the chair he occupied. If the first words of the commissioner appealed at all to his risibilities, he was both too courteous a gentleman and too astute a diplomat to betray any sign. His face was grave to solemnity as he regarded the superb workmanship of the chair upon which he sat, plainly an Oriental interpretation of an American article.

"The chair is comfortable. It serves its purpose and honors its makers," he made reply. "But I desire before presenting my credentials to question the prince-commissioners."

Some one tapped Jiro lightly upon the shoulder. Looking about, he saw that a samurai, half extended through the window, had thus drawn his attention, and he was now making him the peculiar secret sign of the Imperialist, that of dropping suddenly downward the left hand with the little finger extended. Jiro looked into the face of the samurai Genji, where a smile of peculiar meaning shone. In the shock of surprise, Jiro's face was raised so that Genji's eyes gazed closely upon the entire contour, as for a moment the hair fell back from the youth's brow. Instantly the smile in Genji's face changed. His expression became involved. In it, Jiro read surprise, then delight, distrust, and apprehension.

As Jiro's eyes met Genji's again, the crimson flushed with sudden violence the lad's cheeks. His eyes sank. Genji slipped into his hand a tiny roll.

"What is it?" whispered Toro.

"Genji," said Jiro, with an expression of terror; "he recognized me."

"But what did he want?"

Then Jiro recalled the paper in his hands. He opened it with trembling fingers. It was brief, and from Mori, who had evidently trusted his old friend Genji to deliver it to his attendant Jiro.

"*If aught is said of the cause, defend!*" he read.

"What is the meaning?" said Toro.

"Plainly what he says," returned Jiro; "if any one speaks ill of the cause I am to silence and confound him."

Toro smiled with superiority.

"You!" he whispered; "it is for me."

With a passionate movement of negation, Jiro thrust the epistle into his bosom.

"Do nothing," urged Toro; "if you disturb this gathering you are as good as dead. For a samurai it would be a pleasing feat." Toro swelled in appreciation. "But for you—" He broke off. "Mori would not have asked it if he had known—"

"Silence!" whispered Jiro. "Listen."

Several of the Dutchman's translations had been lost by Toro and Jiro, but the interpreter was now speaking again for the American.

"I desire to know," he said, "before I deliver my letters, with whom I am treating—with what Emperor—with which of the two?"

The Japanese were astounded.

"You are dealing with the Emperor of Japan," they responded.

"But there are two. Which one?"

"We are unable to explain," said Aidzu; "we cannot account for your strange belief."

"Perhaps," interjected the wily Catzu, "the Lord Admiral has confounded the head of our religion with the head of our state."

"I must speak," said Jiro, who was laboring under repressed excitement. "It is time."

"Tsh-h!" growled Toro, staying his effort to rise.

"Let the prince-commissioner continue. I have been told that there are two emperors in this land, and that I have been placed in communication with the inferior, who is without authority to ratify his acts."

"I assure you, my Lord Admiral," said Catzu, "that you have fallen into an error common to foreigners."

"Possibly," was Perry's brief assent.

"We have two heads, one a font of wisdom, the other of action. The one is the spiritual head, the divine Emperor; the other the true ruler and Emperor, with whom you are in communication. The spiritual head is without authority in mundane affairs. You make no error, for we, the princes of Japan's real ruler, tell you this."

Despite every attempted restraint of Toro, Jiro leaped to his feet.

"Thou liest! Thou knowest there is but one true ruler in Japan, the Mikado!" he shouted, in a voice that, rapidly ascending in pitch, became femininely shrill.

Every eye in the assembly, foreign and Japanese, turned upon the slight, quivering figure there by the breeze-swept opening. The Lord of Catzu, still upon his feet, stood like a sable statue, his arm still held aloft in the concluding gesture he had used a moment before. The

Prince of Aidzu remained in his chair, seemingly incapable of motion. The American Perry alone preserved his composure, looking from one to the other in a puzzled effort to determine the meaning of this interruption.

The silence within the hall deepened as the startled gaze of the assemblage continued fixed upon Jiro. So still was it that the voices of the samurai outside seemed annoyingly loud, as they floated into the quiet apartment.

There was a long moment of this stunned, bewildered, yet intense stillness. It was broken by Toro, who, ashamed of having been outdone in daring by his slighter companion, threw himself convulsively into the focus of the company.

"Thou, my Lord of Catzu," he shouted—"thou knowest that the youth speaks truth. Banzai the Mikado! Banzai Nippon!"

Another sensational moment! The samurai Genji had placed himself nearer to the two.

The Lord of Catzu broke the spell of wonderment. As he frowned penetratingly upon Toro and Jiro, his face cleared in sudden recognition of his son. He raised his arm in imperative signal to the samurai.

"Eject for me these fanatics," he cried, "and guard them closely."

Instantly the gigantic Genji, leaping through the opening, laid a heavy hand upon the shoulder of the youth. Back to the opening he drew them.

"They are in my custody, my lord," he answered.

While the samurai drew the struggling comrades into the outer air, there was the quick hum of voices over the assemblage that a moment before had seemed as stone. Neighbor conversed with neighbor, the Japanese in consternation, the Americans in wonder.

The interpreter rapidly translated to the American officer the words that had passed between the commissioner and his interrupters. Some of the Americans caught at the drift of events even before their comrades sitting near to the interpreter understood the Dutchman's statements to their commander.

"'Pears to me to be something to this two-king business," said a marine to his fellow.

"We'll leave our bones here, sure enough," was the pessimistic response.

"What explanation can you offer of this?" demanded Perry.

The Lord Catzu lifted his eyebrows.

"Explanation! I do not explain it. They were fanatical priests, madmen, who thought that the head of the church should take over the direction of the state. You have such in your own country?"

The American was not satisfied with this statement. The interpreter informed the commissioners of this fact. Said the Lord Catzu:

"If you do not believe me, I shall, with the concurrence of my colleague, be obliged to declare all proceedings estopped. I cannot continue under such circumstances."

The American saw thus slipping from him the rewards of the labor of months. He might be making a mistake, but he must proceed at once.

"I am ready to continue," he said.

"Very well. You may deliver your letters to the Emperor of Japan," responded Catzu, with great dignity.

At a sign from Perry, two cabin-boys who had remained in the ante-chamber came up the central aisle, closely followed by two huge negroes in marine dress. The boys carried silver and gold salvers, upon which rested the richly set gold boxes containing the documents signed by Millard Fillmore, President of the United States of America, asking consideration of a treaty for open ports.

As the boys reached the red-lacquered box at the head of the hall they stood upon either side, while the negroes stopped between them. Lifting the letter receptacles from the salvers, the negroes deposited them in the red chest indicated by an aide of Catzu. This done, they retreated down the aisle.

"All is now done," said Catzu. "Permit me to inquire when your excellency will return for an answer."

"In some months' time," was Perry's thoughtful reply.

"We need not detain you longer," said the commissioner. "Permit us to express our gratification at meeting you and our compliments for your courtesy."

The American commodore acknowledged the deep obeisance with which the commissioners and their staffs now favored him with a bow as courtly and dignified as their own.

Then foreigners and Japanese filed out from the Treaty House of Yokohama.

XXXII

With the fecundity peculiar to the storm and stress period of a nation's history, the germ almost forcibly implanted into Japanese soil by Commodore Perry waxed strong, came to blossom, fell into seed, and ended by multiplying itself into international form. No sooner had two seaports been opened through signature of the treaty passed by Perry than the English sought and obtained the same privileges. Other nations followed the leaders in timeliness, differing as to their national equation. Then came the establishment of foreign legations and the general introduction into Japan of the hated foreigners. The hermit nation was no more permitted the luxury of the solitude which had made it internally strong.

But now the foreigners were coming to understand the dual state of Japanese government. The treaties which the shogunate had at first attempted to make without Imperial sanction were nominally submitted to the Mikado. In a measure, the brave daring of the boy Jiro was responsible for this latter development.

During all this time Mori had remained in Yedo watching the course of events, and the gradual rise in prestige of the already powerful shogunate.

The policy advocated by Mori was the same outlined by him in his act of instruction to Jiro when he had bade the boy explain to the foreigners the true conditions of government. The shogunate must be embroiled with the foreign powers in such a way that retaliation of the world-powers would fall upon the shogunate alone, destroying it, while at a leap the Imperial party would return to power upon an anti-Shogun basis. This policy he was foremost in pressing upon other leaders of his party, but without avail. The drift of events was too uncertain to permit civil war at this time, his compatriots asserted.

Toro and Jiro did not share the Yedo vigil of Mori. When, upon the evening of the Treaty House assemblage, Genji had brought them to Keiki's headquarters, the Prince had received them as from the grasp of death. The task he had set them, he knew, meant a risk of death, but even a samurai of lesser rank would have welcomed a death decreed by the cause. He had given them up as memories of the past when the great Genji brought them before him.

"My prince," Genji had said, "I have ever been at heart one of your party. As an earnest of my desire to return to your allegiance, I bring you two prisoners, committed to my hands by the Lord of Catzu."

The sight of the samurai Genji had called back into the life and soul of Mori things he had put aside as unfitting his consecration to the cause. Nevertheless, he received him gladly, and made no objection to the proposal of the samurai that he should be permitted to go with Toro and Jiro to the Mori fortress, since longer residence in Yedo was unsafe for the two who had exhibited themselves before the choice gathering of the Shogun's followers at the Treaty House. So it was that for a time Mori remained alone in Yedo.

The continued presence in the Shogun's city of one known throughout the length and breadth of the land as the Imperialist leader could not in the nature of events remain unknown to the authorities. On several occasions he was pressed so hard that he found an occasional sojourn outside of Yedo imperative. It was upon his return from one of these flittings that the Prince Mori found strange news awaiting him.

The Shogun Iyesada was dead. The choice of a successor devolving upon the Regent Ii, a man said to be of low birth, the wishes of a considerable number of the shogunate following had been ignored. Kii, a boy of twelve, had been selected by the Regent.

To make a show of boasted power before the foreigners, now always pressing for treaty privileges, the Regent Ii had ratified with them a treaty then pending, afterwards reporting it tardily to the Emperor at Kioto.

Instantly the city rang with protest, and, following it, the country.

"This Ii would remain alone with a boy Shogun!" cried the nobles of both parties.

Mori despatched instantly to his fortress couriers who conveyed orders to Toro that a considerable body of Mori's troops should proceed at once to Yedo. Before their arrival, however, a crisis had been reached.

Ronins in great numbers had visited the Imperialist headquarters, urging instant action. These roving samurai, having renounced all allegiance to their own lords, had become free agents (ronins), and had sworn never to return to their homes until the shogunate was overthrown.

One Hasuda headed a party that sought out the Prince Mori.

"Let every foreign legation be burned this night," urged Hasuda. "Let us drive into the seas those dogs who already have delayed our action too long. Let it be done to-night."

"No," said Mori, firmly. "Do not let your acts, which hitherto, in spite of their lawlessness, have been tinged with patriotism, be tainted by such action as you now propose. The function of a patriot is not that of assassination, but of honest warfare. Be counselled by me. Do nothing yet awhile. Wait! My men are on the march. They cannot arrive for some days. When they have come, and when our Mikado has given us the signal, let us then attack and expel these foreign barbarians."

"No, no," insisted Hasuda, whose sword itched for action; "the Mikado is influenced by those about him who are hostile to us. He dare not."

"Only by his order will I attack the foreigners," Mori insisted.

"He will not speak," said Hasuda.

"He will," said Mori. "I have assurances to that effect."

Hasuda altered his plea.

"But, your highness," he urged, "what I now advocate is your own policy. The shogunate is responsible to the foreigners for the peace. Destroy their legations and their wrath will descend upon the shogunate."

"Listen; I will not stoop to massacre, but I promise you that upon the order of the Emperor I will fire at once upon their fleets and make warfare against them."

The ronin Hasuda smiled slyly, as with a gesture of resignation he threw his arms aside.

"Your highness," he said, "be it so. I consent, upon one condition. Go thou to Kioto. Obtain at once audience with the Son of Heaven. Secure his consent. Thou hast means within the palace to reach him safely. Do so, then. I will await your return."

"Agreed," answered Mori.

Within a few moments his norimon was carrying him out of Yedo.

Two ronins joined Hasuda near the headquarters half an hour later.

"Your news?" he demanded.

"The Prince of Mori is on the highway to Kioto."

"Good! Then let the bands separate."

The several hundred ronins, divided into parties of some six or seven, set out in various directions. Two hours later they were in the shadow of the Sakurada gate of the Shogun's palace.

A spy from the interior made his report to Hasuda. It was accompanied by many gestures directed towards the wide path which led through the garden to the palace within.

A stately procession was passing down the garden path and had taken the road. It was the cortège of the Baron Ii Kamon-no-Kami, the hated Regent of Japan. Only his ordinary train of attendants and samurai accompanied him. Absorbed in their own personal reflections, they were apparently without suspicion of a planned assault.

Hasuda, in the shadow of the gate and the farther shadow of the cedars which bent their branches over the walls, raised his sword.

"Now," he whispered, in a soft, penetrating voice, insistent as the hiss of a serpent. From the shadows of the walls against which they had stood ronins leaped upon the samurai and attendants about the norimon of Ii. These gave way instantly, some were killed outright, others wounded, while still others were left engaged in deadly strife with ronin adversaries.

"Quick! Forward!" urged Hasuda.

A chosen body sprang out from the ronin ranks, and surrounding the norimon of the Regent, drew him with rough hands out into the road. They dragged him before Hasuda. Within the palace a cry of alarm rang through the night, followed by the hurried mustering of troops.

Outside the Sakurada gate, however, the numerous ronins, showing no sign of fear, proceeded leisurely. Ii had fallen upon his knees. His mute lips moved in prayers for mercy, though no sound escaped them. His lips were livid, his eyes glazed.

At what seemed this manifestation of cowardice the ronins, outlawed samurai as they were, laughed scornfully. They would have died unflinchingly. Ii was not of samurai blood.

"Death to the traitor!" roared a ronin chorus.

"Ay," replied Hasuda—"death!" Then to the Regent: "Ii, thou art a traitor. Rise and receive sentence."

Ii seemed paralyzed with fear.

"Let him die," said Hasuda.

"Let him die," growled the ronins.

Hasuda sent a keen glance over his ranks. He said, quickly:

"Let a samurai volunteer as executioner, but let him remember that he, too, must die, that no Shogun follower may punish him."

A grim, middle-aged ronin pushed forward.

"I was of Satsuma," he said; "that is all you need know of me."

"Do thy office," commanded Hasuda.

The samurai thereupon forced the Regent to his knees, where he cringed trembling and shivering. The sword of the samurai hissed, curved, shone, shot through the air. The head of Ii lay upon the ground.

Hasuda then spoke:

"That no malice may be imputed to us, use thy second sword."

Without a word the Satsuma samurai drew his second sword from his belt. The hilt he rested upon the ground. In an instant he fell upon its point.

The ronins left the vicinity of the palace, carrying the head of Ii with them. This they nailed to a post in a public place of the city.

In a short time, from the newly established foreign quarter of Yedo, flames leaped forth in destruction of the legations. Many foreigners found Japanese graves that night.

Yet, strange inconsistency! the ronins, still under the direction of Hasuda, went about everywhere, crying: "Down with the foreigners! Long live the Shogun!"

Those foreigners who escaped believed that the Shogun had ordered the night's horrors.

At the hour of dawn Hasuda wiped his sword on a foreign fabric. As the morning breezes from the bay cooled his tired brow he laughed grimly.

"Ah," he exclaimed, "what the noble Prince of Mori could not countenance himself has been accomplished; and, being accomplished, I shall find in him no open friend, it is true, but no sworn enemy."

The roar of guns came faintly to his ears.

"To-morrow—to-morrow!" he mused, with a chuckle. "Nay, to-day, the wrath of the foreigners will descend upon the shogunate—the innocent shogunate. Decidedly, it is droll."

XXXIII

It was night when the runners of the Prince Mori's norimon, having travelled the highway to its gated termination, entered Kioto. Uncertain as to his exact course, the Prince was settled upon one thing—haste—haste to arrive in the neighborhood of the Mikado's palace, that he might plan in the shadows his future actions.

He had passed through the city's gates, and with new cries to his runners was again urging them forward, when a cloaked figure, holding in one hand a naked sword, barred to the norimon farther passage. The runners stopped abruptly. Impatiently Mori thrust his head through the curtains.

"What now, you laggards?" he demanded, in no gentle voice.

At the sound of Mori's words the man in the roadway uttered a cry of surprise.

"Thou, Mori!"

"What then?" inquired the Prince, defiantly, preparing to leap to the ground, sword in hand.

"It is I, Echizen. I will join you in your norimon."

"Good!" said Mori. "Urgently I need your advice."

Echizen climbed into the vehicle quickly. With a swift movement he drew Mori's cloak about his shoulders in such a way that it hid his face.

"There is danger in Kioto for you," he said. "Just now as I passed, the sound of your voice instructing your runners struck me with its familiar tones. When you raised your voice I recognized you immediately. You must be more careful, my lord."

"Why should there be danger for me in Kioto?" inquired Keiki, quickly. "I am in my Emperor's capital now."

"But the massacres you have just instigated in Yedo are being used to your disadvantage. Aidzu has come to Kioto two hours ahead of you, and all is known to his Majesty."

"Massacres!"

"Are you ignorant of them?"

"You do not mean—" Keiki paused, a suspicion of Hasuda dawning upon him. "Massacres by the ronins?"

"Yes."

The Prince of Mori groaned.

ONOTO WATANNA

"Hasuda, the chief ronin," he said, "has broken his pledged word to me." He explained briefly to Echizen his compact with Hasuda.

The Prince of Echizen had received a courier who came on horseback but half an hour prior to Mori's arrival. He came shortly after the arrival of Aidzu, who was closeted with the Emperor. The courier's only definite news was that the Regent Ii had been assassinated and the foreign legations burned by a band of ronins under Hasuda, acting, it was believed, under Mori's orders. The ronins had pretended to be the Shogun's men.

The latter information pleased Mori.

"Good!" he said; "the foreigners will lay the blame upon the shogunate."

Echizen leaned from the norimon.

"Proceed slowly," he told the runner, "in that direction," pointing to a quarter of the town distant from the Imperial palace.

"We must adopt some plan of action," he continued to Keiki. "These outbreaks, which I at first thought were at your order, will have fearful consequences. We must plan to turn them to account with the Emperor.

"But he already knows of the massacres."

"Assuredly. Aidzu is governor of the city, and a person of influence with him. He will use the Yedo massacres to your disadvantage."

"But Aidzu is a shogunate."

"True; but lately he has gone over to the Emperor. He is still at heart a shogunate. It is by the order of the Shogun that he has come to the Mikado's court, in fact. He is both a spy and an influence upon the Emperor for the shogunate."

"How do you know all these things?" inquired Keiki.

"Since I left you in Yedo," replied Echizen, "I have made considerable progress in the favor of the Emperor, all for the sake of the cause. I try to set myself against Aidzu."

"Well, and what is the disposition of the Emperor towards my wing of the party? What does he desire us to do? What attitude should we take towards the foreigners and the shogunate at this time? I have a purpose in these questions."

Echizen looked thoughtfully towards the east, where the offshoots of the still distant day were charging the rear-guard of night.

"My prince," he said, slowly, "I feel that this day will be a decisive one in our annals. I feel that there is a great opportunity to be born a new nation to-day."

"Speak on," said Mori.

"The Emperor Kommei is, of course, desirous of regaining the power once held by his ancestors. He knows, as an educated man, that the shogunate has no legitimate right to existence. But he is a man of two natures. Fear, which is not cowardice, and suspicion, which is not discretion, is his ruling motive. He is surrounded by shogunate spies. Every effort he has made up to this time to communicate with us has been frustrated. Were he to put trust in a samurai and think of sending him as a messenger to us, the shogunate straightway removed that samurai."

"By the sword, of course."

"By secret means. In time the Emperor Kommei came to believe that the shogunate held his life in its hands, as it has. He came to distrust all men. He trusts neither Aidzu, his enemy, nor me, his friend."

"What of the foreigners?"

"I believe that he would desire above all things to issue an order for their expulsion, and encourage us secretly to make war upon the shogunate, convinced as he is that his life and the very office of Emperor are at stake."

"Could he be brought to give us secret instructions?"

"He might," returned Echizen, dubiously, "but such is the temper of the man that, while bidding us make war upon the shogunate, he would also warn us that if the shogunate prevailed he could do nothing for us—he would leave us to die."

With knotted brows, Mori considered long. Then:

"You think Aidzu is endeavoring at this moment to discredit me with the Emperor by laying responsibility for Hasuda at my door?"

"Yes, this very instant."

Mori leaned out from the norimon and signed to the runners. They halted.

"One question more," he said to Echizen. "Have you convenient access to the Emperor?"

"At any hour," Echizen answered. Mori bent towards the runners.

"Full speed," he cried, "to the Emperor's palace."

The norimon started ahead.

"To the Emperor's palace?" repeated Echizen. "What are you going to do?"

"To confront Aidzu, my accuser, and urge the Emperor to expel the foreigners," said Mori.

"Perhaps it is the best course," answered Echizen, slowly.

"It is the opportunity of which you spoke," said Mori. "The opportunity for which I have long waited."

XXXIV

The group of buildings set within the walled enclosure known as the Emperor's palace was not surrounded as were many feudal castles of the daimios, and indeed other of the Imperial residences, by a deep moat of stagnant water. The poetic temperament of a people who had returned to the pure Shinto religion, which made Japan a land of gods whose chief was the Emperor, would not permit the Kioto palace to resemble a fortress. It seemed rather a temple, in the atmosphere created in outside eyes by its carved exterior.

The whole interior grounds, in which were the residence buildings, were separated from the city streets only by a heavy wall, rectangular in its completed course. Within, the foliage, set back from the street, rose high above the walls, intermingled with an occasional roof-top.

The wall was entered at intervals by guarded gates, whose porticos protruded into the street. Set out into the street, upon a broad stone platform, approached by a multitude of tiny steps, were two tall pillars, about each of which twined, carved in the material itself, a scaly serpent. Above the serpent, in a carved galaxy of death, were the claws, heads, and bones of wild beasts. Between the pillars and the edge of the wall, and forming the sides of the portico, were two square, wooden panels, upon which were carved dragons, trumpets, and the long-curved, bodied stork. Resting upon the top of the carved pillars and extending over the wall was the sinuous roof, each of whose lines seemed a snake curled in its tortuous travel path.

The roof, made of highly polished bamboo, but preserving its natural form, the little logs being laid side by side, swept up to a curling-point. Over the portico entrance of the gates, two carved, hideously grim faces leered into the faces of any descending the steps. Still higher up, under the shadow of the gabled roof, was the portrait of the Emperor.

The buildings within, set in their gardens and pleasure grounds, had in their roof lines the appearance of the gates. They were of two or three stories, over each of which a gabled, curiously wrought shelf projected from the sides, as a shield from the weather. The windows, small and narrow, were set together in pairs. In the centre of each long side on the lower floor a projecting angle, covered by a triangular roof, made a sort of bay-window. Sliding screens gave admittance to the rooms within.

ONOTO WATANNA

Before the carved gate in the eastern wall the norimon that had brought the Prince of Mori from Yedo discharged its passengers. Echizen and Mori passed into the interior. Once within, Mori, who had approached the structure with the feelings of a devout Japanese, saw that the buildings were set closely together, making an inner rectangular court, in whose exact centre a house more pretentious than its neighbors stood. This he took to be the residence of Kommei Tenno, the Mikado.

To his surprise, Echizen directed his way towards a small edifice set quite without the quadrangle, and of a style more simple and humble than any within the grounds.

"Why are we going this way?" Mori asked. "The Mikado must reside there," indicating the house within the rectangular circle.

"He should live there, it is true, for that is the official residence of his Majesty; but being a suspicious man, he lives in the house least suited to be his residence," returned Echizen.

As if in keeping with the supposed incognito character of the house, there were no guards before it, while the front of the official residence was crowded with sword-wearers.

At the threshold Mori paused.

"Come," said Echizen.

"But a moment," Mori said, in a low tone whose last sound died away in a note of sad, prophetic fear.

He raised his eyes to the trees leafing in the enclosure, and then to the skies. The night mists had passed away, it is true, from the sight, but there was in the air a moistness which the feebly awakened sun-rays had not yet dissipated. A tear of expectation stood in nature's eye. Calm and peaceful the day was dawning, without a sound to ruffle the gentle awakening of drowsy nature. The purple-yellow tints crept up from beyond the horizon, touching the tops of trees and buildings in soft sign of a later imperative sign of action.

Mori bared his head. As he stood there, the longing of the patriotic soul surging through his body until his hands tingled to do noble deeds, the winds gently laved his brow in the cooling of unalterable nature. Mori was praying to his gods, for his country, to the war-god if need be, and to Kwannon, the goddess of mercy.

Then, at the kiss of the wind, a mood, a thought, a picture came to Mori, overwhelming in its potency. The Lady Wistaria! The Lady Wistaria! Her name seemed to sing in his brain. In a flash of thought he realized that, however fierce the action, however great the striving, however complete the attainment, there was no joy in life or death ever for him. The calm of accomplishment meant the wreck of hope.

With a fierce attack upon this memory, Mori drove his faculties back to their duty.

"I am ready," he said.

The two passed within.

A sort of confidential valet stopped them in the ante-chamber. He said:

"The Serene Son of Heaven is closeted with my Lord of Aidzu."

He turned, indicating a closed door.

"You see," whispered Echizen, when the servant's back was turned—"you see they have lost no time."

Then to the servant:

"You may announce to his Majesty that it is I, the Prince of Echizen."

As the servant disappeared behind the door, Mori, on whose brow a slight contraction had come, seizing Echizen roughly by the arm, forced him into the chamber beyond, the secret resort of the Emperor Kommei Tenno.

At the noise of their entrance the slight man who had been pacing up and down the chamber turned in nervous apprehension, his hand seeking uncertainly the naked dagger at his waist. The Prince Aidzu maintained the position assumed by him earlier in the interrupted interview. He was standing easily in an attitude of apparent assurance. An evil smile, meant for Echizen, played over his features as he regarded the future premier and his present rival, for the disconcerting smile of my Lord Aidzu was a trick usual with him whenever an enemy surprised him with his master. It was meant to convey to an intruder intimation of an understanding which might not have been reached prior to the interruption. Echizen met it with the greatest indifference.

For the first time in his short period of vigorous effort in behalf of his Mikado, Mori stood in the presence of the man who was the focus and culmination, the terminal point, of his most honored principle. He saw a slight form which could not be the bodily temple of the vitality of genius. It was that of a man scarcely beyond the thirties, yet there was no promise of the developing years. The features, however, were delicately modelled, the turn of the ankles and hands were exquisite. About the whole manifest personality of the man there was the subtle stamp of effeminacy. The hand, the intelligence within the eye—neither gave hint of action. The brain could not conceive, the hand could not execute.

"Poor lost, poor betrayed cause of Japan," would have been the formulation of Mori's conclusion as these details, tempered by reflection, came to him.

Then there passed through his mind from the little, hidden house of memory all those tales he had heard whispered in secret. The Shogun had bred the Emperor in indolence, in effeminate luxury, so that the war lord of the Mikado might overwhelm his master in the dwarfing shadow of real attainment. There was no hope in this man. Yet the principle was greater than the man, and it was a violation of the principle that had engulfed the man.

These thoughts passed rapidly through Mori's mind as he prostrated himself before the Mikado.

"Oh, it is you, Echizen." The voice, small, without interest, broke upon Mori. "Whom have you there with you?"

"Your highness," answered Echizen, with every token of the deepest respect, "I beg to present to you Keiki, the Prince of Mori."

Mori, who was still on his knees, touched the floor with his head, and remained for a moment in this humble attitude before his sovereign. When he raised his head and looked towards the Mikado he perceived at once that he was frowning, while he made a peculiar movement of understanding in Aidzu's direction, perceiving which the latter shrugged his shoulders. Then, with the decisive cutting of nervous fear, the voice of the Mikado broke the gap of silence.

"We were speaking of you just now, Prince of Mori," he said, with a sinister note in his voice.

The evil smile again crossed Aidzu's countenance.

XXXV

For a moment there was consternation in the breasts of the two men, Mori and Echizen, while the baleful personality of Aidzu, seeming to expand on wings of hate, diffused itself throughout the room.

Mori answered before Echizen could interject a word.

"You honored me by your attention, your Majesty," he said, while still upon his knees.

"Say rather dishonored," said Aidzu under his breath.

"Mori," said the Mikado, with an effort at great sternness, "you have dared to murder the Regent Ii, to burn the treaty houses and legations of the foreigners. What have you to say for yourself?"

"Oh, your Majesty!" was all Mori could exclaim, between his desire to retain his respectful attitude and his impulse to protest against such injustice from the one for whom he had labored long.

"No doubt," continued the Mikado, "you have come to me thinking I shall countenance such an act, and to ask for protection and mercy?"

Mori sprang to his feet. Every nerve in him was tingling and quivering. He heeded not the traditional etiquette to be observed before the Son of Heaven, whereby no man must look the Mikado in the face. Mori was of princely blood himself, and of a lineage as proud and old as his master's. So his own eyes, keen and true as those of a brave and innocent man, met the shifting glance of Kommei Tenno.

"Nay, your Majesty; I come not to ask for mercy, but for justice."

"Justice?"

"Ay, your Majesty."

"But you have committed these atrocious crimes," said the Mikado, his glance wandering uneasily from Aidzu to Mori, "and these crimes will bring upon us the vengeance of these foreign peoples."

"I have committed no crimes, your Majesty. I am innocent of that of which you accuse me."

Echizen interrupted quietly.

"Your Majesty, I do assure you that the Prince Mori is guiltless."

Kommei turned rapidly to the speaker.

"You can explain, Echizen?"

"I can."

"Proofs are many," said Aidzu, thrusting his head forward, "that this young man incited the outrages."

Again forgetting himself, the sensitive and impulsive Mori leaped towards the speaker.

"You lie!" he thundered. Then recalling himself, he turned towards the Mikado.

"I crave your Majesty's pardon, but"—his voice trembled in spite of him—"that worm lies."

The Emperor stared from Aidzu to Mori, then back to Echizen.

"You are prepared to report concerning this?"

"I am, your Majesty," answered Echizen.

"Proceed."

The Prince of Echizen indicated the governor of the city with a slight toss of his head.

"Privily, your Majesty, I beg," he said.

Kommei hesitated. He seemed to be studying Echizen's face. If read correctly, he saw written there so much determination, so much loyalty and faith and truth, that its very expression communicated to him some of its lofty strength and resolve.

"My Lord of Aidzu will withdraw," he said, quietly.

"But, your Majesty—" began Aidzu.

The first expression of imperial command came into Kommei Tenno's face. His head elevated itself, his eyes enlarged and became purple with haughty command.

"I have spoken," he said.

Instantly Aidzu bowed deeply, but into his face there crept a malignant expression. He then withdrew from the chamber. When he was gone, the Emperor made a dignified gesture of permission to Echizen.

"Sire, this young Prince Mori has devoted his life to your cause, as have I," he said, in a low but passionate voice.

"Hush! not so loud," said the Emperor, with a slight shiver. "Wait."

With quick footsteps he crossed to the door and flung it violently aside. There was none without.

"Proceed," he said, almost in a whisper.

Echizen lowered his voice still more.

"Sire, the Prince of Mori did not incite these massacres, but protested strongly against them."

"The proofs! Quick—the proofs!"

Echizen quietly withdrew his sword from his belt. Its point he applied to his own breast. Upon his knees he offered its hilt to his master.

"Sire, my life is at your service, now as ever," he said.

The Emperor bent upon him a gaze that in a man of genius would have shown his soul.

"I believe you," he muttered. Then to himself: "Whom may I, of a truth, believe—whom may I trust?"

The Prince of Echizen, regaining his feet, continued:

"These massacres were the work of a ronin—Hasuda—who is all for the cause, although an unauthorized agent. By this deed, however, he and his men will aid the cause."

"How?"

"They will embroil the shogunate with the powers—the shogunate, which is responsible to the foreigners for the peace."

"But the shogunate had naught to do with these burnings and killings."

"True," said Echizen, smiling slightly, "but think you that the silly foreigner is possessed with your penetration, sire? At the burning of the foreign houses the ronins cried in the name of the shogunate."

"A stroke, truly," said the Emperor, thoughtfully.

And having dared this observation the cautious Emperor hastened to qualifications.

"That is," he began, "that is—" Then, remembering the presence of Mori, "What is his errand?" he asked.

Mori stepped forward. His head was thrown back. The Shining Prince had forgotten again that he was in the presence of the Mikado.

"I have come to urge a national necessity upon your Majesty," he said.

"What is that?"

"To urge your Majesty to give an order for the expulsion of all foreigners within your empire."

"What!" exclaimed the startled Emperor.

Fervently Mori continued:

"The presence of these foreigners makes the re-establishment of your Majesty in your proper position impossible. They distract the Imperialists from their purpose. Fear, or, rather, uncertainty, in regard to them causes the Imperialists to hesitate in attacking the shogunate and forcing civil war upon the country while these foreigners are upon the soil. They have multiplied in such numbers lately that all over the country the people protest against the privileges granted to them by the shogunate."

"This sounds logical," said the Emperor, half to himself.

"Your Majesty, permit me to suggest that the wrath of the foreigners, through the recent acts in Yedo, will fall upon the shogunate. This is well for us. We must take advantage of these very acts of the ronins. Let us follow them up by expelling the foreigner. If thou wilt but issue such a command, a united country will back you. The shogunate will fight because it must, while we will do so for our cause and our homes. Then, the foreigner expelled, thou, sire, thou and the weakened shogunate may reckon together."

Eagerly Kommei listened to the Prince's words—eagerly, and with his eyes fastened upon Mori's face. Down dropped his head in thought.

Echizen, seizing the opportunity, seconded Mori's appeal.

"Sire," he exclaimed, "the shogunate must fall through the foreigner. It cannot rest upon the people. Already is it weakened. Only give the command to expel the foreigner and we will drive him into the seas. He will attack the shogunate, and that once vanquished, thou wilt reign and make peace, perhaps friendship, with these foreigners."

Still the weakened Emperor hesitated.

"I see clearly the results you foreshadow," he said, "but if any detail were to miscarry—" He shrugged his shoulders and shivered.

There was a sound at the door. The confidential valet appeared.

"What is it?" demanded the Emperor, impatiently.

"Your Majesty," said the valet, kneeling, "the Shogun Kii, accompanied by the Lord of Catzu, has entered the palace and craves audience of your Majesty."

The valet backed from the room, drawing the sliding doors behind him.

Mori drew near to his sovereign until his burning eyes held Kommei in an embrace of enthusiasm.

"See—see, sire," he said, slowly, strongly, so that every syllable tore its way to the understanding of the Mikado—"see, the shogunate is already weakened. It comes creeping to Kioto to give that nominal submission to your Majesty ordained by custom to be paid once a year, but deferred up to this day for just two hundred and thirty years. Already the shogunate, needing your divine support, crawls. Crush it, sire—crush it!"

To Echizen the diplomat, this new development in the situation had unfolded itself with intuitive rapidity.

"Sire," said Echizen, "I can tell your Majesty what the shogunate will advocate."

"What?"

"The closing of the ports and the sending away of all foreigners."

"But that is just the policy you advocate," said Kommei. "You will grant me that this is suspicious," he quickly added.

Echizen answered:

"Your Majesty, the shogunate, realizing its own weakness, will outwardly identify itself with a popular policy. In secret, it has its own policy."

"Sire," interjected Mori, beseechingly, "I pray you answer them with the majesty that is Japan, and commit yourself to no policy with them. Once they are gone, command the expulsion of the foreigner, and we, your true and faithful Imperialists, will obey you at once."

The Emperor's faith was still unsettled. Their proposals he respected, but their loyalty he distrusted.

"You, Echizen, and you, Mori," he said, abruptly, closing a period of silence and thought—"I shall put you to the test. Come with me to the audience-hall. If you have fathomed the counsels of the shogunate, it shall be as you wish."

The Emperor left the chamber. Mori would have taken the Mikado blindly at his word and have followed him to the audience-hall, but for the detaining grasp of Echizen.

"His Majesty means," he explained, "that we shall join him in the ante-room of the audience-hall. He regains his own palace by paths of which we must appear ignorant."

Although transported with joy, and in a state of mind that would permit of little restraint, Mori was kept in the room by Echizen until a sufficient time had elapsed. Then Echizen conducted the Prince to his own quarters, where both made suitable changes in their attire. At the end of an hour the confidential servants of the Mikado came in person to summon them to the audience-hall.

Early as was the hour, the whole Kioto court was astir to enjoy a profound sensation—the coming of the Shogun to Kioto. The news ran like fire through the palace, carried by servants and masters alike. Courtiers hastened to seek out the finery they too seldom wore of late. The astute reasoned, and the profound were dumb.

Some rumor of the events in Yedo had gained strength. Even the least consequential felt that a turn in fortune had come.

Within the spacious audience-hall, Echizen and Mori found vantage spots on a side of the Emperor's screen, opposite to that occupied by the sullen Aidzu. Mori now found that he had enjoyed a privilege given to the few in having seen the whole person of his Emperor. Upon state occasions, only the face—or voice, even—gave sign of the presence of the Son of Heaven.

At the head of the hall a raised platform extended across the entire breadth of the apartment. To its edge there hung from the ceiling richly embroidered curtains of heavy silk. The design was that of a dragon whose two frightful bodies met at the head, which occupied the exact centre of the tapestry. The closely observant eyes of Mori detected lines near the head, showing that a square of the material could be removed, leaving a small opening. It was through this alone that the Emperor, as the Shinto deity, received the homage of his court.

There was a signal from the samurai who acted as master of ceremonies. The outer doors were pushed to either side to admit the procession of the Shogun Kii, a boy scarce fifteen years of age, and his numerous advisers, ministers, and court. Among the richly attired crowd of lords about him was Catzu, plainly the virtual Regent, and head of the bakufu.

The Shogun, the Lord of Catzu, and the entire assemblage fell upon their knees at a sign from the master of ceremonies.

There was a pause of expectation. Then the square in the head of the dragon moved aside. Dimly seen, appeared the upper portion of the head of the Emperor Kommei Tenno.

The Lord of Catzu spoke while still kneeling, without daring to gaze in the direction of the Emperor behind the screen.

"Your Serene Majesty, Son of Heaven and Father of Earth," he said, unctuously, "the insignificant shogunate desires, as of old, to render its filial submission to thee, and to give every evidence of its love and devotion."

"It is well," said a voice from within the dragon's head.

"The Shogun," continued Catzu, after a respectful pause, "as war lord of your Serene Highness, desires to ask your Majesty's permission to banish all foreigners now in your imperial realm as most noxious to your Majesty, and to close again the ports of Nippon. The Shogun has sent an embassy to Europe, that this may be done without violence and in dignity."

This time there was no response from the Mikado behind the tapestry. Catzu, having paused an instant, resumed:

"Has your Serene Highness any commands for his war lord?"

The voice issued again from the dragon hangings. It was a trifle raised now, but perfectly clear.

"It is decreed that the Prince of Echizen is made premier to the Shogun, and first minister in all our empire."

Catzu was taken aback. His head, however, was bent to the ground in submission.

"Thou art the Son of Heaven," he said, while rage choked his throat.

XXXVI

At last Prince Echizen, the new premier, and the Prince Mori completed all arrangements for the issue and execution of the order promised by the Mikado.

It was agreed between the two and their Imperialist allies that when the bell within the Emperor's private belfry should sound, the transport of troops and cannon to Shimonoseki, in Choshui, should begin. When the hour struck, a vast army of laborers should move in the same direction, to build fortifications under the direction of Mori, for there a foreign fleet was now lying.

It was also agreed that everywhere within sound of the bell the order of the Emperor for the expulsion of the foreigners should be heralded and placarded by agents in waiting for this purpose.

The Emperor, in spite of the protests of Aidzu, whom he distrusted but dared not remove as yet from his governorship of the city, still held to his promise. Having once gained that promise, Echizen had troubled him as little as possible, knowing that to succeed, he must seek the Emperor last of all.

Mori, on his part, had sent to the forces he had ordered to march on Yedo, other commands that bade them halt until he himself should join them. They would be the flower of his force against the foreigner.

Knowing that Aidzu would interfere with his own person, if need be, to prevent the issuing of the edict of expulsion, Echizen, on the afternoon of the day decided upon, caused it to be whispered about the court that two days hence he would give the signal. He thought thus to put Aidzu off his guard, for he knew that the shogunate meant nothing by its formal request of the Mikado. Meeting popular demand, it had advocated the banishment of foreigners through diplomatic negotiation which signified little. Echizen knew that the shogunate desired open ports, and thought it extremely unlikely that the Mikado would issue any expulsion decrees in response to their statement.

That night Mori and Echizen met the Emperor by secret appointment. Aidzu was not in sight. The three took the way to the belfry, which stood near the outer wall on the western side of the court enclosure. The path lay through a garden little used save by the Emperor alone. Down the hill-side it went through a field of iris to the temple belfry, a low building set on the ground, not in a tower.

The Emperor was still doubtful, even while on the way to issue the order.

"Is it the best thing to do?" he repeated, fretfully.

"The only thing," replied Mori, firmly.

"There is no other course," insisted Echizen.

The wind, stirring in the tree-tops, swayed the shadows gloomily from side to side.

"What is that?" exclaimed the Emperor, halting in alarm.

"Only the wind, sire," answered Mori.

"Come," repeated Echizen.

Arrived at the belfry, the Emperor, gathering his cloak closely about him, stepped gingerly upon its broad platform, and stood there doubtfully regarding the swaying iron chain, from which was suspended, close to the bell, the heavy metal hammer.

"I am to draw this back," mumbled Kommei, stupidly.

"You are to draw it back as far as the chain will permit, your Majesty," answered Mori. "Do, I beg your Majesty, ring; sound the signal at once."

The Emperor, stretching out his hand, reached for the chain with its swinging hammer. A form burst from out the iris bed behind him. In alarm, the trembling Kommei dropped the chain.

"Quick!" whispered Mori, excitedly. "Ring, sire—ring!"

"Ring, sire!" repeated Echizen, frantically.

But the Emperor was staring with fascinated gaze into the face of Aidzu, who stood beside him.

"Do nothing of the kind, sire," he panted, heavily. "Do nothing of the kind. It means ruin to the empire."

"It means ruin to your enemies, sire," cried Echizen.

"It means death," said Aidzu.

"It is the doom of the shogunate," cried Mori.

Still the Emperor hesitated and shivered.

Again there was a sound of running feet. Suddenly a boyish figure leaped into the group of men and sprang upon the belfry platform. A quick hand drew back the swinging hammer to the full length of the chain. Then releasing it, the hand shot the hammer straight and true at the bell's heart.

The signal, reverberating heavily, far-sounding, floated into the distance, filling the air with its sombre zoom! gohn! gohn! gohn!

A slender boy knelt at the Emperor's feet.

"Your Majesty commanded me to ring," said a voice.

Mori, peering forward, recognized in an instant the boy Jiro. A great lump welled up in his throat, choking him with the intensity of his emotion.

"Treason! Kill him!" shrieked Aidzu. "Your Majesty gave no such command."

Nettled at the air of constant authority about Aidzu, the Emperor forgot his caution. Perhaps, too, the deed of the boy had touched him, just as it had relieved him of embarrassment.

"I so commanded," he said.

"But your Majesty spoke no words," exclaimed the infuriated Aidzu.

"The Son of Heaven need not speak by word of mouth to be understood," was the exasperating and perfectly dignified response of the Mikado.

Forgetting himself in his rage, Aidzu turned to Echizen and Mori.

"I will thwart your plans yet, be assured, my lords."

Mori drew himself up proudly, and throwing back his head, surveyed the governor contemptuously.

"It is too late," he said. "Listen!"

From all quarters of the city about the palace there came the sound of stirring movement. At first the noises mingled in confusion and were indistinguishable. Gradually, as their several origins receded and drew apart, they became capable of separate identification. Off to the west a large body of horsemen were fiercely galloping. To the east the tread of men marching in regular formation shook the ground. Farther south there was the indistinct tramp of distant horses, mingled with the metallic clank of gun-fittings. Cannon were being moved.

The march to Shimonoseki had begun.

XXXVII

It was the last stage of Mori's march to his seaport of Shimonoseki. In the extreme rear, with a mounted force lately assembled under the direction of Toro, the Prince of Mori rode. Near him were Jiro and his ever-constant guardian, the samurai Genji, also mounted. An empty norimon, which served as a travelling council-house, was borne by runners in advance of this, the rear-guard.

The march of the expedition was slow, since it was regulated by the pace of the laborers who preceded the main body, as they were to throw up the intrenchments without which the cannon of the Mori foundries were useless.

The division of laborers marched immediately behind the advance-guard. Feeling little apprehension of attack from the objective direction of their march, Mori had thrown his strength to the rear. Here, in addition to the cavalry forces, were the cannon brought from his provinces and those furnished by the Prince of Echizen.

Over all a moon, screened by a filmy cloud, spread its diffused light, which rendered Mori impatient to begin the work of intrenchment, since much might be accomplished before the foreign ships could learn of the Imperialist plans.

When Mori and Jiro, leaving the discomfited Aidzu and the vacillating Emperor together, had rushed from the palace enclosure to mount the horses provided by Echizen just outside, there had been no time for explanations. Mori was not even surprised to find Jiro joined by Genji before they had galloped a mile. He had become accustomed to the association of these two in a convenient comradeship.

The first work of that night had been the posting of mounted guards in advance and in the rear of the laborers, assembled by Echizen. This done, the three had galloped to the division of the cannon, which was hurriedly organized into some semblance of individual batteries and despatched after the proletariat division.

Then in a wild, quick dash across the country the Prince of Mori had marshalled his infantry, swordsmen, and riflemen from the scattered columns into one compact corps. Time was now pressing, but the Shining Prince had yet to converge his parallel lines of cavalry.

Fearing that the unstable Emperor, in some new doubt of

expediency, might yet despatch other troops to recall him, Mori placed his strongest cavalry body under the command of Genji in the rear.

While waiting for one of these divisions to file past him, Mori, turning suddenly to Jiro, asked:

"How came you into the Emperor's palace, Jiro?"

"It was simply done," replied the lad. "I returned with the couriers sent by you to your forces from the fortress of Mori."

"You came in good time," Mori said, in quiet commendation.

The distribution of the various forces completed, Mori, ordering Genji to exercise a general oversight until his return, had turned to gallop back to the palace. He had gone but a short distance, however, when he found that the lad Jiro was close behind him.

"Return to Genji's cavalry division," he ordered, briefly.

"But, your highness, I am your personal armor-bearer; I must accompany you."

The hard-riding form of Genji at this moment had dashed forward. Mori was astounded at this singular disobedience.

"What, you!" he had cried. "You leave an army to care for itself!"

"But the lad—Jiro," said Genji.

"Is he, then, so precious that you endanger the safety of a whole cause? Return at once, both of you, to your stations."

Without a word more, Mori rode to the palace to confer with Echizen. He found the premier greatly troubled.

"Mori," he said, "I cannot prevail upon the Emperor to make me his own premier as well as that of the Shogun. Already he is weakening. You must expect little aid from me now, since I will be under the Shogun. I may aid you unexpectedly, but rely upon nothing more than my willingness. Undoubtedly, efforts will be made to interfere with you, but disregard them. Obey the order you have received, and allow no Shogun to countermand it. The foreigners once aroused, the rest will come in time."

So it was with an anxious heart that Mori rode in the rear of his forces on the last stage of the journey. Up to this time nothing untoward had occurred. He had met and joined to his army the forces under Toro, ordered earlier to proceed from the Mori fortress to Yedo. All was well with them.

The melancholy of the Prince was broken by the entrance through a sudden opening made in the group of his horsemen of some strange samurai. Straightway these samurai, having delivered to him some rolls of parchment, were dismissed to the advance.

The general staff of Mori, which included Genji, Toro, and the boy Jiro, were summoned about the Prince for council.

Mori, who had dismounted from his horse, spread out upon the ground and examined by the light of a lantern the plans of the heights overlooking Shimonoseki. Quickly he marked upon their surface black spots.

"Here you will dig your trenches," he ordered Toro. "It is time for the work."

The heights overlooking the water below were entered first by the advance-guard, now under Mori in person. A cordon was placed about them, with every approach from the land guarded. Into the large circle thus formed Toro led the laborers under their direction. At once the trained pioneers began the erection of earthworks upon a system imparted by Mori to Toro, and from the latter direct to the chief pioneers. The entire space of the immense circle was soon filled by the burrowing, grubbing laborers.

While these were sinking holes on the landward side, it became apparent that no raised fortifications were to be made a target for ships. The hills themselves were cut into, but always upon the landward side, leaving their natural elevation towards the sea. Thus the guns would lie in a pit below the surface of the highlands. The walls were all within.

Mori's next task was the formation of the infantry into another circle to the landward of that occupied by the pioneers. Into the centre of it the cannon were drawn, where they were to remain until the trenches were ready for their occupancy. The remaining force of cavalry was massed at a convenient station, whence they could be sent quickly to any desired point.

Now at last there came a period of inaction for Mori. The pioneers were making full speed, but nothing further could be done until the trenches were completed. In this breathing space Mori rode apart from all his forces, dismissing his temporary staff to their tasks of oversight.

Upon a lonely bluff the Prince dismounted, where he was able to make out indistinctly the foreign ships of war at anchor below. Concerning their identity he was little informed. He knew several nationalities were represented, since the advent of the Americans had drawn English, Dutch, French, and Russian men-of-war to the coast.

ONOTO WATANNA

At least four nations must be represented in the little fleet that stretched out yonder over the water.

"It little matters," said Mori. "They may be American, English, French, or Russian, but they are all foreigners, and desire to encroach upon our sacred realm."

As he turned away from the water a young officer of his staff saluted him.

"Many trenches are now prepared, your highness," he said.

At once the task of installing the guns was begun. Out from their guarded circle they were drawn. The horses originally transporting them were aided by the cavalry mounts, while footmen pulled enthusiastically at the wheels as they sank into the trampled mire or were blocked by natural obstructions.

Once within the pits destined for their reception, the guns were levelled and adjusted by men from Mori's works. The crews appointed to each gun were composed of the followers who had come from the Mori fortress.

Dawn found much of the work completed. The trenches were fashioned, the guns within the pits, and the cavalry in their appointed station. The outer cordon of guards was instructed to dismount and to recline, horse and man, so that nothing suspicious could be seen from the decks of the vessels below.

Within the trenches the adjustment of the heavy pieces was in progress, together with the levelling of a gun platform or the furtive sighting of a gun. Such of the infantry as were not engaged in this employment were thrown out as scouts on the landward side, that no Shogun force might attack them in the rear.

Mori now made a round of inspection within the fortress. Seeing that a number of the guards were in position for their final firing elevation, the Prince called Toro to him.

"Let the crews be drilled," he ordered, "but without raising the guns above the tops of the trenches."

The young and impetuous Toro gave his orders speedily. The crews were thus familiarized with their pieces.

During the course of the forenoon it was observed that the foreign fleet changed its position, standing off from land, and that two vessels left the squadron and disappeared around the headland.

"They are in communication with the Shogun's people," said Mori, aloud.

"Catzu will be upon us shortly," said a voice at his elbow.

Turning, Mori found the youth Jiro. His eyes warmed with interest as he regarded kindly the boy who, with the spirit of a samurai, had never faltered in his service. Feeling strangely drawn towards Jiro, the Prince looked about him for some piece of especial employment to give him as a token of favor.

"Ah, my boy," said he, "there is a rare spirit within thee. Would that thou wert a man."

Hot blood colored the cheeks of the boy.

His eyes clouded, then his head drooped forward.

"My lord," he faltered, almost tremulously, "I am indeed a man, I do assure you."

Mori smiled.

"Only a boy, Jiro, that is all. But see yonder, they are bringing in the last and largest of the guns. Do thou attend its mounting."

"And after," asked Jiro—"after it is mounted, my lord, who is then to have charge of it?"

"Perhaps thou also," replied Mori, still smiling.

"I thank thee, my lord," said Jiro, bowing deeply and hurrying away.

The Prince was still standing there, smiling across the water, when Oguri, his chief of staff, approached him, and bowing low, awaited his pleasure.

"What is it, Oguri?" he asked.

"Your highness, the Lord of Catzu is at the outer guard-post, announcing that he comes with a message from the Shogun."

Mori's brows darkened.

"Tell him," he ordered, "that we know no Shogun here," and turned again to the water-front.

In a flash he saw that the foreign fleet was approaching a spot opposite his position.

Oguri maintained his place.

"Will you not see him?" he asked.

The sight of the fleet changed the determination of Mori.

"Tell my Lord of Catzu that I will see him outside the works, as Lord Catzu simply. Have him conducted outside, if you please."

The Lord of Catzu was brought to the spot mentioned by the samurai deputed by Oguri. Mori met him coldly. When Catzu offered credentials from the Yedo government the Prince waived them aside.

"No credentials are necessary, my lord," he said. "I receive you as a private individual."

"I come as an official," returned Catzu.

"What is it you wish to say to me?" inquired Mori, in as haughty a tone as his own.

"As a representative of the Shogun, I order you to disarm. The shogunate alone makes peace and war."

"I have the sanction, the command, of the only master I acknowledge—his Serene Majesty the Mikado."

Catzu still breathed heavily from his labored ascent of the hill, for the Mori men had refused to permit him the attendance of even his runners.

"Do you still refuse to obey the august Shogun?" he cried, testily and with difficulty.

"I obey the Mikado," returned Mori.

"Disarm!" roared the now infuriated Catzu.

Mori raised his hands as though in preparation for a signal. He held them aloft as he shouted:

"I shall give you my answer with awful effect, your highness."

Sharply Mori lowered his hands. The sally-port facing them crashed sharply open, disclosing the interior of the lately erected fortifications.

"Look, my Lord of Catzu."

In trepidation Catzu looked about him. The silent, absorbed patriots were at their guns. Directly across from the sally-port within the works the gun of Jiro had been placed in position. The youth bent forward, was sighting the piece, while Toro, arms akimbo, stood back, approval written upon his face.

"Guns and men," muttered Catzu; then, catching sight of Toro, he almost rushed upon him. Toro, surprised, turned about and faced his father.

"Thou recreant son!" roared the senior Lord of Catzu. Meeting his father's eyes squarely, Toro kept silence.

"Thou art," said Catzu, "truly a vicious product. Hast thou forgotten all the precepts of honor taught thee from childhood? Thou art no son of mine, nor indeed of Japan, for what man can be a patriot with honor who sets his father at defiance? It is admitted by even those more ignorant than thou that a true son owes his first allegiance in life to his parent."

"Nay, my lord," replied Toro, quickly. "You do labor under a mistake. The first allegiance a son of Japan owes to any man is that claimed of him by his supreme master, the Emperor. Banzai, the Mikado!"

Mori stepped quietly before the enraged Catzu.

"Now, my Lord of Catzu," he said, "you shall have my answer."

As he spoke, he caught up a light rifle from a guard at the gate and fired into the air. Instantly the crews, with hoarse cries, elevated their pieces until their muzzles stood above the breastworks; carefully they trained them upon the ships.

"Ready, my lord," shouted Toro.

"Ready, my lord," echoed Oguri.

Mori made a sign. Instantly a heavy discharge rent the air and shook the ground whereon they stood.

Jiro, at his gun, directly before Mori and Catzu, himself applied the match, and then, stepping back, squinted along the piece to see the effect of his fire. The ball broke a foremast on the leading vessel. In consternation Catzu left the place, the design of the crafty Mori to embroil him with the enemy through his accidental presence dawning upon him.

For upward of an hour the firing continued. At the end of that period the ships drew off from range. Mori, elated at having held his own against the foreigners, and now certain of the consequences of his action, withdrew his people from the batteries. That night the army rested, for Mori knew that the foreigners would lay the cause of the bombardment to the shogunate and make new demands upon it.

The next day a courier from the Kioto court entered his works.

"It is some new mark of the Mikado's regard," cried Toro, impulsively.

Sadly Mori smiled.

"I fear me it is," he said.

With a calm face and firm hand Mori opened the despatch. His face darkened.

"What is it?" cried Toro.

"We are branded as outlaws," answered Mori, his spirit quite gone, a deathly pallor creeping over his face. "We are forbidden to approach the Imperial city."

"Aidzu?" whispered Jiro, almost in tears.

"Yes, Aidzu," repeated Mori.

A GARRISON WAS LEFT IN the works in charge of Oguri, who was to make more intrenchments. Mori, with his cavalry and footmen, accompanied by Toro, Jiro, and Genji, returned inland that night to the fortress of the Prince.

XXXVIII

Without the Imperial city of Kioto, in an open field, lay encamped a little army of thirteen hundred men. It was some months following the decisive action of Mori at Shimonoseki. Imperialists of the neighborhood could not have told who the commander of this force was. They were known simply as the "Irregulars."

Small as was the force, it was admirably trained and drilled in all three of its divisions of cavalry, infantry, and artillery. Each division was the flower and choice of some larger body. The force, which had remained in inaction for a considerable period, showed nevertheless a state of ruling vigilance, whether for attack or defence could not have been told from its appearance.

The camp was in the shape of an elongated circle, whose circumference was regularly defined by field-pieces set at regular intervals, and trained to oppose any invading force. Near each cannon were tethered the horses furnishing the motive power. Hard by, stretched upon the ground, or lounging within the scant shadows of the gun-carriages, were the artillerymen. Infantry guards, in armor, and for the most part armed with rifles, patrolled the space without the circle. Other soldiers and samurai, armed only with swords, sat in the openings of tents assigned to their division, or occupied the time in sword exercise in the open spaces between their shelters. Near the centre of the encampment were assembled the horses of the cavalry division, saddled and in complete readiness for their riders, who lounged near by.

Within a short stone's-throw of the horsemen was pitched what seemed, from its commanding position on a little eminence, the tent of the commander of the "Irregulars." Close by its entrance stood an enormous samurai, whose naked sword was held lightly, carelessly, in his hand. In conversation with him stood a hardy youth, attired as a cavalryman.

The curtains of the tent on the eminence were parted deftly, and the slight figure of a boy hastened towards the two.

"My Lord of Catzu," he said, "the Prince Mori desires your presence, and that of you also, Sir Genji."

Toro smiled at the youth's ceremoniousness.

"Is there news, my Jiro?" he asked.

"Oguri, as you know, has arrived from the south, and our enemies have reported concerning the condition of the city."

The three hastened within, where they found Oguri and Mori.

"Now, then, Oguri, your news," commanded Mori.

"Your highness," said Oguri, "the British have bombarded Kagoshima as a result of our attack upon the foreign fleet."

"Kagoshima!" exclaimed Mori—"the capital of our old friend Satsuma. Then, indeed, have we brought trouble upon our allies."

Other members of Mori's staff sent through Kioto reported the results of their investigations. The premier Echizen had abolished the custom of the daimio's compulsory residence in Yedo during a portion of each year, and now all these territorial lords resided in Kioto. Within the Imperial palace of Kommei Tenno the Lord Aidzu appeared to have controlling influence. The Lord of Catzu was there with him in consultation. Troops of the Aidzu clan had arrived at the palace in great numbers and were encamped in the flower-gardens. Though loathing the shogunate, the Mikado appeared to be completely under its control.

Having ascertained these facts, Mori dismissed all the staff save Oguri, Toro, Genji, and Jiro.

"No answer has come to our petition?" he asked.

The four shook their heads.

"None," they said.

"You have heard the reports," continued Mori, "and will perceive that the Aidzu-Catzu party, now in possession of the Emperor's person and the palace, are determined upon something. These constant arrivals of new troops, the silence of the Mikado to our petition, the crowding of the palace with armed samurai—all these things mean that we are to be punished for having petitioned the Mikado to remove from us the ban of outlaw."

"Then, your highness," broke in Toro, "since the petition was not signed by you, but came from us, your followers, they may now know of your arrival here, and may be preparing to send out an expedition against you in the south."

"No," replied Mori, "I think they know I am here with you, and propose to attack me at once here in my camp. Now, my friends, the time has come for me to disclose to you the real purpose of this expedition. We have respectfully petitioned the Mikado to admit us again to his favor. He is silent. He is surrounded by his enemies. We must attack the palace and rid it of the Aidzu-Catzu combination, thus allowing the Mikado once more to become a free agent."

Oguri and Genji leaped to their swords.

"Now, on the instant, my lord," they cried.

Mori answered, calmly:

"No; we must first gain some knowledge of the exact plans of those within the palace. I want a volunteer for this service."

Simultaneously the four cried out for the service. Mori considered.

"No, not you, Toro; you would be recognized too quickly; nor you, Oguri, for you are needed sorely here. Perhaps you, Genji, but you are too large."

"I am small. The task is mine," broke in Jiro. "I will go."

"Not without me," said Genji.

"Why not without you, Sir Genji?" inquired Mori, mildly. "The boy Jiro needs no guardian. He has proved his valor and discretion upon many an occasion."

With a smile whose influence was ever potent with the Shining Prince, Jiro moved nearer his commander. He said, gently:

"Permit Sir Genji to accompany me. I have resources within the palace I need not speak of now, which will insure me complete safety, but I would ask that the samurai be placed"—he smiled boyishly—"under my command, so that if I am forced to remain within the palace he may carry to you whatever news I may gain."

"What do you mean?" inquired Mori. "What resources can you have in the Mikado's palace?"

The lad, stammering, blushed.

"My lord," he said, "you know I visited the palace before, and—and—"

He broke off in confusion.

"As you will," said Mori, turning aside.

An hour later the samurai Genji strode through the eastern gate of Kommei Tenno's palace, accompanied by a young woman with the air of a princess. They were allowed to pass, while Genji answered the challenge of the guard readily.

"Of the household of the Lord Catzu," he said, pointing to the young woman. "My lord's apartments?"

The guard indicated the house in which the Lord Catzu had temporarily taken up his residence. Without further challenge, the two reached the door of Catzu's private apartment. The guard at the door, recognizing the two, ushered them into the presence of the Lord Catzu.

They found him before a table on which were spread plans and letters. In irritation at being disturbed in the midst of some important employment, Catzu glanced up from his scrolls.

His face became purple with astonishment and mingled emotions. From the caverns of flesh surrounding his puffy cheeks his little eyes gleamed. He stared at the two with his mouth agape. They regarded him smilingly. Finally Catzu gasped out:

"By the god Bishamon!" and again lapsed speechless.

The woman, advancing, knelt at his feet.

Catzu lifted her into his arms.

"Wistaria!" he exclaimed.

"Yes," she smiled up at him. "It is indeed Wistaria."

Catzu held her at arm's-length.

"Ah, my lady," he chuckled, wagging his head at her, "it is plain to be seen that a religious life has dried your tears and honorably mended a foolish heart-break. The mountains have made you as rosy as its flowers and as strong and hardy as its trees."

"And thou, dear uncle?" she inquired. "Thou, too, seemest in good health and spirits."

Catzu sighed, somewhat out of keeping with his fat and happy appearance.

"Alas, my dear Wistaria," he said, "your poor old uncle has suffered much."

"But how?" asked Wistaria with feigned surprise.

A tear appeared in Catzu's eyes and rolled over his puffed cheeks.

"I have lost my graceless son," he said.

"My uncle!" said Wistaria, sympathetically, while she looked past him at Genji with a knowing glance.

Catzu also turned towards Genji.

"And you, Sir Genji, what became of you? Now, sir, tell me how it comes that you are here with my lady niece."

"My lord," answered Genji, "I joined my lady, summoned by a messenger at Yokohama, on the day of the reception in the Treaty House. I turned my prisoners over to another. I trust they were deservedly punished for their offence."

"Nay," said Catzu, "they escaped. But no matter. And you, Wistaria, have you any love left for that husband of yours who deserted you on your wedding-day, or have the mountains and the gods taught you of his baseness?"

Wistaria's features darkened in seeming hate.

"I could kill him," she said. Under her breath she added, "Forgive me."

The Lord Catzu appeared satisfied and turned to Genji.

"You may resume your old place in my train. There will be work for you soon."

Genji bowing, withdrew.

"Uncle," said Wistaria, "tell me what your words just now meant?"

"Presently, presently," returned Catzu. "I have good news for you. But, first, what of yourself?"

Wistaria shrugged her pretty shoulders.

"Oh, of myself there is little to tell. I grew tired of the service of the temple. Thou knowest that I was never meant for a priestess. Thou didst use to declare," she added, smiling roguishly, "that the gods designed me for the court."

"True, true," said Catzu, regarding her fondly, "and more than ever I declare it. Thou hast budded into a very beautiful woman, my little niece. But continue. Thou wert tired of the temple—yes?"

"Well, I thought I had surely offered up sufficient supplication to the gods to have saved a hundred ancestors and parents' august souls. So I sent for Genji, and have, as thou seest, returned unto thee."

"Thou didst well. And, what is more, it shall be my task to punish your husband."

Wistaria averted her face for a moment. Then seating herself on the floor, comfortably against his knee, she raised to him innocent eyes.

"Punish him? Why, how can that be, honorable uncle?"

"He is encamped near by with a rebel army," said Catzu, lowering his voice confidentially; "the day after to-morrow we send an army of chastisement against him under the valiant Prince of Mito."

"The Prince of Mito," repeated Wistaria, half aloud.

"Yes, a brave nobleman I desire to become your husband in time. You will be free ere long, I do assure you." Catzu chuckled confidently.

"What is the offence of—of—this rebel?"

"Your husband dog? He conspires against the Mikado. Oh, we shall drive him out."

An attendant, interrupting them, ushered in Aidzu. Wistaria slipped to the door. Catzu recalled her.

"Thou mayest remain, niece. Hear our plans. They closely concern thee."

"I will return in a moment; but Genji has my perfume sack, which I desire."

Outside the door, Wistaria spoke in an excited whisper to Genji.

"Quick, Genji, you must hasten back to the camp without delay. Tell the Prince that an army of chastisement under the young Prince of Mito will attack him the day after to-morrow. You yourself have seen the forces in the gardens. Go to the camp at once. Make your report and return then to me."

"And thou, my lady?"

"I cannot return at this time without exciting suspicion, perhaps hastening the attack upon my lord by a day. I must remain. I can be of service here."

"I like not to leave thee," said Genji, in great doubt and perplexity.

"Nay, you must do so; I insist."

"I cannot. My duty—"

"Ah, Genji," remonstrated Wistaria, "the devotion of a samurai is best proved by his obedience. Go thou to the camp of my lord; do, I beg—nay, I command thee."

Genji bent his forehead to her hand, then very slowly turned and left her.

Her uncle, grown impatient for his niece, came into the ante-chamber.

XXXIX

T he report of the samurai Genji caused an instant stir of preparation throughout the camp of Mori. The commanders of the batteries inspected their pieces carefully, giving orders for hurried repairs where necessary; horses were examined foot by foot, and within the tent of the Irregulars' leader a last council of the staff arranged the details of an early morning march. Then the rank and file were sent to sleep upon their arms.

"You are certain Jiro is in no danger?" Mori asked, just before the samurai's return to the palace.

"None whatever," answered Genji, "even if I am not with him, your highness. He has friends at court and may yet serve us further."

Relieved in mind concerning the safety of the youth, in whom Mori placed deep confidence and for whom he had great affection, the leader of the Irregulars returned to his tent. There he found his staff, the leading kuge of Choshui, still gathered, though the morning's attack had been thoroughly ordered.

Seating himself, Mori began the composition of a memorial to the Imperial throne. Glancing up, he saw his officers silently watching him.

"What is it?" he inquired.

Oguri stepped forward. There was a strange gravity and even sadness in his face as he bowed deeply before his superior.

"Your highness," he said, "our cause is just, and history should accord us our proper place when the anti-Shogun government is established."

"Yes."

"But it is of the present we think."

"Speak on."

"The present esteem of our friends in the Kioto court—we must advise them of our purity of motive."

Mori held up quietly the scroll upon which he had been engaged. He replied:

"I have thought of that. At this moment I am inditing a memorial to the throne, begging his Imperial Majesty's pardon for creating a disturbance so near to the base of the chariot (throne), but declaring that we do it that he may rule without a Shogun, the sole and Imperial master of his own empire."

The officers looked at each other with solemn expressions of approval.

"My lord," said Oguri, "we would wish also to write letters to our personal friends at the Imperial court. May we have your august permission to do so?"

"Do so at once, my brave men," returned Mori, "but do not forget that we cannot send them this night, since that would warn them of our contemplated attack. Leave your letters with me. Write them here, if you wish, and I will be responsible for their delivery."

Then the company, careful of their honor with their friends and foes alike at court, set to their task. With tears in their eyes, the patriots traced upon the paper words of devotion to their country and their cause. Soon a little pile of epistles lay under Mori's hand. Their valor was in no way diminished by this satisfaction of their honor.

During the night Mori obtained some rest, which was broken at intervals when bands of ronins, who had devoted themselves since the Yedo troubles to the extermination of anti-Imperialists, came to his encampment, offering their services in any movement against the Aidzu-Catzu combination. So small was Mori's force that he would have been glad of their aid, but for his unwillingness to stand sponsor for their unlicensed acts.

At the hour when the Lord of Catzu was unsealing a letter from his son, Toro, justifying all his actions in the past, and at the same time beseeching his father's forgiveness, the little force of Irregulars encircled the Imperial palace.

The Lord of Catzu had read enough of the letter to understand its import, when the movements of the army without, accentuated by the sharp cries of the guarding samurai, came to his ears.

"There has been some strange treason here," cried Catzu, wildly, as he summoned his followers to arms.

Mori's plan of battle was simple. The force had been divided into three divisions, commanded by himself, Oguri, and Toro respectively. It was not without misgivings that the Prince had intrusted the command of a division to the rash Toro, but the reflection that his very temerity might be a valuable element in the day's events had decided him.

Each of these divisions was to proceed to a different gate, through which a simultaneous attack upon the inner palace was to be made. Those within were to be driven out by the infantry into the streets, where cavalry and artillery would cut and pound them to pieces.

The artillery was upon no account to be directed against the palace itself, since the life of the Son of Heaven and the safety of the charging forces within might thereby be imperilled. A portion of the artillery was given to each division; the cavalry, acting as one body, was to act as the circumstances might require.

To himself and a band of chosen samurai, Mori reserved the capture and guarding of the Emperor's sacred person.

At the western gate Mori halted the van of his division, while the cavalry, closely compact, rested on his right in readiness for their orders. At his left was his artillery force, so arranged that their fire should cut obliquely the line of entrance.

The Irregulars who faced the samurai guarding this port of entrance presented a far from uniform aspect. They, the infantry of his force, were all in armor, but their weapons differed. Some carried rifles, others were armed with spears, swords, and bows and arrows. They were gathered into corps according to the nature of their arms, but all were infantry.

At a signal from Mori a rifle volley cut down the samurai at the gate. Those who were struck dashed through the portals, whence issued audible proofs of the alarm felt within.

Instantly the ranks of the infantry parted to permit the passage of a body of laborers and sappers, who, attacking the gate with their tools, gave promise of a speedy breach.

At the moment when one of the doors gave way, when the infantry, straining every nerve, waited couched for the charge, when Mori in their rear gathered about him the picked samurai he was to lead, there thundered from a point across the palace directly opposite the heavy detonation of artillery.

The commander was thrown into grave anxiety. From its volume he knew that one of his lieutenants, disobeying his orders, was shelling the Imperial palace. The safety of the Emperor, and his own good faith, were equally endangered, since the death of the Mikado would make him and his men choteki (traitors) in the eyes of the nation.

Mori came to an instant decision. Even at the cost of the utter failure of the storming of the palace, such a false position must be avoided. Committing the assault of the western gate to a young officer, and bidding his picked samurai follow him, he seized the horse an attendant held for him, and galloped around the angle of the palace wall.

When he came within sight of the central gate of the eastern wall, Mori saw that Toro, wearying of the slowness of his pioneers, had ordered his artillery to batter down the doors. One small volley had been fired when the Prince, riding fiercely at the men serving the guns, beat them down with the flat of his sword.

"Remove these guns at once," he shouted; "you must not fire."

Sheepishly the gunners picked themselves up, as the horses dragged the pieces to one side. Mori, dismounting, strode up to Toro, now standing abashed before the very gate he was to storm.

"You are superseded," roared the enraged Mori. "I give the command to—"

With a quick, almost superhumanly nervous movement, the gates were thrust aside from within. The black muzzles of cannon threatened the now disorganized division of the Irregulars.

"After me," cried Mori.

A flying leap carried him across the line of cannon. Out from their mouths belched their fire. The invaders were swept aside. Mori, striking terrible blows about him, ordered his men to advance, when the Shogun cannon were withdrawn, and a body of horsemen, with savage cries, rushed from within the palace, driving before them and scattering the survivors of Toro's division.

A horse felled Mori and tossed him aside. As he struck the ground a gigantic samurai seized his motionless form, threw it across his shoulder, and carried it into the group of palaces.

The body of chosen samurai who had followed Mori, more slowly because on foot, now came up, and made a disheartening stand. A terrible cry arose that carried dismay, disorganization, and defeat to all divisions of the Irregulars.

"The Shining Prince is taken! Mori is killed!" was shouted by some witless member of Toro's division.

Taken up by others, the report came to the officers in whose charge the various divisions had been placed. Although Oguri made every effort to carry cohesion throughout the force, the shout had done its work. Mori, the Shining Prince, their invincible leader, was dead, thought the rank and file. All was lost. With such a spirit to combat, the officers could do nothing.

A superstitious fear that the gods had deserted them entirely for their sacrilegious act of attacking the palace of their representative on earth, the divine Mikado, added terror to the Irregulars.

Some little advantage was gained here and there by charges into the gardens of the palace, but the great force of Aidzu easily repelled them. Then pouring out into the streets, the army of chastisement, under the young Prince of Mito, cut asunder the already divided and leaderless force of Choshui. Away from the vicinity of the Imperial enclosure the centre of battle rolled. The cavalry of Mori, dashing about compactly, made charges that were intended to rally the men of Choshui, but fruitlessly. They alone, of all the bodies of the Mori army, hung together.

The Shogun troop, having seized the cannon of Toro's division, turned them upon the Imperialists. Fresh troops, ordered to the palace some days before by Aidzu, now arriving, overwhelmed by sheer swamping effect the artillery of Mori, once their fire was drawn. Most of Mori's artillery was now in the hands of the shogunates.

As the flood of fighting men surged through the city of Kioto in diverse, disintegrating directions, fire ingulfed large portions of the city. A gale sprang up from the west, fanning the work of incendiarism and cannon. Houses, squares, streets, yashishikis of the visiting daimios, whole districts were destroyed, while the bakufu followers cannonaded and beat to pieces the public store-houses, lest some Choshui men should find hiding there. The lowly Eta in their peaceful villages were driven out and their houses consumed before the breath of angry war. An Imperial city fell almost to ashes and ruin in a day and night.

But scattered and isolated as they were, the valorous men of Choshui, once they recovered themselves from the disaster of the palace, made a last, wild, determined resistance.

A party under Toro, now insane with grief, occupied house after house and building after building, as with their rifles they brought down the enemy during a slow retreat, when they fired every edifice they were forced to abandon.

Darkness drew no kindly curtain over the red-heated stage of action. The light of vast conflagrations gave sufficient illumination for sword to meet sword in a shock broken only by death. The houseless, homeless residents of the city, non-combatants, fleeing to the hills for their lives, deepened the tragedy of the scene.

In the confusion of this isolated series of battles, Oguri had come upon the cavalry division. Vaulting into an empty saddle, he took command. Diffused as the avenging wave of the young Mito had now become, it could be broken through in some single spot, Oguri believed. The bakufu men thought only of attack, not of being attacked.

Through a quarter of the town as yet untouched by the fury of either party, Oguri led the cavalry back towards the palace. Coming upon Toro's party, he added them to his forces. But with his meeting of

Toro he had chanced upon a fighting zone. Through the cleared space on which still smouldered the ruins of buildings fired by Toro, Oguri directed a charge against the infantry opposed to him, and passed on. In this way, Oguri gained gradually a passage towards the palace. Whenever he came to a region of houses from which he was attacked, Toro and his followers, become pioneers and sappers, levelled and set fire to them, clearing the way for a new charge of Oguri's horse.

Slowly, still undiscovered by the main body of the enemy, they reached the palace.

Gray, dismal, haggard dawned the day, as though fearing to look with sun eyes upon the horror wrought by dark night. From the burning city great mists of smouldering débris hastened to veil, as though in sympathy, the eyes of the lord of day.

Within the palace Mori came to consciousness. He lay in a chamber looking upon what he recognized as the inner court of the Imperial palace. One hand wandered in convulsive movements down his person. He found that his armor was still upon him, though loosened. Upon the floor by the side of his divan lay his swords and helmet. Mori fell, rather than rose, from the divan, and stood dizzily, uncertainly erect. Then attempting to raise his sword, he fell from weakness.

At the sound a woman came forward from the recesses of the apartment. Mori regarded her with delirious eyes. She seemed a white phantom who had risen up in his path to taunt him with her wondrous loveliness. But over her there was the gauzy cloud of falsity. She was a vampire.

"You are yourself?" she breathed, in soft question.

Sullenly, dizzily, Mori raised himself, and, with the motion of a drunken man, stooped to his sword and helmet. Obtaining them, he turned on the woman burning eyes.

"Touch me not," he muttered. Then flinging aside the door, and seeking the stairway as if by instinct, he tumbled rather than walked down the stairs.

He heard the tramp of horsemen without. Brandishing his sword, he rushed into the gardens. He was in the midst of Oguri's horsemen. The leader flung himself from his horse and threw his arms about his disabled chief.

Mori tottered into the arms of the chief of his staff.

"Seize the Emperor!" he half moaned, half gasped, in command; "then—retreat—south—back—to our provinces."

Anxious to retrieve himself in the eyes of the army whose destruction he laid at his own door, Toro set off for the building within the court, shouting to his men, as Oguri received the swooning Mori into his arms.

"Follow me! To the Emperor!" shrilly cried Toro.

If any of the bakufu troops still remained within the palace they did not show themselves while Oguri, busied with Mori, let his cavalry stand idly by. The footfalls of Toro's party resounded through the inner quadrangle.

Within an inner chamber, crouching in seeming fear, Toro found a figure dressed in the garments his knowledge told him were Imperial. He knew that the central, palace was the Mikado's residence. To the crouching figure Toro made respectful obeisance.

"Oh, Son of Heaven, yield thyself to me. I shall care reverently for thy person," he said.

The figure raised a pallid face, while trembling lips murmured:

"Wouldst thou lay profane hands upon the sacred person of thy Emperor?"

"It is he!" cried Toro, delighted. "Seize him, my men, and carry him off." He modified his command to add: "Touch him with respect, I command you."

To Oguri they bore the still trembling man. The lieutenant ordered him placed in a norimon, where his sacred person might be shielded from the scrutiny of his men.

"Is it indeed he?" Oguri questioned Toro.

"No doubt of it," returned Toro. "He himself admitted it."

Oguri and Toro now consulted together as to their next course. Mori was still insensible, despite their efforts to arouse him. In the reduced condition of their force, Oguri did not deem it wise to remain longer, lest returning bakufu hosts should spoil all. He could not spare the men to carry an additional norimon. He spoke thoughtfully:

"His highness, our beloved Prince of Mori, is of royal lineage and blood himself, as thou knowest, my Lord of Catzu. It will, therefore, be meet that we place him within the same norimon with the Son of Heaven."

The body of their senseless leader was placed in the norimon, while Oguri, in order to attend to his wishes when he should regain consciousness, was forced also to crowd into the vehicle. Eight strong samurai lifted the carriage.

"Back to Choshui," ordered Oguri, mindful of the last order of his chief. Moreover, the long march back to their base of supplies was the best, and indeed the only course left to them.

Three miles outside the city, Mori, moaning, struggled in the arms of Oguri.

"All is lost! All is lost!" cried Mori, with heart-breaking bitterness.

"Nay, my prince, my dear lord," said Oguri, in a voice as tender and soft as a woman's, "all is not lost. We were but a portion of our one clan of Choshui. Our southern allies, our friends, are only waiting to rally to thy aid. Moreover, we have achieved a great triumph over our enemies." He lowered his voice. "Your highness, we have honorably captured the person of the Son of Heaven. See!"

He lifted with one hand the head of Mori, while with the other he parted the curtains of the norimon, letting in the strong light of day, which shone upon the face of the figure reclining on the opposite seat in the norimon.

Painfully Mori looked. His head fell back.

"Fools! Fools!" he mumbled. "You have been tricked by the cunning Aidzu. That is not the Emperor."

XL

For two days the fleet carrying the flags of four foreign nations had bombarded Mori's intrenchments on the heights of Shimonoseki. Towards the evening of the second day, Mori cast up the results.

Guns dismounted by the foreign fire lay in heaps of débris, the dead and the wounded impeded the steps of the living, and fully half of the guns were out of action. Yet steadily and fiercely the foreign vessels, sweeping across the fort's line of fire in a wide circle, one by one emptied their guns into the fortress. Only a third of the garrison now remained to Mori.

Again the Prince drew from his breast Jiro's brief letter, sent to him by Oguri, in charge of the Choshui fortress, whither it had gone from Kioto.

"My lord," wrote Jiro, "your honorable family, together with the two cadet families of Nagate and Suwo, has been stripped of all its titles. An order has been issued for every loyal clan to march against you in your southern stronghold. They are sending a vast army against you. Be warned. It has already departed for your province. Yet a little cheer—a small light appears to me. The Shogun's troops, my lord, are garbed in Japanese fighting attire. They are, moreover, far from being a united or happy body of men. There is sore dissatisfaction and unrest among them. Many dislike the prospect of the long journey to your province, many are secretly opposed to the chastisement, many Kioto men are entirely unfit for service. If you will permit your insignificant vassal to suggest, I would remark that it will be well for your highness now to avail yourself of your many years of labor in the perfection of the training of your troops in the arts of Western warfare. When the shogunate troops finally reach the south, take advantage of their weakness."

It was the month following Mori's disastrous expedition to Kioto, and the letter was now many days old. As Mori bent his head in restoring the letter to its place, a dull impact shook the fortress. A shell from a heavy foreign gun, striking the long cannon erected by the youth Jiro at the previous bombardment, bursting, rolled the bronze tube from the carriage and swept it into a little knot of pioneers, crushing and killing the majority of them outright.

A bitter smile, torn from the heart of the commander, curled his lips.

"Having defied the 'civilized' world, I little fear the shogunate," he said; "and yet I cannot spend more time here. Our guns are dismantled. That is an omen for retreat. It was Jiro's gun, and here is Jiro's letter."

Summoning his officers, the Prince gave the order to evacuate the works. Horses were attached to such of the guns as were worth saving. Then, with these in the rear, the remnant of the Shimonoseki garrison began the march to the Choshui fortress.

Upon rejoining his chief in the latter's private apartment, Oguri had news to impart.

"It is a strange army, truly," he said, "that the Shogun has sent against us. They are encamped near the highway, a good day's journey north of us."

"A strange army, you say?" inquired Mori, mindful of Jiro's letter.

"Ay. Though all the clans were ordered to march against us, but few have done so, and they are sick, silly fellows, growling at having to leave the court and its pleasures."

"How are they armed? With rifles?"

"Some."

"Artillery?"

"The pieces taken from us in Kioto."

Mori was lost in reflection for some moments. Then:

"Let all retire to rest at once."

It was the middle of the afternoon.

Mori added, without pausing to explain to his puzzled chief lieutenant the reason of his strange order: "At dusk report to me."

However large an army the Shogun might have sent against the men of Choshui, the fortress defenders with its attendant army went to their unaccustomed rest without the slightest fear. The fortress might now well be considered impregnable. In addition to its regular defensive works, constructed immediately upon the return of Mori from his melancholy wedding-day, there were now a deep moat of great width constructed about the whole region of the fortress, gun-factories, and the works built by the Prince of Satsuma.

All that afternoon the army of Mori slept. The first hour of darkness saw a departure from the fortress. First rode six companies of horsemen, from whose body scouts were thrown out. Next marched two thousand infantry, all with rifles. They wore no heavy armor, and as their company commanders gave their orders, their tactics were seen to be modelled upon European forms. Finally, in the rear lumbered sixty field-pieces. Oguri rode with the cavalry, directing the route of the army. Close behind him was Toro, who, since the affair of Kioto, was on intimate terms of good-fellowship with the chief lieutenant.

Mori, attended at a distance by his staff, rode in the centre of the infantry division. The entire direction of the current routine he left to his subordinates, riding moodily apart from all. The men marched with firm and light step. On their own soil they were more assured and hopeful of the issue.

"Oguri," asked Toro, as in perfect quiet they advanced with their cavalry—"Oguri, how may I atone for Kioto?"

"By following my orders closely," answered the serious Oguri. "You, with the cavalry, are upon no account to charge before cannonading begins."

"I swear by the god of war I will not," promised Toro.

"You must move to the west at least four miles, throwing out your scouts regularly."

"I will. Only give me the chance. Was not I responsible for the failure at Kioto?" said Toro, his face quivering in spite of himself.

"Yes and no," said Oguri; "but, at all events, his highness has not held it against you. He told me that after-events justified you, since the enemy had artillery at your gate."

"But he allowed me no chance to explain that I ordered the pioneers back when I heard their artillery being brought up. I wanted to check them at once."

"The Prince has nothing but affection for you," said Oguri.

"Ah!" cried Toro, in delight.

The other smiled, half paternally, half reprovingly, at the enthusiasm of youth.

"But you must restrain yourself during the first half of your manœuvre," said the chief lieutenant; "during the latter part you may give free rein to your impetuosity."

As the first sharp light of the September day began to make visible objects along the highway, Oguri held out his hand to Toro.

"Now go," he said, "and remember all I have said to you. Now is your opportunity."

Toro dashed a sleeve to his face. Then, turning to his cavalry, he raised his sword in command.

"Forward!"

Sharply turning, the six companies wheeled due east, to disappear in the distance. The main body advanced for two hours. Then Oguri saw that Toro had reached the spot settled upon in their plan of battle.

Mori, leaving the centre, came briskly up with his staff, to assume the ordering of the formation. The infantry were set out in two close ranks. Back of them, in the centre, the sixty field-pieces were assembled, their horses tethered close by.

"Scouts!" called Mori to Oguri.

Scouts and skirmishers were thrown out. All rested upon their arms.

The place was a broad and level plateau, through whose middle the highway ran. Back of Mori's artillery rose a steady height which the army had crossed. Facing the force, resting upon its arms, the plateau stretched out for a mile until a sharp descent came into view. Up this the army of the bakufu must climb, since the great highway was also there.

It was a time of idleness for Mori's troops, until towards noon, when the outposts reported to the main body:

"The enemy is approaching."

Mori issued a number of orders, the effect of which was instantly seen. The artillery horses were attached to the guns, the infantry closed ranks. All stood at arms.

Oguri approached the Prince.

"Shall I send the guns to sweep them down before they can gain the plateau?" he asked, in excitement, as the natural advantages of the place seized upon him.

"No, let them reach the plain and form in their best order. I wish to crush them completely."

Even when the first ranks of the enemy appeared, Mori remained inactive. They formed quickly and advanced. Still Mori remained impassive.

When the bakufu troops had advanced half of the mile separating the two armies, Mori, turning upon the little eminence, whispered in the ear of his youngest lieutenant. The young man rode off at full speed to the artillery.

A moment more and the lines of infantry split apart to allow the passage of forty guns. At full gallop they rushed towards the enemy, sending up great clouds of dust from the dry plain as they sped on. Their carriages swayed from side to side without disturbing the pose of the impassive men seated there. The postilions lashed their horses.

Mori faced his staff. He smiled with a quiet smile.

"Now we shall see, my lords, how the line holds."

The officers addressed, thinking he referred to the cannonading, looked for an unexpected fire from the batteries. None came. Straight and true towards the heart of the enemy's lines, the artillery, drawn by foaming horses, rushed. The enemy's lines held. But a hundred yards separated them. It held at eighty; it wavered; at sixty—it broke.

As if in answer to his unheard command, his flying batteries whirled in irregular curves, stopped, unlimbered, fired, then with the speed of wings were off again, this time in retreat.

Again Mori's infantry lines parted. Out went the twenty remaining guns, straight for the enemy.

Mori's lips poured out a stream of orders. His staff flew over the ground. The whole army advanced to support the artillery attack, while the boomerang batteries were recovered.

"To the left wing," cried Mori to Oguri.

Oguri placed himself to the left of the centre, while Mori took the right. Still in one compactly joined front, the infantry advanced.

"Now, now," moaned Oguri. "Toro—where is Toro?"

As the line advanced, the artillery, having reloaded, bore down again upon the enemy's centre, pounding it.

The infantry neared the bakufu. Mori despatched an officer to silence the batteries.

Now was the crucial moment. Broken and scattered like a herd of untrained cattle was the bakufu's centre.

A cheer sounded in the enemy's rear. Just at the proper moment Toro's cavalry charged the rear, dashing through the centre.

Now a movement of division took place in the forces of Mori. Oguri's left divided on the centre and swung to the west, while Mori's right swung eastward. The artillery became two corps, one for each of the divisions; the cavalry, divided, also followed the direction of the two leaders.

Mori's forces had sundered the centre of the bakufu and were rolling up on either side, driving in two opposite directions the immense army of the shogunate.

As panic and fear spread through the poor-spirited forces of the bakufu, the cavalry withdrew to pursue fugitives. Mori's infantry in its two divisions was now sufficient for the isolating and destroying of the two segments of the enemy.

At last it was done. The forces of the shogunate were routed or destroyed at the first battle.

With every mark of his favor, Mori received Toro into his circle of officers. Toro's face, black and grimy from the smoke of cannon and the dust of action and the road, nevertheless was shining.

"My lords," said Mori, "we are now at the crucial time in our career. We must advance instantly upon the capital. This time no small force will be sufficient. The entire army must accompany us to Kioto. Oguri, you take the cavalry. You know the country well. Ride forward to Kioto at full speed. Then throw out a long skirmish line and capture every fugitive from the bakufu, that the news of our advance may not reach Kioto. We shall give the depleted army of the shogunate now in Kioto a noble surprise."

Mori drew Toro to him.

"Return thou, Toro, to the fortress. Take every available man, leave only the company of the governor of the fortress, and march speedily to join me on the highway."

XLI

Days went by. The entire force at the command of Mori moved slowly in the direction of the Emperor's capital of Kioto. As the days stretched into weeks and months, still the army moved without haste. Mori was now in communication with the other leaders of his party, through runners. All were concentrating upon the capital.

Echizen, moreover, had sent word to Mori by special courier. The boy Shogun was dead, and the young Prince of Mito, who had headed the army of chastisement against the Imperialists in Kioto, had been appointed Shogun. But Echizen's tidings of death did not stop here. The Emperor Kommei Tenno had succumbed to disease and oppression, and upon his death, his son, young Mutsuhito, a youth of sixteen, had succeeded to the throne.

When Mori learned of this latter event he despatched long epistles to each of the leaders. He urged that all should concentrate their forces in small parties, whose approach should be gradual upon the Imperial palace. Once having possession of the Imperial city and the palace, the Aidzu-Catzu supporters would be instantly expelled, and Mutsuhito, the new Mikado, should be proclaimed sole ruler of Japan.

To this all assented. The 3d of January was settled upon as the day.

Dividing his force into small parties, who were assigned a rendezvous in Kioto, Mori continued his advance. Then came the news to him from Echizen that the Prince of Mito (now the Shogun) had been persuaded to resign his office. Now there seemed small obstacle in the way of the Imperialist plan.

On the day appointed, the various relays of Mori's force which had preceded him to Kioto met and joined his personal following. At the hour of noon they marched in perfect order to the western gate. Each of the nine gates was taken without force by a large body in command of one of the Imperialists.

Two hours later Mori, Echizen, Oguri, and the other leaders were in full possession of the Mikado's person and policy. The shogunate was declared abolished. An edict was issued declaring the Mikado the sole ruler, and a government was created. Aidzu and Catzu had been expelled from the palace.

It was reported to Mori that the ex-Shogun, Mito, had left Kioto in anger, and that, regretting his resignation, he was gathering troops about him to dispute the *coup d'état*.

Wearily Mori assumed command of some two thousand troops, went to Fushimi, where he met the Prince of Mito, with an army much larger than his own. After three days' fighting the ex-Shogun was driven back to Ozaka, whence he departed for Yedo on an American vessel. Mori followed more slowly.

He was now embarked upon the most desperate stage of his undertaking. Mito possessed in his capital, Yedo, forces, ships, and resources in great excess of any belonging to the new government. Nevertheless Mori marched upon Yedo steadily. At the gates of the city the senior Lord of Catzu met Mori.

"How now, my lord?" demanded the Mikado's defender. "Are you come again to bid me lay down my arms?"

"No," said Catzu, almost humbly, "I am come to offer you the submission of the Prince of Mito."

"Ah!" Mori veiled his satisfaction.

"Under my counsel," continued Catzu, "his highness the Prince of Mito has seen his error. Never again will he take up arms against his sovereign lord the Mikado. I but beseech you now to spare the city of Yedo."

"My business here is done," was Mori's reply.

"Stay, my lord." Catzu entwined his fingers in an effort to conceal a strange nervousness.

"I await your words, my lord."

"Thy wife—" began Catzu.

The brain of the leader became clouded and dark with passion.

"Another word, my lord," he replied, haughtily, "and thou and Yedo shall both be put to the sword. Having found my armor invulnerable to the darts of your spears and arrows, you think to advantage yourself by an ancient weakness of mine. Be assured that I am as invincible in that regard, my lord, as in the matter of warfare."

At the end of twelve days Mori was again in Kioto. The surrender of the late Shogun had not carried with it the submission of Aidzu, who had fled to his province. The Prince despatched Oguri into the highlands of Aidzu to complete the unification of the country. Eventually Oguri fulfilled his mission, bringing complete victory to the Imperial cause.

In the Kioto court the new party wrought speedy change. The daimios, or territorial lords, were summoned, and resigned into the hands of the Mikado their feudal possessions.

At one of the last councils attended by Mori, the Shining Prince made an address of deep import.

"Your Majesty," he said, "may not be insensible to the changes forced and hastened in your country by the advent of the foreigner. I have been fighting feudalism, the bakufu, and the shogunate with the civilization and weapons of the foreigners. Through them we have conquered and prevailed. Since we owe our supremacy to their rifle and cannon, a conviction has forced itself upon me. Your Majesty no longer lives behind a screen, seen by a few eyes only. Your Majesty is a world power, and must have relations with other nations. We must assimilate foreign civilization, if only to combat the foreigner."

Thus Mori came to the spirit of New Japan, speaking almost the identical words uttered by Iyesada long ago.

Having accomplished his share of the establishment of the new government, Mori felt that he could now turn his attention to the welfare of his faithful followers.

He set a day for a final interview with them, when he should bestow such rewards as were now in his power, as chief adviser to his sovereign, to give.

For himself, an important cabinet portfolio had been offered, but he had come to no decision. He felt that his work was done. He desired only peace. He was not ready to think further.

Realizing that the lost Jiro, if alive, must be in some portion of the palace, Mori caused him to be sought for.

On the evening prior to his final meeting with his officers, Jiro came to him as he sat alone in his chamber. The sight of the lad affected the Choshui Prince peculiarly. He realized in a moment of self-revelation that the feeling of loneliness and isolation among his officers had first manifested itself just after the departure of Jiro. While his relations with the youth had not been of an intimate nature, still Mori felt that he had ever sought and found tacitly a silent, unspoken understanding and support of his purposes from him. He felt drawn towards the boy as one great soul seeks the penetrating sympathy of another. A longing, throbbing into wistfulness, pervaded him. Wearily, yet patiently, he regarded the youth.

"Jiro, my boy, why have you left me so long?" he said.

The boy flushed slightly as an eager delight betrayed for a moment his pleasure in Mori's words.

"Have you, then, missed me?" he began, in a warm voice, to break off abruptly as a forced coldness took possession of him. "I have been much engaged, my lord," he said, without enthusiasm.

"Ah!" said Mori, quietly, noting his flushing face; "and I am ready to wager it was with a maiden."

"It was, my lord."

"Ah!—thou, too, Jiro," said Mori, sadly. "A youth, thou hast come to the gates of love, to enter paradise—or hell."

"It was not an affair of love, my lord."

"No?"

"I have been endeavoring to right the wrongs of a woman—a very near kinswoman. But I find that I am without power to proceed further."

"Nay, tell me, Jiro, thy troubles, and those of thy kinswoman. I am not without power now, and may assist thee."

Mori smiled pitifully at thought of his power and the poor satisfaction it held, now that its great consummation had been crowned.

A slight nervousness fell upon Jiro. While his hands tremblingly fingered his obi, there came into his eyes and his voice a suggestion of something ulterior, something beyond.

"My lord, my kinswoman loved a man and he loved her," he said, pausing.

"Sad," murmured Mori, with the cynicism of his broken mood.

Without noticing the Prince's comment, Jiro continued:

"My lord, has not a parent the right to exact obedience from his child, even though that obedience lead her to utmost misery?"

"Such is the Japanese idea," returned Mori.

"Then, my lord, the parent of my kinswoman exacted a task from her. He forced her to betray her lover, though she, ignorant that he was the person implicated, yet sought to warn him of the danger to himself and the unknown."

Mori's eyebrows contracted darkly. He half rose from his seat. Then with a forced calm he dropped back into his place.

Jiro's face was now flushed a deep scarlet. He seemed to be using all his strength in an effort to control his emotions.

"My lord," he added, "my kinswoman was not only forced to betray her lover by her father, but she was driven further—into marrying, and, consequently, degrading him, because only in that way could she save his life from the hands of the public executioner."

Mori was white to the lips with his anger. But he controlled himself strongly. Jiro had claims upon his gratitude.

"You have failed to tell me," he said, coldly, "in what way I can serve you—and your kinswoman."

"My lord, the lover put away my kinswoman, being in ignorance of the treachery of her parent. Yet so grievously is he wounded that he could not be approached by one so slight as I. He would not listen to truth."

Impenetrability masked the face of Mori. His thoughts were veiled behind a set countenance.

Half abashed, and fully shaken in his late confidence, Jiro spoke trembling words.

"Do you, my lord, speak to this lover—tell him that it was the fault of their fathers, and that his lady, indeed, loves him and has always loved him."

Still silent and motionless remained Mori.

Jiro faltered. "I have served thee," he said, as he went a step closer to Mori; "do thou this now for me."

Mori spoke.

"To-morrow," he said, "I take farewell of my officers. My worldly tasks are then finished. Then I will endeavor to serve you, Jiro—to-morrow."

"But, my lord, thou speakest of thy worldly tasks. Wilt thou, then—?"

"Nay, Jiro, I will not take my life, I promise thee, before I have seen thee. To-morrow."

"To-morrow," repeated Jiro, and was gone.

Near the iris field in the Emperor's garden there is a slight hill, set upon whose sides are a number of fanciful shelters. Under one of these, upon a bench that night long sat Prince Mori Keiki. Above him the bare trees supporting the structure twined their naked boughs together into what in the leaftime was a natural roof. This night, bare of leaf, they were as open to the cold as the structure's side, yet Mori seemed unaware of the season. There was no chill upon his limbs. A strange smile flitted across the features of the solitary Prince.

With a shrug of the shoulders he glanced at the slight structure under which he sat.

"It is a summer-house," he muttered, "and it is now winter. Fitting—fitting."

Farther up the hill above him, within the shadow of another similar structure, a slight form crouched, while burning eyes were fastened upon Mori. With chilled and shivering being, the youth watched.

"He must not depart this life," said the little watcher on the hill; "he must live—and believe. Oh! all the gods, lend me the strength and power to convince him!"

XLII

Alone in his deserted apartments the Mori sat—prince no longer, for with other nobles and daimios he had resigned his fief into the Mikado's hands. The officers had long ago departed, to enter upon the new courses the parting benefits of their leader had determined for them. Some were already upon their way to the provinces, the offices of Mori had procured for them, as governors appointed by the Mikado.

Toro had gone to Catzu, to govern for the Mikado the territory his father had administered for the Shogun. Father and son had been reunited. The Lady Evening Glory had long been dead, and Catzu was without a mistress.

Yet Mori had detailed for Toro what he considered a greater reward.

"Toro," said Mori, "you will deliver this order, signed by me, in person to the Lady Hollyhock, directing her to cease forthwith her mutinous rebellion, and to render herself as a conquered province into thy hands."

"But, your highness," said Toro, "I do not desire an unwilling bride, who yields herself but to superior command."

Mori's smile had within it the tinge of a satirical wisdom.

"Toro, my comrade and friend," he said, gravely, "I do assure you that you will not need that order. The heart of the lady is yours. Only her coquetry holds out, and finding in my writ a convenient pretext, she will gladly go the way the heart has long directed."

With exuberant joy Toro had started from the apartment.

"Yet, once again, Toro," said Mori. "While I aid you with the Lady Hollyhock, I warn you that you will never find your complete happiness in a woman. After the first days you must look to the faithful administration of your province for your chief satisfaction in living."

"I do not agree with you, your highness," Toro replied. Then he added, with a cheery laugh:

"But there will be some satisfaction, truly, in administering my province, and mine ancient, rebellious sire."

Before the officers departed, Toro, as their spokesman, had presented to their old commander two swords, richly wrought, the usual token of the samurai as their parting tribute.

"I do assure you," Mori had responded, "that in giving me these swords you have not merely given me a reminder, as your spokesman has said, of our services for the New Japan, but you have given me as well the conquest of a newer, higher, more happy universe. As a citizen of a greater universe, I thank you."

In these words, and in every act of the former Prince that day, the officers, save the delight-blinded Toro, had observed a touch of finality, the savoring grace of a farewell to earthly things, that, samurai as they were, had not failed to move them. Plainly their lord contemplated something that their order called honorable; yet they shuddered at the thought.

Now they were all gone out of Mori's life, into the new life he and they had created together. The Shining Prince was left alone—alone with two swords that lay upon a low table at his side.

The moment long waited by Mori had come. The Mikado had been restored to his ancient sovereignty; peace was once more upon the land. The great purpose of his efforts was attained; every thread connecting Mori with this new order of things had gone from his opponents— from his life—save two swords alone, which he had said were means for another conquest.

Yet in spite of the atmosphere of finality that he felt pervading his apartments, Mori was not thinking of the termination he had set to his activities. His thoughts carried him beyond the black period he had said should close his sentence. Over into regions of life across finality his imagination strayed. The Lady Wistaria came back to his memory, his mind, his heart—occupied his whole being with the force of the magic spell she had woven about him.

When Jiro had made his plea the day previous Mori had instantly recognized its meaning. It came with no joy to him. His course of thought and heart had been too long bent in one direction for the timid, blind words of a youth to swing it abruptly.

"It is one more device, perchance, of my enemies," he had said, dully, in the first bitterness that came when the lad's words had touched his heart.

Now, when all was over, he was again, in spite of his will, weighing the possibilities. Of course there might be truth in what Jiro had said, but it could not be determined save in the eyes of the Lady Wistaria herself, and now the lad Jiro had not come, as he had promised.

With a profound sigh, Mori, raising his head, caught sight again of the two swords. Yes, they held their meaning for him. Jiro's words were not worthy of belief. He stretched out his hands to the swords.

"She was false—and Jiro lied!" he muttered.

His hand sought and found the hilt of one of the swords and grasped it firmly, stiffened, and fell to his side. Suddenly the face of the Lady Wistaria with its all-pervading purity and truth-compelling quality arose before his vision. As he regarded the unsought vision which had come to his uncontrolled imagination, it dawned upon him with a sudden, great light that he had been wrong—wrong. Back to his consciousness floated that dark night by the side of the stagnant moat, the memory of the tortured white face that shone out from the interlacing boughs of bushes about them, the trembling hands and the little water-soaked feet. Were she utterly false as he had thought, would she have thus come to him to warn him of the danger that encompassed the one she did not know was he himself?

A great upheaval arose in Keiki. The rush of emotions ingulfed him. A cry, a groan, escaped him, as, burying his face in his arms, he threw from him the swords.

"She was truth itself," he said. "It is I who have wronged her—I who have been unworthy."

"Too late!" a voice within his world-dulled soul said. He recalled now the intelligence he had heard somewhere many months before. The Princess of Mori had become a priestess of the Temple Zuiganji.

"My lord!"

The voice behind him, vaguely familiar, passed into that of the boy Jiro.

"My lord," repeated the soft voice, "it is I, Jiro, returned to thee."

Mori answered:

"Alas, you come too late, my Jiro. Thou canst tell me nothing now, for I know that she was guiltless. I was at fault. The gods alone can forgive me."

Again he bent over the swords. The figure behind him moved from its position. It stood before the bending Prince now. A white robe reached to the floor, brushing his hand and covering the swords at his feet. Impelled by a force he could not resist, Mori raised his head. Wistaria—Wistaria in her bridal robes, with white flowers in her glorious hair, stood before him.

Mori started to his feet.

"Jiro—Jiro—"

He looked about the room, as though he still thought the boy within the apartment. Was he dreaming, or had he actually heard the voice of the boy Jiro, saying:

"It is I, Jiro, returned to thee."

But where was Jiro, and who was this white being who had taken his place? Not the Lady Wistaria, she who had become a priestess because of her wrongs. Then her lips framed themselves in words that reached his consciousness.

"If it please thee, my lord, I am Jiro."

"Lady Wistaria!" he gasped.

"I am Wistaria," she said.

Slowly, with the movement of one dazed, Mori moved towards her. Her exquisite hands she held out to him. He seized them with his own. For a moment he held them in a close, spasmodic clasp, then suddenly he sank to the floor, burying his face in the folds of her kimono.

But the Lady Wistaria was upon her knees beside him, her hands upon his head.

A NOTE ABOUT THE AUTHOR

Winnifred Eaton, (1875–1954) better known by her penname, Onoto Watanna was a Canadian author and screenwriter of Chinese-British ancestry. First published at the age of fourteen, Watanna worked a variety of jobs, each utilizing her talent for writing. She worked for newspapers while she wrote her novels, becoming known for her romantic fiction and short stories. Later, Watanna became involved in the world of theater and film. She wrote screenplays in New York, and founded the Little Theatre Movement, which aimed to produced artistic content independent of commercial standards. After her death in 1954, the Reeve Theater in Alberta, Canada was built in her honor.

A NOTE FROM THE PUBLISHER

Spanning many genres, from non-fiction essays to literature classics to children's books and lyric poetry, Mint Edition books showcase the master works of our time in a modern new package. The text is freshly typeset, is clean and easy to read, and features a new note about the author in each volume. Many books also include exclusive new introductory material. Every book boasts a striking new cover, which makes it as appropriate for collecting as it is for gift giving. Mint Edition books are only printed when a reader orders them, so natural resources are not wasted. We're proud that our books are never manufactured in excess and exist only in the exact quantity they need to be read and enjoyed.

bookfinity™

Discover more of your favorite classics with Bookfinity™.

- Track your reading with custom book lists.
- Get great book recommendations for your personalized Reader Type.
- Add reviews for your favorite books.
- AND MUCH MORE!

Visit **bookfinity.com** and take the fun Reader Type quiz to get started.

Enjoy our classic and modern companion pairings!

Classic & Modern